Palo Alto City Library

Still Life

STILL LIFE

by
Rick Hanson

KENSINGTON BOOKS

For Jerry Kreiter
My Captain. My confidant. My brother.

KENSINGTON BOOKS are published by

Kensington Publishing Corp.
850 Third Avenue
New York, NY 10022

Library of Congress Card Catalog Number: 96-075285
ISBN 1-57566-041-5

First Printing: June, 1996

Printed in the United States of America

Chapter
One

Happiness is a large check for a little effort. This was told to me once by either a wise man or a U.S. Senator, I can't remember which, but I took it to mean that being paid well for doing something you enjoy is a good thing. I was getting very close to that definition of happiness as I ambled across the Taos Plaza with a pair of freshly made burritos, extra hot.

I felt pretty good about myself, content with my station in life. The New Mexico sun warmed my face and the clean dry air filled my lungs. All around me tourists spoke in accents from every corner of the world, and over their voices I could hear the low, soothing melody of an Indian flute. Since leaving the Marine Corps, more years ago than I cared to think about, this was the most foreign place I'd ever been. The architecture in Taos reminded me more of Mexico than Mexico itself. In my home town of Portland, Oregon, I didn't get to see much adobe, except for the occasional Taco Bell. Taos was a town full of Taco Bells of all shapes and sizes. Pueblo Indians sat cross-legged on flannel blankets on the sidewalk. Some sold jewelry of silver and turquoise and some just sold a few minutes of their time for a photograph or a quick sketch of their weather-worn faces.

I was here on business. The potential for making large bucks selling my sculptures was extremely promising. And I was having fun.

As I approached the Bent Street District, I could see Alison Brooks standing in the arched, adobe entryway of the Sundog Gallery. She wore a black gauzy blouse, off the shoulder, and a flowing skirt of black and turquoise with matching earrings, bracelets and concho belt. She motioned for me to hurry up.

Through her Art Gallery in Portland, Alison had arranged to have six of my sculptures displayed at the Sundog Gallery for the Taos Art Festival, the last two weeks in May. At first, I wasn't too hot on the idea. After all, people who shop art in Taos wouldn't be looking for my kind of stuff, dolphins and orcas and such. But Alison had been quick to point out that we had several friends in Oregon whose homes were decorated in a southwestern motif. So why wouldn't the inverse be true? She had also said that this was an international affair of high regard and only an idiot would decline such an opportunity. Since I was undeniably in love with Alison, I did not wish to be seen through her eyes as an idiot, so after prolonged deliberation, I accepted.

As I stepped into the gallery, Alison's green eyes flashed hungrily. "Adam, I'm so glad you're back. I'm starving. Is one of those burritos for me?"

Actually, they were both for me but this was a good chance to turn a thoughtless oversight into a sweet and generous act. "Be careful," I said, handing her one of the spicy morsels, "they're hot."

"I like my burritos like my men," she said, taking the first bite. "Hot and spicy." A translucent film of reddish brown ooze dribbled onto her chin and she dabbed at it with a paper napkin.

"And greasy?"

"Especially greasy," she said seductively.

I had peeled back the foil wrapper on my own lunch and was about to dig in when Alison seized my arm.

"Come with me," she said. "There's someone I want you to meet." She led me to the back of the gallery where a European-looking gentleman, dressed elegantly in a white linen suit, poured red wine into crystal glasses.

"Adam," Alison said. "This is Jacques LaFraque. He owns a fabulous little gallery on the Left Bank near the Rue des Rudes. Jacques, this is Adam McCleet."

"Of course he eez," Jacques said, never bothering to take his eyes off Alison or offer his hand in greeting. "You have zee reum in Taos, mon cher Aleezon?"

"Sadly not," Alison said, nibbling at her burrito. "We'll be staying at a friend's house outside of town."

I just about had my lips around my own burrito when Jacques grabbed me by the arm and said, "Mais non! Why eez zees? You are keeping her to yourself? You fear zee competition, no?

"No." I bantered as burrito grease dripped onto the front of my "Rob Me—I'm A Tourist" T-shirt.

Alison explained, "Adam's sister has offered the hospitality of her hacienda at Mesa Rana—"

"Rana means Frog in Spanish." I emphasized frog. "You wouldn't like it."

Come to think of it, I wasn't sure if I was going to like it. The downside of this trip was that I'd waited so long to make up my mind about coming, that all of the inns, hotels and motels in or around Taos were booked. As fate would have it however, my over-bearing sibling, Margot The Malignant, needed someone to check out this piece of property that she'd taken away from ex-husband number something or other in a divorce settlement.

Margot had never visited the ranch, but she had a stack of color photos of the Spanish-style hacienda. It looked like the Nixon estate in San Clemente, white stucco and red terra-cotta everywhere, about four thousand square feet of main house. Alison fell in love with the place, so my rule about never involving myself in anything having to do with Margot carried little or no weight. It wasn't just that I didn't like Margot, which I didn't. Over a period of more than forty years, I had compiled sufficient data to prove that wherever Margot McCleet-Zarabi-Hammer-schmidt-Luciano-Stang sailed, pain and heartache roiled in her wake.

Since Alison and Jacques had begun to chatter in French, I decided it would be safe to have a bite of my lunch. But before I could get a taste, Jacques asked, "McCleet? Zees name is known to me. Zees sister of yours? Her first name eez . . ."

"Margot," I said. "Margot McCleet Stang."

"Oy vay," Jacques exclaimed, slapping his forehead, "I know zees femme. Monsieur, you have my deepest sympathy."

"Thank you," I said and bit a substantial chunk out of the burrito. It was hot—spicy hot—just the way I like 'em. As I chewed, I thought that it was possibly a little hotter than I expected.

"Delicious," Alison said as she finished the last of her burrito. "How's yours, Adam?"

"Delicious," I wheezed, fighting back a tear. "Could I have a glass of that wine, please?"

I wouldn't have minded telling Alison that the burrito was unquestionably the hottest fucking thing I'd ever put inside my head in my entire life. She'd seen me make a fool of myself plenty of times and loved me in spite of it all. But the Frenchman was a snob of the highest order and I wouldn't give him the satisfaction of hearing me whimper.

"Not too hot is it?" Alison said as she handed me the wine.

"Oh, no," I said. I tried to remain calm, but my hand was trembling as I took the wineglass from her. I was afraid I'd spill it on myself before I got the glass to my mouth. I poured the cool liquid over my tongue as quickly as possible without looking too obvious.

"You like?" Jacques asked. "Theez wine, eet eez très expensive but worth every franc. An amusing little Bordeaux with a slightly fruity bouquet, no?"

"More," I gasped as I tore the glass from his hand and gulped it.

Instead of quenching the fire, the wine acted like a combustion accelerator. The inside of my mouth turned into a blast furnace. I looked cross-eyed at my nostrils to see if steam was coming out.

Jacques cradled the bottle protectively. "I think maybe you like thees wine too much."

My attempt at sophistication ended in mind-numbing panic. Rivulets of sweat dripped off my brow. If I didn't extinguish the inferno, I was going to die. "Ambulance," I croaked.

"Calm down, Adam." Alison tried to reason with me. "Nobody ever died from eating a burrito."

What did she know? "Nine-one-one."

"Adam, please stop."

I grabbed the neck of the bottle and lifted Jacques off his feet.

He struggled, kicking his feet inches off the floor. "Monsieur, s'il vous plâit, thees wine, it must be savored."

I wrenched the bottle from his hands, upended it and glugged until the wine was gone. I took a deep breath and exhaled slowly. I could feel my face again. The back of my throat was as raw as an underwear commercial in France, but the fire was out.

"You peeg!" Jacques screamed. "Thees was an 1891 Bordeaux."

"Eighteen ninety-one?" I reached into my pocket for a twenty and handed it to him. "No problemo. Keep the change."

"Adam," Alison said. "I think we should be going now."

She took my arm and guided me out of the Sundog Gallery.

"Second turn on the right and straight on 'til Mornin'." Tobacco juice dripped from the old man's leathery lips and ran ran down his stubbled chin as he stared into the passenger-side window of our rented New Yorker and barked the instructions at Alison. She turned to me with a look in her green eyes that said: Help me.

"You had to ask," I said. We had followed the instructions Margot had given us, as best we could, but after making four consecutive left-hand turns, I was certain that she'd screwed me up again. I planned to initiate an expanding radius search pattern until we found a geological formation that resembled a frog with the Nixon estate mounted on top, but Alison had another idea.

She held out her map toward the old timer. "But there is no Morning on this map."

He didn't spare a glance for the neatly folded colored paper in Alison's hand. He wiped his chin with the back of his dusty jacket sleeve, spat a stream of black juice at the ground and wiped his chin again. "Just 'cause Rand MacNally don't know where it is, don't mean it ain't there. The trouble with maps is, you got to know where you are if you want to figure out how to get anywhere."

I leaned across Alison and asked, "Once we get to Morning, how do we find Mesa Rana?"

The old guy raised his bushy gray eyebrows. Though his clothing had the disheveled look of a derelict, his blue eyes were bright and alert. He was no fool. "It's too confusin' to try to tell you from here," he snapped. "You'll just get yourselves lost again."

"We're not lost," I informed him.

He spat again and said, "Then I guess we don't need to be havin' this conversation." He tugged at the rope lead to his heavily loaded burro, which had been patiently nibbling at the dried grass on the side of the road. "Let's go, Laddie. We ain't needed here. You folks have a nice drive."

"Wait," Alison said, "we are lost. Where do we go from Morning?"

"You're the smart one, ain't you?"

Alison answered too quickly. "Yes."

Though I couldn't see her face as she looked up at him, I'd have bet a trip to Disneyland that she smiled and winked at the old fart.

His cackle turned into a squawk that sounded like a buzzard claiming fresh road-kill. Once he'd regained his composure and wiped the tears from his eyes, he pointed to the north and said, "When you get to Mornin', you go to Stoker's Feed and Seed. You can't miss it. You go inside and find the biggest, stupidest lookin' man in there. That'll be Melvin Stoker. The big stupid lookin' woman standing next to him, doin' all the talking, will be his wife, Nelda. You tell 'em that Dental said they should take you to Frog Mesa. You'll probably have to give Nelda a couple of bucks for gas, but she'll have stupid Melvin lead you there." He spat again.

Alison thanked him then turned to me. "Give him some money, Adam," she whispered.

I reached for my wallet, but Dental said, "I won't take your money. Save it for Nelda. You'll need it."

I pulled away slowly so as not to stir a cloud of dust around Dental and his burro, Laddie. "Do you see why I don't like to ask directions from strangers," I said to Alison.

"No. Not really."

"Second turn on the right? Straight on until Morning? Those are the instructions on how to get to Never-Never Land." I quoted, "Second star on the right and straight on 'til Morning. Doesn't that seem strange to you?"

"At least he didn't tell us to say hi to Peter and the lost boys," she said. "And you're a fine one to talk about strange after your performance in the gallery. You shotgunned a five-hundred-dollar bottle of Bordeaux. The only way it could have been worse would be if you'd offered him twenty dollars for it. And you did. So, please don't talk to me about strange."

As we approached the second intersection, a sign read: Morning Next Right. I switched on the turn indicator a full five seconds before Alison said, "Turn here."

We covered the next three miles of unimproved road in relative quiet. Alison had fallen silent under the spell of a lingering Kodachrome sunset.

I fiddled with the static on the radio, but before I heard an intelligent word, a group of signs came into view at the crest of a small rise in the road. The first sign warned: Stop Ahead. The second sign spoke volumes in a few words—Welcome to Morning, Population: Yes. If the third sign had been shot full of any more bullet holes, it could have been a basketball hoop, but the octagonal shape and the fact that it was positioned at a three-way intersection said, Stop, to me. So I did.

Alison came to life. "There it is," she chirped, pointing out the feed store a few seconds after I'd spotted it.

"The crusty old guy was right," I said. "We couldn't miss it."

The building was a large, one-story box of turquoise stucco patches plastered over more mismatched shades of green and aqua stucco patches. The words, Stoker's Feed and Seed, were hand-painted in white, block letters over the double door. A rusting yellow school bus, equipped with a tin smokestack and cinderblocks where the wheels should have been, protruded from the near side of the feed store—as if it had crashed through the old building, and the inhabitants of Morning had simply decided to leave it there. On the side of the bus, crude cursive lettering spelled Espresso, in green spray-paint.

There was one other permanent structure. A single, defunct gas pump stood in front of a smaller stucco building bearing a hand-lettered sign of its own, Morning Cafe-Tavern and Jail. Five mobile homes, each equipped with large piles of rusting refuse and barking dogs, were scattered around the central business district. I felt like we'd just driven onto the set of a cheap spaghetti Western. Not _The Good, the Bad and the Ugly._ More like, _The Old, the Neglected, and the Funky._

Alison cleared her throat. "This is very—"

"Please don't say quaint."

"Weird, is much closer to what I had in mind," Alison said as we climbed out of the New Yorker, which now looked as sleek and futuristic as a lunar lander in a Yugo factory.

I followed Alison into the Feed and Seed, watching the motion of her hips, swaying seductively under her long black and turquoise skirt. Her back view was always a treat, even now as she strode recklessly into the very heart of weirdness.

Inside the Feed and Seed, I heard Nelda before I saw the woman. Her voice was loud, twangy and incessant.

"Well, look here, I do believe we have a couple of strangers, come all the way to Morning. Now what can we get for y'all? How's about a cappuccino? Or a nice tall iced latte with some Nestlé's syrup to sweeten the milk? It's two percent."

She paused for breath and Alison said, "You must be Nelda."

"Aren't you the cutest little thing! Just a little ol' ladybug. A tiny, itsy-bitsy—"

When I saw Nelda, an event I likened to Ishmael sighting the great white whale, I knew why she made such a big fuss about size. Everything must seem small to this woman. She stood at least as tall as me, about six feet, two inches. She was broad-shouldered as a linebacker. Tucked into her long denim skirt was a flowing, white muslin blouse with a loose neck. Her breasts were the size of basketballs. From the neck down, I wanted to sculpt the woman. She had the shape and form of Mother Earth. From the neck up, she was moon-faced with tiny close-set eyes and a broad, cavernous mouth that never stopped flapping. "—how'd y'all figure out I was Nelda, huh? Are you one of them psychics?"

"We met a man on the road," Alison said quickly. "His name was Dental."

"That old fart is all over the place, popping up from behind the mesquite at the darndest times." She yelled over her shoulder, "Hey, Melvin! These folks were talking to your daddy."

His daddy? I digested the news of that relationship slowly. Dental had referred to his own seed as big and stupid. The man was either incredibly cruel or firmly convinced. After a few minutes with his daughter-in-law I began to suspect the latter.

I looked toward Melvin—another large person with thinning strands of hair plastered across the top of his head. He didn't bother to interrupt his wife to greet us.

And she continued to talk about the weather, the water table and the delights of living in a big city as compared to Morning. Her words faded to a monotone "blah-blah-blah" in my head.

Melvin leaned across the countertop, lifted his big hand and waved. Then he went back to his whittling. I knew right away that this was more than a hobby because the display case nearest the door held a crowded display of Genuine, Hand-Made Kachina Dolls. No doubt these crudely whacked bits of wood that had been spray-painted white then scrawled with little faces were Melvin's work. Several of the kachinas had Nelda's features, and I wondered if he occasionally took them out and stuck pins in them. Or taped their mouths closed.

In addition to the dolls, the Stoker Feed and Seed store offered shelves full of dusty souvenirs welcoming tourists to New Mexico. There were also T-shirts, canned goods, baseball caps, fishing tackle, a cooler, hunting knives, plumbing supplies and candy bars, also dusty. I didn't see anything that resembled seed or feed.

Alison was being taken on the grand tour by Nelda, and I just stood there, nearly as big and stupid as Melvin. I walked around a circular barrel that held a huge supply of tenpenny nails and joined him at the counter. "We're looking for Mesa Rana," I said.

"Why?"

"The hacienda there belongs to my sister, Margot," I explained. "We're staying there for a week or so."

"Why?"

"Art show in Taos."

Apparently that satisfied him because he nodded. "Okay. I'll take you there. Going to cost you twenty dollars."

I'd been told that people in this part of the country liked to barter. "Five," I said.

"Eighteen." His blue eyes glittered with a spark of the intelligence I'd noticed in Dental, his father. "You'll never find it by yourself."

"Six bucks," I said. "I figure it's a deal to get you out of the store for an hour."

"But I'm fixing to close the store in five minutes. So, it'll be seventeen to you, stranger."

After more cagey haggling on my part, I had the price of the trip down to ten dollars and seventy-five cents.

Nelda and Alison came to the counter. She zipped open her little purse, took out a twenty and a five and slid the bills toward Melvin. "This should cover our trip to Mesa Rana."

"Just so," he said, pocketing her money and grinning at me.

Nelda was bustling toward the door, with a "Closed" sign in her hand. "I think we're going to be shutting down the store for the night, Melvin. It's been a real long day. I don't think I remember a day that was so blah-blah-blah."

When Alison and I stepped out on the attached porch that ran the length of the boxlike structure, the weirdness had not gone away, but it was more natural out here. The display of sunset colors continued, lingering in the desert air.

I've always been a water person. My studio in Portland is on the banks of the Willamette River, and my favorite recreation is sailing. Being in the high plains of New Mexico felt like a visit to another planet. Therefore, I wasn't surprised when two people seemed to materialize from nowhere, walking from opposite sides of the mesquite-dotted landscape to meet in front of us.

One of them wore shoulder-length hair and a flowing robe that appeared to be made from a flowered sheet. Riding low on his hips was a hand-tooled belt and holster that looked like they came straight out of the Old West.

The other wore blue jeans and a brown uniform shirt with a silver star pinned over the pocket and a police belt rigged with a holster. An official of some sort, maybe the guard from the Morning Cafe-Tavern and Jail. As the twosome turned and came toward us, I could see that the uniformed person was a woman with her hair tucked up inside her wide-brimmed Stetson.

The robed individual, darkly tanned as any southern California beach bum, raised his hand and spoke in a voice that could only be described as mellow, "I knew you'd come. I am Robinson Crusoe." He nodded toward the woman. "And this is—"

"Let me guess," I said. "Your girl Friday?"

Her right hand gripped the heft of her six-shooter. Though the gun stayed in the holster, she leveled a dark-eyed glare in the direction of my lower torso that made me want to protect my groin. "Never call me girl."

Not much of a sense of humor.

"He didn't mean any offense," Alison said.

Her tone implied that she spent the better part of her life apologizing for my moronic behavior. I hated when she referred to me as "he" when I was standing right next to her.

"Really," she said. "I'm sure he was just trying to make a little joke."

"Well, it's not funny," the woman said. Still, she let her hand fall away from the gun. "I'm Shirley Gomez-Gomez with a hyphen."

If I'd been armed, I would have snickered. But I held my smirk inside.

Alison said, "What an interesting name."

"Both my parents were Gomez," she said. "I'm the sheriff around here, plus I own the Cafe-Tavern."

"With a hyphen," I said.

The sheriff eyed me another contemptuous glare. I wondered if levity had been outlawed in Morning.

"What's your business around here?" she demanded as if we were some kind of nefarious characters instead of the most normal-looking individuals within twenty miles.

Alison ran through our introductions. "We're going to be staying at Margot Stang's hacienda. She's Adam's sister."

Gomez-Gomez stuck out her chin. "You got some ID?"

A little bit of her attitude went a long way, and I was tired of being treated like a criminal. "Tell you what, Sheriff. We promise not to shoplift or jaywalk while we're in Morning, if you'll back off. Lighten up."

Her dark eyes flashed and she unleashed a rapid-fire burst of Spanish. My comprehension of the language was pretty much limited to the menu at Taco Bell, but I managed to pick out a few choice phrases that might have translated to something about the son of a coyote dog or Charo's brother. I think she said that I had spicy _cojones,_ that meant balls. Or tiny _cojones._ That seemed more likely.

She slapped her holster and marched stiff-legged toward the Cafe-Tavern and Jail.

Her robed companion shook his head as he watched her go. "Seems that you've made an enemy, Adam."

I shrugged. Why stop with Gomez-Gomez? I might as well offend Robinson Crusoe as well. "So," I said, "what's with the sheet?"

He laughed. "Simple dress does not always indicate a simple

mind. My people choose to discard the accessories of main-stream society that impede inner cognition."

"Hmmm," I said. I had already noted that he wore leather boots and Levi's under his sheet. Apparently, those didn't count as accessories. "Your people? You mean, your family?"

"In a way, yes."

All through this conversation, he continued to smile pleasantly, and his bland spirits were beginning to annoy me. I couldn't decide if he was the idiot older son of some otherwise normal Crusoe family or if he belonged to some lunatic cult that had taken up residence in Margot's backyard. "And who are your people?"

"There is no label for us. We exist as a symbol."

"Like the artist formerly known as Prince?"

Melvin stomped out onto the porch beside me. "I'll bring my truck around and you follow me." He nodded to the sheeted one. "Hey, Rob. How's it going?"

He inclined his head and thought for a moment, then said, "Excellently well."

"That's good." He ambled down the step toward an incredibly beat-up truck.

"I sense," Rob said, "that you will be receptive to my offer, Adam."

"And what offer is that?" I asked. Had I missed a step?

"My people wish to purchase the land that belongs to your sister." He bowed, traced a figure eight in the air with his finger and stepped back. "Adam, let's do lunch."

Suddenly, I understood Robinson Crusoe's particular brand of weird. "You're from Los Angeles," I said.

"Of course," he said as he drifted toward the Cafe-Tavern and Jail. "I'll see you tomorrow."

Under my breath, I muttered to Alison, "Tomorrow, let's call around for a motel room. This place is too damn strange."

"Adam, you're an artist. I'd expect you to be more tolerant of unusual behavior."

I slid behind the steering wheel and followed Melvin's cloud of dust. Her reasoning made sense. Most artists operated in a separate time zone, some sort of creative hyperspace. But I was different. I wasn't born with a silver sculptor's chisel in my mouth, hadn't gone to school to learn technique, hadn't spent a lot of time in trendy cafes discussing theory. During the very early seventies, when most artistic types were growing long hair and beards, I was a Marine in Vietnam. I followed up that background with a fifteen-year stint as a cop on the Portland PD. When it comes time for reckoning who's weird and who's not, I stand solidly on the side of "not."

The sunset left fading streaks in the dusky skies as we trailed Melvin down a road that wasn't much more than a path. It was looking to me like Margot's promise that the hacienda would be well cared for was a pipe dream. She'd promised strawberries and champagne. I figured we'd be lucky to get peanut butter and running water.

After a brief ride, less than two miles but slow, we bounced across a ravine and inched along a graded driveway that was at least sixty-percent pothole. At the end loomed the sprawling outline of Margot's hacienda. Totally dark.

"I hope there's electricity," Alison said.

"Gosh, that would be neat. I hope there's a bed."

Melvin was out of his truck and waiting when I parked beside him. Taciturnly, he plodded toward the arched entryway.

I had to admit that the exterior was promising. Though night was settling, the white stucco seemed in fairly good repair.

When Melvin pushed open the front door, he turned on a light. The tiled entryway was swept. On either side of the door were large earthenware pots holding bright red and violet blooms of bougainvillea. The flowers were plastic.

I looked at Melvin. "You have a key?"

He placed it in my hand.

"Why?" I asked.

"There's an Indian who takes care of the place. He kept losing the key and having to break in. So, Nelda and I hold onto the key for him."

That was the longest sustained speech I'd heard from Melvin. Since he seemed to be the sanest person in Morning, I encouraged him to continue while Alison bounded through the door and entered the hacienda. "How come this caretaker kept losing the key?"

Melvin pantomimed drinking from a bottle. I guessed that he was done talking.

I asked, "Does this guy live in the hacienda?"

Melvin pointed toward the dark, angular outline of a trailer, about a hundred yards from the entry. "Over there."

From inside the house, Alison was exclaiming delightedly. Oohing and ahing as if she were on tour of the Sistine Chapel.

I asked Melvin, "Does this caretaker have a name?"

"Whiney."

"Because he drinks a lot?"

"His Indian name is Hokanto Pos Quanto Yoyo Ma."

"Yeah?"

Melvin smiled. "It translates to Whines For No Reason."

Alison reappeared in the entryway, grabbed my arm and dragged me inside. "Adam, this place is wonderful!"

Melvin waved good-bye and disappeared into the darkness as I was sucked into the interior of Margot's desert home. The architectural design of the living room was unusual, using the stucco and adobe in a flowing whirlpool with curved arches above every door. Even the ceiling was arched. There were rounded fireplaces in two corners. I couldn't spot a right angle in the place. The walls in the living room were painted a rosy color. It felt like walking into a womb.

The furniture was, appropriately, all pillows and rugs in

Southwestern designs, and the place looked fairly clean. Apparently, Whines For No Reason took his job seriously. "I'm surprised," I admitted.

The kitchen was huge, as large as the living room. Though the appliances were an unfortunate shade of olive green, the white walls appeared to be relatively free from grease and grime. Inside the refrigerator was a six-pack of beer, a four-pack of bottled Perrier, an extra large package of bologna, tortillas, bottled salsa, cheese and eggs. "I'm impressed," I said.

"There's more," she said, leading me through a narrow, tunnel-like passageway.

I should have ducked when I entered the passage, but I didn't and I whacked my forehead hard enough to see a couple of stars. This place must have belonged to one of Margot's shorter husbands. I wished that I could recall which one. There had been five, and one of her marriages only lasted a few weeks before the man came to his senses, realized that he'd wedded a harpy, and hurled himself through a seventeenth-story window.

The first thing I saw in the bedroom was a giant scorpion. It was the granddaddy of all scorpions, six feet tall and painted on the white wall. Other critters danced around it in a spiral.

Alison stared at the wall with rapt attention. "Excellent display of primitive art," she said. "Just excellent."

It wasn't my taste, but Alison knew more about painting than I did. She had done the whole educational, philosophical thing before inheriting Brooks Gallery from her father. Fortunately, when she took over the running of the gallery, her business sense emerged with a vengeance. She made art profitable, which was no mean feat in this day and age of slashed funds, the heritage of Newt's Congress.

I almost looked forward to the times, like now, when her artistic sensibilities became evident. Her green eyes sparkled with appreciation. As she whirled and raced toward the bedroom door, her shoulder-length auburn hair danced with a vitality that was matched by her graceful gestures.

"Every bedroom has a mural," she said. "Not all scorpions, of course. There's a sunrise landscape with cactus. And a ritual dance of some sort. And a huge flower, not a Georgia O'Keefe style, but splintered, as if you're looking through a kaleidoscope. Adam, this place is a living gallery."

She was all the art I wanted. "I'll see them in the morning."

Instantly, her excitement turned smoky and hot. I knew that good art turned her on. "Before we make love," she murmured, "tell me that I did the right thing in coming here."

When she rubbed up against me, I would have told her anything. "You always do the right thing, Alison. You're brilliant."

"Even when I make you stop to ask directions?" She stroked my cheek, teased the lobe of my ear with her fingernail.

"Even when you treat me like a senile old coot."

"Senile, maybe. But you're not that much older than I am."

Eight years was a long time, and lately I'd been feeling every minute of our age difference as I pushed at the gateway to midlife. My rising hard-on reminded me that I wasn't quite dead yet. "I feel eighteen," I said.

"And randy as hell," she murmured, placing my hand on her beautifully rounded breast.

We collapsed onto the bed and made love in the intense silence of a windless desert night.

Afterwards, I slept heavily, wakening to a squawky noise and Alison punching my rib cage. "Adam," she said. "Adam, there's something out there."

"It'll go away." I rolled over.

"Go see what it is." She snuggled up against me and punched again.

"Ow! Stop that!"

"Come on, Adam. There's something out there."

I listened. It sounded like a rusty hinge on a gate, squeaking and squawking.

Alison dug her sharp little fingernails into my side and complained, "I can't sleep with that noise."

I could have slept. But she wouldn't let me. If Alison was being kept awake, I would be kept awake. Groaning, I dragged myself out of the bed, pulled on my Levi's and loafers and my shirt, which I left unbuttoned.

I staggered out of the bedroom, clunked my forehead on the low ceiling of the tunnel hallway and trudged through the hacienda's front womb to the entryway. I'd made the mistake of turning on lights and I was blinded by the electric glare as I stared out into the black New Mexico night.

Outside, the noise was louder. And it was chilly. From what I understand, high plains deserts are like that. The sun goes down and the heat goes off. I shivered and stumbled in the direction of the noise.

There were an amazing number of stars overhead, but they seemed to shed very little light. The moon was a sliver. I hobbled toward the noise and recognized the source.

"Laddie?" I stared at the burro that had belonged to the old man, Dental, who directed us straight on 'til Morning. "What the hell are you doing out here, Laddie?"

The beast made a squeaky hinge noise, so I continued our conversation. "Hey, Laddie, where's Dental?"

I could have sworn that the animal said, "Dental? Who the hell is that?" But I wasn't sure because the next thing I was aware of was a swish of air on the nape of my neck and a hard thump on the back of my head. I'd been whacked on the head enough times to be familiar with the procedure for brain concussion. The stars swirled, then blurred. My knees buckled. I swooned, then recovered. My knees buckled again. I was falling, almost uncon-scious, I stuck out my arms out to brace myself, but the ground went away. I landed in a heap. Say good-night, Adam.

Blackness filled the inside of my head as I muttered, " 'night."

Chapter
Two

I was drooling. My tongue was glued to the roof of my mouth, but when I swallowed, there was no saliva, only the grit of a dirt sandwich that went down hard as sandpaper on the walls of my gullet.

I sucked in enough air to jump start my brain. My nostrils burned with the stench of shit, sweat, blood and dirt. I groaned, not wanting to puke. More than anything, I didn't want to go through the agony of coughing up a dirtball. When I tried to move, intense pain radiated from the base of my skull and wrapped around my head like a blanket of nails.

My eyelids peeled open, and I realized it was dawn. I blinked through a veil of dry New Mexico soil and stared at a wall of dirt.

Under my nose were a pair of battered boots, coated with dust, muddy with dew. Inside the boots were feet. Attached to the feet, legs. I was lying on top of someone, and it wasn't Alison.

"Oh, shit!"

I grabbed at something firm and smooth, a handle of sorts,

and used it to leverage myself up and out of the shallow grave.

On my hands and knees, I found myself staring into the brown eyes of Laddie the burro. Last night, I remembered having a brief conversation with the animal, who seemed none the worse for wear.

Reluctantly, I peered down into the hole, knowing what I was going to see. Dental Stoker lay stiff with rigor mortis. His gnarled fists were clenched. His body had collapsed inside his clothes. His face was covered by his beat-up cowboy hat and dried blood marked the filthy white of his long-sleeved thermal underwear shirt. He was undeniably dead. Much as I hated to, I needed to contact Sheriff Gomez-Gomez right away.

With a labored moan, I stood upright, leaning heavily on the wooden handle I'd found in the grave. It was a pickaxe, and the business end was smeared with the sticky residue of drying blood.

I staggered into the house, discarding the pickaxe at the patio door, and went to the nearest phone. It was dead, of course. No one really lived here, so the phones weren't operational. This meant I would to have to drive into Morning and get the sheriff.

As I fumbled toward the bedroom, I realized that I couldn't greet Alison looking like I'd just climbed out of a grave. And I sure as hell couldn't pop in at the Cafe-Tavern and Jail like this.

I headed toward the shower, tearing off my clothes as I went, and turned on the faucet. The shower worked surprisingly well, and I stepped into a hard, hot pulsing spray. It felt good, chasing the chill out of my bones. I wanted to stay longer, but there was a dead man in my backyard and, therefore, a certain need for urgency.

The bathroom door swung open just as I turned off the water.

"Buenos días, Señor McCleet." The harsh female voice of the Señorita Sheriff Gomez-Gomez echoed off the bathroom tiles.

I had wanted to see her, but not just yet.

_____

Nonchalantly, I grabbed a fluffy pink towel and wrapped it around my waist. "Sheriff," I said. "There's a—"

"Move slowly, McCleet. Keep your hands where I can see them."

I didn't know exactly what she expected me to do with only a towel for a weapon, but she kept her heavy-duty pistola aimed directly at my crotch as she said, "You are under arrest."

"What are the charges?" I asked.

"Murder."

"Wait a minute." I shook my head, aggravating an excruciating headache. Quietly, I said, "Why are you here? What's going on?"

"I came this morning to investigate."

"Investigate what?"

"Holes. People keep digging holes on this property."

It was a typically weird form of Morning vandalism, but the gun pointed at my private parts kept me from commenting on the aberrant behavior of the natives. "And?"

"I saw Laddie. I saw Dental Stoker, dead."

So far, so good. The sheriff and I were on the same track. There was only one difference of opinion. I asked, "Why would you assume I killed him?"

"When I came to the door, your girlfriend answered. She said you weren't in bed last night, that you had gone to check on a noise. I saw the bloody pickaxe. I followed the trail of bloody clothing. To here."

I had to admit that she had grounds for suspicion. Still, I tried to explain, "This isn't what it looks like."

I told her my side of the story, but she already had the scenario figured out, and she didn't want to hear my part of it.

"Adam, what's going on?"

When I heard Alison's voice, I felt somewhat reassured. Much as I seem to have the innate ability to piss off authority figures, Alison is a natural-born soothing influence. She could tactfully explain to the sheriff that I was basically harmless.

She stepped into the bathroom, I felt a familiar warmth. Everything was going to be okay. Gomez-Gomez would see the error of her ways, and I would be free to take Alison to Taos where I would become internationally famous.

Alison glared at the sheriff and repeated, "What the hell is going on?"

"I'm arresting him. The charge is murder."

"Murder?" Alison pulled together the gaping front of her black silk kimono. She was visibly shocked. "Who's been killed?"

"Dental Stoker," I said.

"That old man we spoke to on the road yesterday? He seemed so harmless. Who would want to kill him?"

"Looks to me like your boyfriend did it," the sheriff said.

"Don't be an idiot," Alison said. "Adam used to be a cop. He's one of the good guys. He didn't kill anybody."

"But the evidence—"

"Damn the evidence." Alison took my hand. "Adam, come into the bedroom and get dressed."

"Stop!" Gomez-Gomez snapped. "I'll give the orders around here."

Alison and I looked at her expectantly.

"McCleet," she said. "Go into the bedroom and get dressed."

Both women followed me into the bedroom and stood there watching as I rummaged in my suitcase for a fresh shirt. I wanted to ask them to turn around, but I was afraid that I'd sound like Alison's maiden aunt from Walla-Walla.

In a no-nonsense tone, Alison demanded, "Now, Sheriff, why on earth would you suspect Adam of murder?"

"Dead man in a shallow grave. Bloody murder weapon. Trail of blood leading to your boyfriend's shower," Gomez-Gomez said. "This is an open-and-shut case."

"And I suppose you've had a lot of experience with murder investigations," Alison said sarcastically. "I'll bet Morning is a real hotbed of crime."

"I can handle this."

While they bickered, I yanked on my Jockeys and jeans. I turned around, buttoning my shirt and saw Shirley Gomez-Gomez scowl at me. Clearly, the feminist sheriff was not impressed by the firmness of my bare ass. She said, "Let's go, McCleet."

I didn't see any percentage in refusing to cooperate. She had the gun.

We trooped through the house and out the door. The sunrise had become morning and I could already feel the heat rising in waves as we left the shadow of the house and walked into the sunlight.

"You can't do this," Alison protested. "We have to be in Taos."

"Are you telling me how to do my job?"

"Perhaps someone should. That poor old man has been murdered, and you're wasting your time with us."

I cringed. Where was the famous Alison Brooks charm? Instead of gently persuading the sheriff, Alison was coming after her with a sledgehammer.

Evilly, Gomez-Gomez said, "I think maybe, Ms. Brooks, you are an accessory to murder."

"Don't be absurd."

"McCleet. Brooks. Both of you turn around," the sheriff ordered.

"Why?" Alison demanded.

"I'm arresting you. Both of you. Now, turn around."

When we didn't move, she punctuated with a blast from her pistol. The dirt at our feet sprayed up. I grabbed Alison and turned her.

"Hands behind your backs," said the sheriff.

"Do it," I told Alison. It didn't take a rocket scientist to figure out that Ms. Sheriff was plenty mad, and I really didn't want to see her use force on Alison.

While the handcuffs pinched onto my wrists and Alison rattled off a few choice threats about false arrest and harrassment and F. Lee Bailey, I stared past the foxhole where Dental lay. Last night, in the dark, I hadn't appreciated the surreal aspect of the lands surrounding the hacienda. The primary landmark was a fat stand of rock that must have been Mesa Rana. I tried to imagine a frog in the formation and failed, unless the frog was lying on its back and had wings. Across the mesquite-covered land leading up to the mesa were dozens of holes like the one that contained Dental. The land was pockmarked. If Dental had been prospecting here, it was an odd method.

Gomez-Gomez directed us to her vehicle, a sleek-looking white Lumina with police lights mounted on the roof. None too gently, she pushed us inside.

Alison's lovely face was red with fury. The front of her kimono hung open, revealing a flimsy black nightgown with lace across her perfect breasts. "I can't believe this," she muttered.

"I can." The fact that my sister, Margot the Malevolent, owned this place was enough for me to believe the hacienda was irreparably cursed. I turned to Alison. "This might not be the best time to mention it, but I actually did remind you, yesterday, about the problems I seem to have when Margot is involved in my life. I remember that I told—"

"Don't say it. Don't you dare say that you told me so."

"Okay." I knew when to quit.

"Now what?" she demanded.

"We go to jail, directly to jail."

The interior of the Cafe-Tavern and Jail was predictably crude. I didn't mind the decor at all. There was something friendly about this style, which was best described as Vintage K-Mart.

Gomez-hyphen-Gomez hustled us through a large square room with plastic booths, formica tables and plastic posies in beer-bottle vases. The only customer was a small, gnomelike man with a dirty white beard and a battered hat. Uninterested in our dramatic entrance, he sipped his coffee and turned another page in the book he was reading.

The sheriff directed us past a long counter that doubled as a bar, and into the kitchen where a softer, more feminine sēnorita tended sizzling bacon on a grill. She looked up, raised her dark eyebrows and asked, "What's going on?"

"Dental Stoker is murdered," the sheriff informed her. "Go back to work, Consuela."

"Dental?" Consuela traced the sign of the cross on her gently rounded breasts. She was wearing a crucifix but not a bra. "Who are these people?"

"The killers."

"No," Alison said. "We are not. At best, we're suspects."

"Then you admit it," the sheriff said.

"Can't you get it through your thick head, you hyphenated bimbo!" I had never heard Alison so outraged. Maybe it was the handcuffs. "We didn't kill anybody. Why would we? We don't even know you people!"

Consuela's dark eyes widened, then she nodded sagely. "A psycho murderer. I've read about this sort of person in the _National Enquirer._"

The old man stuck his head into the kitchen. He held his book against his skinny chest, marking his place, and I could read the title: _The Joy of Quantum Physics_. "My bacon?" he said.

Ignoring the charring strips, Consuela went to him. Her full bosom heaved with compassion. "I am so sorry, Dr. Gunter, but I have sad news. Your friend, Dental Stoker, has been murdered."

"Oh." He shrugged and shuffled back into the other room.

Consuela and the sheriff exchanged a meaningful glance. Unfortunately, I couldn't guess at the meaning until I heard a crash from the restaurant portion of the Cafe-Tavern and Jail.

An ancient voice rattled against the thick adobe walls. "We must build him a funeral pyre. Light the way to Valhalla."

The sheriff and Consuela hurried into the cafe.

Gomez-Gomez reprimanded him like a mother talking down to a kid, "Dr. Gunter Bjornsen, you put down that chair. Right now!"

He ignored her, much as a kid ignores his mom.

From the kitchen doorway, Alison and I watched as Dr. Gunter Bjornsen worked to pile all the Formica tables and plastic-covered chairs in a stack in the center of the scarred linoleum floor. For such a small person, he was surprisingly strong.

"Valhalla!" Gunter shouted. "A hero's death deserves a hero's burial."

To Alison, I said, "He seems to be taking it well."

Again the sheriff asked him to stop.

Then, Consuela, wringing her hands, asked him to stop.

But the doctor was a perpetual-motion machine, shoving and stacking. The pyre was almost up to the ceiling. I wondered if he intended to torch the chairs. All that plastic and Formica would make a hell of a stench.

Gomez-Gomez stepped up to the doctor, who was barely as tall as she was. "For the last time," she said, "are you going to stop?"

"Never."

"Sorry, Doctor." When he turned his back on her, she pushed off his hat and conked him on the back of his head with the heft of her pistola.

The doctor set down the chair he was carrying, spun around and stared at the sheriff. He raised one finger, as if to make an important point. Then, he crumpled.

Consuela bustled toward him.

Gomez-Gomez hitched up her gunbelt and swaggered back to us. "Let's go," she said.

None too gently, she pushed us toward the rear of the kitchen. We went through a heavy wooden door. Using her key, she opened the door to the single jail cell and shoved us inside. The cell door slammed shut with the discordant clank of metal against metal.

Gomez-Gomez pivoted, apparently planning to leave us there while she dealt with the more immediate crisis in the other room.

"Sheriff," I said. "What about the cuffs?"

"What about them?" She slammed the heavy wooden door and left us behind thick iron bars.

There were three resting places in the cell, a single bed and a bunk bed. Alison sank down on the single. "I've never been in jail before."

"You get used to it," I informed her. "If I had the cuffs off and a harmonica I could make this place homey."

"Don't joke, Adam."

"Yeah, you're right. We should probably be weeping and moaning."

"We should probably be calling an attorney. Don't we get one phone call?"

"Supposing that there was a phone," I said, "who would you call?"

Alison thought for a moment, then said, "Margot."

I shuddered convulsively. "Why Margot? Isn't life rotten enough?"

"If anybody knows lawyers, Margot does."

Alison had a point. My sister's multitude of divorces had caused her to compile a fairly impressive list of attorneys nationwide. Besides, when all was said and done, I was sure that the blame for this whole fiasco would rest squarely upon Margot's fashionably padded shoulders. Somehow, I knew this was her fault.

"Okay," I said. "We call Margot, get sprung from Morning, and then . . . Can we go to Taos like sensible people?"

"Not until I find the artist who did the walls in the hacienda."

"What?"

"I think this person might be a major talent. Primitive, of course, but there's a purity and a—"

She halted. Her gaze riveted to the bunk bed on the opposite wall.

There was movement on the upper bunk. We weren't alone in the cell.

A big, round head appeared. The features were heavy. Long black hair tangled around his scrawny neck. His voice resonated with a particularly irritating nasal squawk. "Hold it down," he said, "I'm trying to sleep."

"Sorry," I said.

"I have such an ache in my head." He sat up, dangling his skinny legs over the edge of the bunk. "And my stomach hurts. I'm hungry. You wouldn't believe how miserable I am. You've probably never been sick a day in your life."

"Maybe one day," I said.

"You don't know how it is. I just want to die. My eyes itch. I wish I had my toothbrush. I'm so dirty. I really need to floss. Why doesn't anybody ever pay attention to me?"

I knew who he was. Meeting his gaze, I smiled. "You're the caretaker at the hacienda."

"How'd you know that? Who are you? I'm so tired. Why are you bothering me?"

"Alison," I said, "I'd like you to meet Whines For No Reason."

Chapter
Three

The Indian, Whiney, climbed cautiously from his top bunk. "Whenever I spend the night," he informed us, "I sleep on top. I have an allergy to dust."

He hobbled across the cell floor, sat, peeled off his moccasin and stuck his foot toward Alison. "Does that look like a tumor?"

"No," she said. "Are you really the caretaker at Mesa Rana?"

He twisted his foot around, trying to see the bottom of his heel. "It won't go away. I've had it for weeks, and it really, really hurts."

Alison made the mistake of paying slight attention. "Have you tried an antiseptic?"

"Have I ever!" He rolled his eyes. "Vitamin E and aloe and alcohol. Everything." He dropped his foot, grabbed his forehead and groaned. "Have you ever had one of those headaches that pound and pound? Well, this is ten times worse."

"Hangover?" I suggested.

Whiney was immediately defensive. "I have to drink. It's the only thing that takes my mind off my problems. I'm dying, you know."

"So are we all."

That was my benediction on the subject, but I doubted that my wisdom would stop his nasal-voiced complaining.

Alison tried to switch subjects. "Tell me about the hacienda. Do you know who painted the murals in the bedrooms?"

"Why?" His eyes narrowed suspiciously. "Who are you and why is it any of your business?"

"I'm Alison Brooks and this is Adam McCleet," Alison said with a polite formality that was totally out of place in a jail cell. "We're staying at the hacienda. Adam is Margot's brother."

"Margot," he said with a reverence that I found particularly disgusting, especially when applied to my sister.

"Miss Margot," he repeated, then frowned. "I work my fingers to the bone keeping that place clean and tidy, and does Miss Margot ever come to visit? No, she does not."

"But we're here," Alison said, "and we really appreciate your efforts. Don't we, Adam?"

They both looked at me expectantly. And Alison should have known better. I didn't care about Whiney's housekeeping skills. He could be a Picasso of the vacuum cleaner, and I wouldn't be impressed.

But I did have questions. "Out at the hacienda," I said, "there were a bunch of holes on the grounds."

"Margot can't blame me for that," Whiney said. "People are out there digging all the time. I can't watch the whole acreage twenty-four hours a day, can I?"

"What are they looking for? Buried treasure?"

"Nothing so simple." Whiney wheezed like an accordion, with a laugh that turned into a cough. "No treasure. Everybody around here—everybody but me—is searching for the answer to an ancient Indian legend, one of those Anasazi things."

"The what?"

"The Anasazi," Alison informed me. "They were a mysterious

tribe of Native Americans who completely vanished several hundred years ago. Anasazi legends are very New Age."

"That's probably why I haven't heard of them." Years ago, I had come to the conclusion that the quest for total enlightenment was very time-consuming, and not near as much fun as having a life. Though I try to keep an open mind, the only Shirley MacLaine-ish theory I can really embrace is: If you meet the Buddha on the road, kill him."

Alison continued, "Some people compare the disappearance of this advanced culture to the disappearance of Atlantis."

I glanced over at Whiney. "So, what's the legend? How come people are digging holes?"

"They seek Tonna-Hokay-Pokay-Lawnchair-Yada-Yada."

"Could you be a little more specific."

"He Who Shines At Night." Whiney pulled a ragged television schedule from his hip pocket and asked, "What day is it?"

"Tuesday," Alison said.

He consulted the schedule and wailed, "I missed the Laverne and Shirley retrospective."

"You must watch a lot of TV," I said. He probably watched so much that he couldn't separate fact from fiction in his alcohol-soaked brain.

"I don't have a TV," he moaned. "It's broken."

"Why carry a television schedule?" Alison asked.

"I have to. How would I keep track of what I'm missing if I—"

"That's very resourceful," I said. "Tell us more about the legend of Glows In The Dark."

"Shines At Night," Whiney corrected.

"Whatever. Who's digging all those holes?"

"Rob Crusoe and his no-names are the worst," Whiney said. "They creep around with their shovels hidden under those sheets they wear, and they dig. I've asked them not to. Even told the sheriff, but she doesn't do anything. Nobody ever pays attention to me. Besides, I think she's sweet on Crusoe."

I encouraged him to gossip. "Why's that?"

"All the chicks are. It's his hair, you know." Whiney picked up a lank end of his own tresses and held them in front of his eyes, staring cross-eyed. He sobbed, "I have split ends."

"You poor dear," said Alison. "Listen, Mr. Whines For No Reason." She paused. "Is that your real name?"

"Whiney will do."

"Whiney," she said, "I own an art gallery."

"Who doesn't?" He mumbled under his breath about Taos and the intrusion of artists. "Taking over everything, that's what they're doing. First, it was the Mexicans. Then, the artists. Then, the sisters. It all belongs to my people, you know. I'm Pueblo Indian, born on the res. I should own the hacienda, not just take care of it. If I wasn't such an even tempered person, I'd be—"

"Stop!" Alison interrupted. "Did you do those paintings?"

"I think I'm going to throw up."

"Me, too." She looked at me and whispered, "I really hope it wasn't him. I can handle most people, but this guy?"

"Let Monte take care of him," I said. Pure evil caused me to suggest this pairing. Monte, Alison's assistant at the Brooks Gallery in Portland, was the most flamboyant individual I've ever known, also the fussiest. He was one of those guys who never belch. Monte didn't sweat, he got moist. And he had accompanied us to Taos.

I figured that Whines For No Reason would drive him crazy with grotesque imagery of tumors, phlegm and loose stools. Maybe Monte didn't deserve being saddled with the Native American crown prince of hypochondria. But, after the morning I'd had, I felt like spreading the grief around.

The heavy jail door crashed open. Consuela and Gomez-Gomez marched through. "Ms. Brooks can go," the sheriff announced. "But you stay McCleet. I'm not turning a murderer loose."

Whiney squeaked, "Murderer? He's a murderer?"

While Consuela unfastened our handcuffs, Gomez-Gomez helped the barely conscious Gunter Bjornsen to the lower bunk and laid him down.

Whiney hopped back and forth on one foot and the other. He whined, predictably. "You can't leave me locked up with a murderer. He might hurt me. Please, Sheriff, please let me go."

"Go," she said.

Whiney grabbed his moccasins and fled. Alison was right on his heels. At the door leading to the kitchen, she turned back toward me. "I'll arrange for bail as soon as I can, Adam."

"Fat chance," said Gomez-Gomez. "You're not getting out of here, McCleet. Not as long as I'm in charge."

"Adios," said sweet Consuela.

And then, they were gone. Everyone but Dr. Gunter, who lay, still and silent, on his bunk.

I followed his example and winced with pain as the back of my head pressed against the hard mattress. A medical person would probably say that I should get up and move around before I lapsed into a coma. But as I saw it, a coma would be a good thing.

I was just beginning to drift into cloudy dreamland when I was aware of movement in the cell. The little skittering noise was either rats, lizards, or Dr. Gunter. I looked up into the small man's face.

"Did you kill him?" he demanded. "Did you kill Dental Stoker?"

"No."

"Who do you work for? It's some government agency, isn't it? Or Los Alamos? Don't deny it, young man, I can spot a G-man at a hundred yards."

"Young man?" I grinned. It had been a while since anybody

called me young. Of course, Dr. Gunter was probably a hundred and ten so his judgment wasn't objective.

"The military," Gunter said. "Of course, you're with the the military. Army Intelligence? Navy?"

"I'm an artist."

The doctor launched into a muttered tirade. "Well, you're not getting your hands on my discovery. Not after all these years. Dental and I were close, extremely close. But why would you kill him?" He paced the cell floor. "Why? Unless Dental had found it." He whipped around and faced me. "Is that what happened? Dental actually found it and you killed him?"

"Believe me, Dr. Gunter, I'd really like to hold up my end of the conversation. But I don't know what you're talking about. And I didn't kill Dental."

"Did you see it? By God, man, have the decency to tell me. I've been searching for eight years."

"It? What?"

"The alien."

"Are you talking about a person who carries a little green card, or a person who's little and green?" His answer was going to make a lot of difference in how the rest of our discussion would unfold.

"Little and green?" His eyes burned question marks in my forehead. "Then, you've seen him! He exists!" Gunter clasped his hands and rejoiced, "Tonna-Hokay-Pokay-Lawnchair-Yada-Yada exists!"

"Glows In Dark is an interplanetary traveler?"

Of course, I thought dismally. This ancient Anasazi legend couldn't have pertained to something as interesting as an ancient statuette chiseled from a shard of phosphorescent rock or the ghost of a white buffalo.

"Good God, man! You've got to let me see him."

I spoke slowly and calmly. "I don't know what the hell you're talking about."

"Of course, that's what you'd say." He winked slyly. "That's the good old standard government line, isn't it? But we know better, don't we?"

I wanted some ideas to sleep on, any piece of the puzzle. But I didn't think cluttering my throbbing brain with little green spacemen would be productive. "Go away now," I advised. "You've had a severe blow to the head, and you need rest."

"I'll cooperate. I'll do anything you ask, sign any kind of waiver. But please, you've got to let me work on this."

"Sure," I promised expansively. "You have my word, Doc. If there is an alien, he's your baby."

"Thank you, sir. You won't regret it. I have a theory about extraterrestrial matter and magnetization."

"I'll bet you do." I closed my eyes and slept.

My next encounter with consciousness was when Alison returned. She was fully dressed and businesslike as she stood outside the cell with her graceful hands wrapped around the bars. "I have bad news, Adam."

Why wasn't I surprised? "Yeah?"

"I contacted my attorney in Portland who gave me a name of an attorney in Santa Fe. When I talked to him, he said that Morning isn't even on the map. This is an unincorporated sector of Rio Arriba County. And there's a district circuit judge who sets bail, but he's on vacation and—"

"Bottom line?"

"Gomez-Gomez is in charge. And, Adam, she doesn't know what she's doing."

"Why am I not surprised?"

"She hasn't called the state police or a coroner or a district attorney or anyone." Alison chewed on her lower lip for a few seconds and added, "She wrapped that poor old man's body in butcher paper and stuffed him into the deep-freezer on the back porch of the cafe."

I considered the implications of Alison's news. With Gomez-

Gomez doing her worst to contaminate the evidence, it would be difficult to convict me or anyone else of Stoker's murder. In the meantime, the trail to the real killer was rapidly cooling.

"There doesn't seem to be anything I can do," Alison said. "I even called Margot. She was furious about the holes. She said, 'She'd get to the bottom of it.' "

I didn't really expect she'd be concerned that her brother was in jail for murder. "Did you call anyone else?"

"Monte in Taos. He said your sculptures are receiving a lot of attention, but it would be better if you were there. And he had some great ideas about how to generate more interest in your work."

"What kind of ideas?"

"He didn't say." Alison squeezed my hand. "Adam, I'm worried. Maybe I should contact the state police."

"Not yet," I said. "If you call in the big dogs, I'll still be the number-one suspect. Let me think about this for a while." Maybe the sheriff would come to her senses. Maybe the real murderer would come forward. Maybe Elvis Presley would stop by for a jam session. "It's okay. I wasn't really looking forward to being internationally famous at the Taos Art Show anyway."

"I'm sorry, Adam."

"Hey, don't worry about it," I said. "I've got Margot and Monte on my side. What more could a boy ask for? I'll just stay here and sleep." The bunk had worn to fit my silhouette. The pancake-thin mattress wasn't all that uncomfortable. Plus, I reasoned, I was safer in here than at Margot's hacienda.

"I guess I also ought to tell you that the sheriff is really serious in her suspicions. I thought she was just being vindictive, but she really thinks you killed the old man."

"As long as the locals haven't organized a lynch mob, I'm okay."

"Can I get you anything? Food? Clothes?" She frowned. "This isn't like you, Adam. You're so calm."

Maybe I'd been clunked on the head one time too many, but I just didn't care. All I wanted to do was lie back and let the world go by. Maybe it was age. Maybe I'd finally gotten past the midlife crisis that everybody gave me such grief about and had taken my first doddering steps toward peaceful senility.

I laced my fingers with Alison's. The feel of her warm flesh, and my response to the glow from her green eyes reminded me that I wasn't completely over the hill. "Don't worry about me," I told her. "As long as I'm locked up, nothing else can happen to me."

She pressed up against the bars and I kissed her lightly. She seemed especially soft and gentle. "I'm getting you out of here," she promised. "One way or the other, I'm getting you out of jail."

"I'm really okay."

She kissed the tip of her finger and touched the end of my nose. "Trust me, Adam. You shouldn't be here."

She pivoted and strode out of the jail, full of purpose and determination. That made one of us.

I settled back to sleep some more.

The next visitor wasn't for me. I wakened to see Dr. Gunter, standing in the middle of the cell with his arms folded over his chest. "Prove it," he demanded.

"He says he's your daughter's fiancé," Gomez-Gomez said. "His name is Dustin Florence."

"And I still say that he must prove his connection with my daughter."

I glanced outside the cell where a Dockers-wearing prepster stood beaming like one of those idiots who bounds into a room and asks, "Tennis, anyone?" His baby blue cashmere sweater draped casually over his shoulders with sleeves knotted at his throat. This was a style I found particularly annoying, almost as irritating as the polo pony logo on his burgundy cotton shirt.

With a confident smile, he dug into his trouser pocket and produced a wallet that was a slim calf leather model of efficiency, including Day-Timer, credit cards and a calculator that was thin as an invoice.

"Well?" Gunter stuck out his whiskered chin. "Why, in the name of Odin and Thor, should I believe you are the betrothed of my beloved daughter, Freya?"

"You are a character, sir."

Dustin had an undefinable accent, not British and definitely not Hispanic. I decided that his heritage was probably a variety of too-rich, too-tan and too-blond to be poor. He held out a sheet of pale melon-colored paper. "Here you are, sir. A letter from Freya. She's awfully concerned about you, Papa Gunter."

"Don't call me Papa."

As Gunter studied the sheet of paper and muttered under his breath, I couldn't help but notice that the sheriff had opened the cell door and was standing aside. She instructed Dustin, "Step inside."

"Thank you, Ms. Sheriff, ma'am. You're too kind."

As soon as she closed the door behind him, Gomez-Gomez announced, "Dustin Florence, you are under arrest for the murder of Dental Stoker."

"Excuse me?"

"You are a stranger in town. This gives me cause for suspicion."

The sheriff turned on her heels and left.

Aghast, Dustin stared at me. "I'm under arrest? Why? Whatever for?"

"Ever heard of being in the wrong place at the wrong time?" This was the cosmic anomaly that ruled my life.

Gunter glared at him. "This note is from Freya, all right. Why'd she send you out here?"

"I'm under arrest?" Dustin couldn't seem to grasp his plight. If he hadn't been such an obviously overprivileged, candy-ass, I might have sympathized.

Still aghast, he continued, "But I just got here. I was having a latte in the feed store and I mentioned your name and the proprietor said you always had breakfast here."

Gunter grabbed the knotted arms of his sweater and pulled him toward a bunk. "Sit."

Dustin obeyed.

"Why did Freya send you?"

"Well, Freya has been dreadfully concerned about you, sir. As I'm sure you are well aware, she hadn't heard from you in nearly five years. So, when she received the letter, detailing your progress and mentioning a place thirty miles northwest of Taos, she asked me to find you."

"Why? The last I heard of Freya, she was in Vienna studying waltzes or some such. The girl hasn't laid eyes on me since her thirty-first birthday when she destroyed my vintage Rolls Royce."

His vintage Rolls? Who was this little Viking?

"She requests the honor of your presence at our wedding. Two months from yesterday."

Sneering, Gunter looked down at the prepster sitting on the jailhouse bunk. "I don't much like you, Dustin. I think you will have to prove yourself in a test, a heroic feat, before I'm willing to bestow my blessing on these nuptial rites."

"A test?" He sprawled backward on the bunk. "Oh. My. God."

"Let's see." Gunter was pacing on his short, muscular legs. "Walk across hot coals? Scale a mesa? Wrestle a rattlesnake? No, those won't do." He pointed one stubby finger toward the ceiling of the cell. "If you get me sprung from this jail—me and Mr. McCleet who is sitting over here—I'll bless your marriage to Freya."

"I can do that." He sat up straight. "I was in law school for six and a half years."

The door to the jail swung wide and the sheriff ushered Melvin and Nelda inside.

Melvin shuffled, head down.

Nelda, predictably, protested, "Shirley, honey, you can't arrest us. Who's going to run the store if we're in jail?"

"I'll get Consuela to go over and lock up."

"Consuela? You tell her not to mess with the newspapers. She always does that, comes in and reads the *Enquirer* without buying it. I'm not a library, you know. I'm not blah-blah de-blah."

The cell door opened extra wide to allow the two gargantuan Stokers to lumber inside.

This time, I stepped up to the bars, "Sheriff? Are these two also under suspicion for murder?"

"That is correct. They would stand to inherit from Dental, which makes them suspect. Always look to the family." She tossed her head. "You can tell your friend, Ms. Brooks, that I'm doing this investigation by the book. Gathering evidence."

Having spent fifteen years of my life as a cop, I knew the difference between gathering physical evidence and arresting everybody in town. But I didn't criticize. "Does this mean I'm not the main suspect?"

"You did it, hairball. You're the perp." She smiled at her own utterance of the efficient TV cop-speak. "But I must cover all the bases so I can show the state police, when I call them in, that I investigated impartially and thoroughly."

Trying not to offend her, I suggested, "You might want forensic specialists to fingerprint the axe."

"I know whose fingerprints are there. Yours."

"Yes," I agreed, "but there might be—"

"Don't tell me how to do my job." She left.

Dustin had gallantly stepped aside so that Nelda could sit on the bunk, and she made herself as comfortable as her massive womanly figure would permit. It took awhile to adjust her watermelon-sized breasts, presumably so she wouldn't be overbalanced, and topple. All the while, she was chattering about what a tragedy it was and how it was bound to happen sooner or later.

"What was bound to happen?" Dustin asked.

"Violence," she said. Her piggy eyes squinted to slits. "The kind of random violence they show on the television in the cities and even in smaller towns. Blah-ditty-blah. Mark my blah, blah. . . . matter of time before Morning would have a crime wave. Teenagers. Gangs. Blah. Blah. This is just the beginning."

To be sure, it was the beginning of something. As the afternoon progressed, Shirley Gomez-Gomez also arrested Robinson Crusoe and three teenagers from the no-name cult compound.

The jail accommodations, which were not spacious to begin with, now resembled nine clowns in a Volkswagen. But I wasn't exactly feeling _Fahrvergnügen_ about the experience. Crusoe and his three acolytes sat Yoga-style against the bars and quietly meditated. I sat next to Rob. "What are you in for?"

"Murder," he said with a calm that suggested it wasn't his first time behind bars. "I'll be out of here by eight o'clock tonight."

"You have a lawyer?"

"I have a date," he said. "With the sheriff."

"Ah," I said. "Does she actually have any kind of reason for suspecting you? Or were you arrested as part of the round-up at the Morning Corral?"

"Dental and I were not on the best of terms," he said. "The old prospector kept trespassing. He claimed that he didn't see the signs outside our compound, but the acreage is clearly marked."

"Liar," said the mini-Viking professor. "You and your sheet-wearing hoodlums were the ones who kept following Dental. I wouldn't be surprised if you killed him to get his piece of the map."

"The map?" I questioned. "Does this have something to do with the alien?"

Talk about a conversation-stopper. The cell went as silent as if I'd mentioned Dean Witter. Even Melvin, who had been curled up lumpishly in a corner, looked up.

Nelda leaned forward, dragged almost prone by the weight of her titanic breasts, and asked, "What do you know about the alien?"

"He's valuable," I said.

They all exchanged murmurs and nodded their heads.

I tried another guess. "He might be buried on my sister Margot's property."

Again, there seemed to be agreement.

Slyly, Nelda asked, "Can you tell us something we don't already know, hon?"

Since I seemed to be batting a thousand, I gave it another shot. "He glows in the dark."

"Have you seen him?" Nelda demanded.

"Stop!" Gunter stepped forward. "Don't say another word. This man, Adam McCleet, is a G-man. He's from the government, and if he finds the alien, he'll take him."

Dustin Florence fought his way to the iron bars and shouted, "Let me out of here. I don't belong here."

I felt much the same way. "I'm not from the government. I'm a sculptor. I've got a showing in Taos at the Sundog Gallery."

"What an obvious alias!" said Robinson Crusoe.

"Why?"

"Artists are as common as cactus in New Mexico," Nelda informed me. "Anybody can say they're an artist. What branch of the government do you work for?"

They were looking a bit surly and there were enough of them to do just about anything they wanted. I decided to cooperate. "I did work for the government at one point in my life. A long time ago. I was a Marine. Vietnam."

With a surprising agility, Melvin hauled his large butt off the cell floor and came to stand beside me. "Welcome home, brother." He wrapped his large arm around me and gave me a bearhug. Squeezing extra hard, he asked, "By the way, did you kill my father?"

"No."

He dropped his arm and turned to the others. "Leave him alone."

"But Melvin, honey," Nelda said, jiggling to her feet. "He knows something about the alien. And he does have a kind of government look about him. I really don't think you should allow your old loyalties to get in the way of—"

"Shut up, Nelda."

She went silent. I suppressed a hoorah.

The jailhouse door opened, and we all groaned. What poor fool had Shirley Gomez-Gomez brought, to further stuff this bulging can of mixed nuts? The local high-school football team? A bus full of tourists, wandered off the beaten path?

But it was pretty little Consuela who bounced inside. In her hands, she held a Polaroid. "Everybody come up near the bars. I want a picture."

"Certainly not," said Gunter.

"Oh, please."

She fluttered her thick velvet black eyelashes, and it occurred to me that the women in New Mexico were truly remarkable creatures. Since I lived near the ocean in Portland, I tended to think artistically of women as water sprites, rising from the waves, but these were women of the land. There was Consuela, dark and lovely as a night dream. And Nelda whose giant body personified Mother Earth. Even Gomez-Gomez had a certain exotic mystery about her. I felt that itch to create, to fondle these women in clay.

"Please," Consuela begged prettily. "This is the most people we've ever had in the jail at one time."

"I'll cooperate," said Robinson Crusoe.

When he smiled at Consuela, she almost blushed. Old Rob must be quite the ladies' man in these parts. I almost envied him.

"All right," Consuela said, stamping her foot. "If you don't pose for me, I will not feed you tonight."

Everybody shuffled together at the bars and I wondered if they knew that Dental's corpse was stored in the cafe's freezer.

She aimed her camera. "Okay, smile." The camera flashed.

Before the floating colored spots in front of my eyes had a chance to fade, she focused the lens directly at my face and flashed again.

"Thanks everybody."

As the others shuffled back to their former positions, she came close to me. "Your friend, Alison, she says you are a world-famous artist."

"My friend is exaggerating."

"*Qué?* But you have a show at the Sundog Gallery in Taos. This is true?"

"A show doesn't mean you're famous."

"Maybe you will be." She cast me a sensual smile, whirled and left the jail, ignoring the plaintive wails of Dustin Florence who promised that he didn't belong here. He knew his rights. He was almost a lawyer.

The afternoon dragged into evening with the only interruptions being several one-at-a-time trips to the bathroom and the serving of a greasy but well-meaning enchilada dinner. Everybody but Nelda was fairly quiet. No one had informed her of proper jail etiquette, and she was delighted to have a literally captive audience. After she ran out of gossip, Nelda launched a blow-by-blow description of a talk show I had never even heard of.

After dinner, at exactly eight o'clock, Gomez-Gomez came into the jail and unlocked the cell door. Her movements were sloppy. Her breath smelled like the bottom of a tequila bottle. "All right, Rob. You're out."

"I'm sorry, Shirley, but I can't leave while my three young friends are still in jail."

"Well, I can't let them go. They're suspects."

Nelda was at the bars. "Let me and Melvin go. Come on, Shirley, have a heart. We have conjugal reasons."

There was a frightening thought. I imagined the mating of behemoths.

"We promise," Nelda said, "not to leave town. Where would we go, anyway?"

"Okay, you go. But don't leave town."

As the Stokers waddled past her, Gomez-Gomez stared at Rob. "Are you coming?"

"Not without the boys."

"Then, rot!" She slammed the cell door with a resounding clang. "I've had a really bad day, you bastard. I'm not going to forget this."

He shrugged. "We do it my way, Shirley. You know that."

"Pig!" She staggered out of the cell. Without the incessant blabber of Nelda, the night settled quietly on Morning's jail.

It must have been near midnight when I heard a voice outside the window's thick iron bars. "Adam?"

Who was that?

"Yoo hoo, Adam, are you in there?"

I knew the voice. It was Monte, Alison's flamboyant assistant at Brooks Gallery. He was one of the only individuals in the free world who would actually say "yoo-hoo."

I stood on my tiptoes and looked out. In the moonlight, I saw him. He wore a white ten-gallon hat, tight white Roy Rogers-type trousers and a red satin cowboy shirt that matched his fancy tooled red boots. He posed, thrusting his arms out to the sides and doing a pirouette. "Don't you love the Old West."

"What the hell are you doing here, Monte?"

"I've come to break you out of jail."

Chapter
Four

Though I was determined not to get involved in any idiotic jailbreak scheme, especially not an escape engineered by Monte, the other occupants of the cell were curious. They took turns at the window, stretching up on their toes like ugly ballerinas, trying to get a look at this Monte person.

After each of the inmates caught his first glimpse of Monte's satin and stretch-pants version of a cowboy, they discussed the pros and cons of the great escape.

Dustin from Boston was emphatic. "I say we do it! We go for the gusto!"

"Perhaps," Rob agreed. "It doesn't seem that Shirley has the intention of being fair or reasonable." He turned to me. "Adam?"

"No," I said. "Breaking out of jail is definitely illegal."

"We're already accused of murder," Dustin reasoned. "How much worse could it get?"

"Very rational," Rob complimented him.

"Why, thank you. I was almost a lawyer, you know."

After a minimal debate, Dustin Florence and Rob Crusoe

agreed that Monte just might be a reincarnation of Roy Rogers who had come to save the day, and we should take advantage of his presence. Crusoe's three teenage disciples didn't know who Roy Rogers was, but they all concurred about getting out of the Morning jail.

One of them said, "I mean, the geek outside looks like one of those country-western singer dudes. But I say we go for it."

Gunter, who was too short to ever have a prayer of seeing out the window, was frustrated. He tried to jump up but the soles of his boots barely left the floor. "Roy Rogers? The real Roy Rogers? Let me see."

Noticing Gunter's plight, Rob Crusoe tossed his well-conditioned mane of hair and said, "Poor old Gunter. I'd forgotten that you were height-impaired."

"I'm what?"

"Boys!" Rob snapped his fingers and the three young men came to attention. "Lift him."

The three young men responded immediately and without question, circling Gunter and trying to get a hold under his short arms.

"Stop it," Gunter protested. He flapped as angrily as a flightless bird. "Don't even try to pick me up. It's not dignified."

The teenager looked confused. "But Rob said lift."

His buddy concurred. "We got to lift you, Gunter dude."

"Back off, you brainless ninnies." Gunter took a swing at one of them. "Do you do everything Rob says?"

"You got that right, man."

Rob placed a restraining hand on one of the boy's shoulders. "I have another idea."

The kid was looking at his leader with the sort of vacant expression I have come to associate with adolescents. But there was obedience, too. A scary, mindless obedience. What kind of power did Rob Crusoe have over these kids anyway?

Rob squeezed the boy's arm. "Down on your hands and knees, Jason. Form a human step."

Fascinated, I watched and waited for the kid to rebel. Down on your hands and knees? No self-respecting, innately obnoxious teenaged boy would go along with that order.

But the kid dropped without a single comment.

Rob Crusoe gestured graciously to Gunter. "Stand on his back so that you might see."

Gunter was understandably hesitant, but he climbed aboard his human step stool. Finally casting his gaze on the stranger outside the jail, the short Viking said with great disappointment, "By the Gods . . . that's not Roy Rogers."

"Yoo hoo," Monte called out again. "Yoo-hoo, Adam."

When Gunter and the weirdly obedient youth moved out of the way, I returned to the window. "Go away, Monte. I don't want to get sprung."

"Now, Adam, you old cowpoke. Don't be a sourpuss." Monte ran to the trunk of the New Yorker I had rented. "Alison told me to do whatever it takes to get you out of here."

"Including a jailbreak?"

"Not exactly, but I tried to get some legal action going, but you know . . . everything is _mañana_ down here. You could be stuck here for days, and you'd miss your big showing."

He opened the trunk with a dramatic flourish and pulled out a length of heavy manila rope. After getting tangled in the rope, practically strangling himself with it, he held an end up to me. "Tie that around the bar."

"No."

"Listen, Adam, you could be convicted of murder. After all, you are the prime suspect. Even Alison says so." Monte played with the pearl buttons on the front of his satin shirt. "Always nice to be number one, isn't it?."

Oh, yes, being numero uno suspect in a murder case had to be the pinnacle of my aspirations. "Leave me alone, Monte. If you break me out, it's going to look like I'm running away because I'm guilty."

"Come on, Adam. It'll be fun."

"Fun?"

"Just like Butch Cassidy and the Sundance Kid. I get to be Robert Redford."

I pushed the rope out the window. "Go away."

Dr. Gunter Bjornsen stood beside me. "I think you should seize this opportunity, Adam."

"Wait a minute, Doc." All of a sudden, we were buddies? What was going on here? "I thought I was a G-man who couldn't be trusted."

"I've reconsidered," he said. "Do you recall the conversation we had before all these other suspects were incarcerated. About the location of the you-know-what?"

"The alien?" I said. I could feel my jaw begin to tighten. Was there no sane person in Morning? "Glows In The Dark?"

"Shines At Night." He laughed genially, but his gaze was hard and determined. "Break out. Do it."

"Perhaps we're being hasty," Rob said. "If we break out, we look guilty, and Shirley will track us down like a mudslide in Malibu."

The three teenaged boys echoed his comment, but punctuated it with "dude" and "wasted" and "grip of shit, man."

"However," Rob continued, "if Shirley has already concluded that Adam is the murderer, it doesn't really matter what the rest of us do."

I thanked him for his vote of confidence. It seemed to have slipped everyone's mind that I wasn't the only suspect who had been incarcerated in the Morning Jail. One of us might actually be a cold-blooded murderer that we would be setting free.

On the other hand, while I was locked up, I wouldn't have a prayer of figuring out who had done it. I couldn't clear myself.

Dustin flashed his tennis-anyone grin and said, "I say we make a run for it. Let's give it the old college try."

"Right," Gunter said. "Let's win this one for the Gipper."

When Monte held out the rope again, Dustin grabbed it, looped it around the bars and began to weave an incompetent wad of macramé so pathetic that I couldn't stand to look at it. I'm a sailor. I know knots. "Give me that."

I used a simple clove-hitch backed up with a half-hitch then peered out the window.

Monte frowned at his end of the rope. "What do I do?"

The sleek Chrysler had no convenient appendages for towing. I called out to him, "You'll have to get under the car."

"I'll get dirty," he complained. "But, all right. I hope you appreciate the sacrifice I'm making. This is my Texas outfit. I always wear it when I go line dancing with Carla Jean."

"In Portland?"

"Corpus Christi."

Amazingly, Monte had a woman in every port. "Who are you seeing in Taos?" I asked.

"Marlena Montoya." He fussed around under the rental car. "An incredibly talented woman. She's a flamenco stripper. Oh, God, Adam. I hate this. I'm all greasy."

When he finally stood up, his gleaming white pants were dirty, his butt was saggy and he was grumbling. "Well, Adam! I hope you're satisfied."

"I am. What's a flamenco stripper?"

"She taps her heels really hard and fast." He illustrated by clicking the heels on his fancy red boots. "And she vibrates right out of her dress."

It was a startling mental picture, and I contemplated the potential attributes of Marlena Montoya while Monte climbed behind the steering wheel of the New Yorker and slowly crept forward until the rope was taut. His skill surprised me. In the years that I had known Monte, I had never before detected the slightest modicum of mechanical ability. He was brilliant at keeping track of the artwork and promotions at Brooks Art Gallery, but he was incapable of holding a hammer peen-side down.

Easing the car forward, he gunned the motor. And the bars began to creak against the heavy adobe wall.

The crew of jailed suspects stepped back against the jail door and watched. It was fairly amazing that neither the sheriff nor Consuela had noticed this intrusion. We weren't exactly being subtle. The only explanation was that Shirley Gomez-Gomez must have drowned in her tequila.

The car engine whined.

The cult teenagers started a chant. "Go, Mon-tay. Go, Mon-tay." It sounded like a rap. "You go, Mon-tay. You go, boy."

The bars on the window shuddered. And then, with a lound *sproing,* they tore loose, ripping out a substantial chunk of wall along with them.

Adobe and stucco crashed loudly as an earthquake, and I knew there wasn't much time. The demolition was enough noise to wake the dead or the drunk. I bolted through the hole in the wall. Gunter was right behind me.

I knew from past experience that allowing Monte to drive would be an exercise in frustration. So, I went to the driver's-side door and opened it. "Move over."

"I did it, Adam. Wasn't that spectacular?"

"Right. Now, move over. I'm driving."

"If you insist."

Gunter was in the back seat.

I looked back at the jail where Rob and the boys and Dustin were peeking out through the hole. Why weren't they coming with us?

I saw the answer. A staggering Gomez-Gomez shoved past them. Though she reeled unsteadily between the broken wall and the tail of the New Yorker, she was still dangerous. Dropping to one knee, the sheriff aimed her pistola and fired. The back window of the car shattered.

I floored it. Now, I was a fugitive.

We tore along the rutted roads leading away from Morning. Gunter cackled gleefully in the back seat. Monte took off his cowboy hat and waved it out the window. "Hi-ho, Silver! And away!"

Gunter joined in with his own victory cry, "Hi-ho, Odin!"

I whipped along the unlit roads at an unsafe speed, dodging potholes the size of canyons. Behind us, the iron bars of the jail, still attached by the rope, bounced and clattered.

"Turn left here," Gunter instructed. "I know a place where we can hide out. There's a road. About fifty yards."

I peered through the darkness. "I don't see an intersection."

"Trust me," he said. "Another twenty. Ten. Here."

Blindly, I swerved over the ditch at the side of the road and plummeted along another pathway through the sagebrush that aimed directly at a long flat-topped mesa. Hoping that the imminent crash was only an optical illusion, I kept driving at top speed. The road swerved suddenly, almost at a right angle. On pure survival reflex, I veered to the right, and we were in a ravine between two mesas.

"Stop," Gunter said.

"Why?"

"If we stop here and let the dust settle, Shirley won't see any sign of where we are." He opened his car door. "Let's untie the bars, shall we?"

His plan sounded logical, but still I asked, "Won't the sheriff know about this place?"

"You're in New Mexico, lad. This is only one of a thousand hidden ravines and canyons. The only way Gomez-Gomez is going to locate us is if she gets reinforcements from the state police, and I really don't think she'll do that."

Neither did I. In my opinion as an ex-cop, Sheriff Shirley

Gomez-Gomez had screwed up in just about every way possible. She'd stashed the corpse in a freezer without forensic investigation and, as far as I knew, without even an okay from a coroner. Whimsically, she'd arrested half the population of Morning and then—just as nonchalantly—had let some of them go.

But I didn't think her incompetence was the reason she wanted to avoid the state cops. Was it stubbornness? Or something else?

Monte cantered up beside us. "I told you, Adam. Just like Butch and Sundance and the Hole in the Wall gang. Do you remember that part when the posse was closing in and they jumped off the hundred-foot cliff?"

"We're not going to do that, Monte."

"Of course not, but it was ever so dramatic."

When I detached the rope, I saw that Monte had held true to his nonmechanical nature. He had tied his end of the rope to the axle which was now twisted like a corkscrew. Given the damage, we'd been lucky to make it this far. I didn't know how many miles we could log without the rear end falling off the rental car.

Gunter started up the angled slope of the mesa. His short legs churned and loose shale broke away beneath his boots, but he progressed like a powerful tractor, in complete command of the terrain. He was squat with heavy chest and shoulders, but his agility defied his age.

"Come on." He waved for us to follow.

Monte did so, with great enthusiasm. He even got a couple of picnic blankets from the trunk.

I was less excited. Playing fugitive from the law went against my basic nature almost as much as deliberately setting my face on fire. However, now that I was sprung, I needed to waste no time in finding the murderer, proving my innocence and getting back to being famous.

_____

I climbed up on the mesa and stood beside Gunter. "Who do you think killed Dental?"

"Lie down flat," he said. "From up here, we can keep an eye on the road."

Monte spread his blankets and the three of us lay in a row on our bellies, staring at the stark New Mexico landscape of terraced mesas and flat stretches of mesquite.

Apparently, it had taken the sheriff several minutes to subdue the other suspects before she set out to search. There were no headlights in sight.

"Gunter," I said, "who killed Dental?"

"If you didn't do it, I don't know who did. It's a damned shame that he died. Dental Stoker is a fallen warrior."

"Don't start," I warned. "Don't even think about a Viking funeral pyre."

"No. Not now. But, someday, I will send his spirit to Valhalla with the rich ceremony he deserves."

"Valhalla?" Monte questioned. "Are you really a Viking?"

"My heritage goes all the way back to Eric the Red," he said proudly. "The Vikings were explorers. And, in my twentieth-century manner, so am I."

My recollection of Viking lore included a fair share of plundering, raping and conquering as well as some ill-advised journeys across the oceans to look for more people to rape and plunder and conquer. I decided not to incite the small Norse man with insults to his heritage. "What are you looking for?"

"My quest is knowledge. I have doctorates in archeology, anthropology and language. For most of my life, I stayed sequestered in a university, but I tired of seeking in books. Sixteen years ago, I embarked on field work. But nothing has been as satisfying as the last eight years when I have been searching for the you-know-what."

"Glows In The Dark. The alien."

"Shines At Night," he corrected.

"An alien?" Monte stared at Gunter and then at me. "A real alien from outer space? Oh, my God, this is too good."

I could see dollar signs behind his fluttering eyelids.

"Whatever you're thinking, Monte, stop it."

"Do you know how much free publicity we could get if you found an alien? It's too fantastico. I keep telling Alison that the only way we're going to make your name really big is with some publicity. Of course, the murder charge is a fine start. But an alien is way better."

"What publicity?" I asked dourly.

"Notoriety, Adam. It's million-dollar fame. Your name on the lips of the general public. I mean, publicity is the only way we can distinguish you from all the other sculptors."

"Silly me, and I thought I could distinguish myself with my artwork."

"Step into the twentieth century." He snapped his fingers in my face. "If you find an alien, you'll be a star."

A click in the back of my head told me he was right, and I didn't like the implication. I had never aspired to the lifestyle of the Rich and Famous, and I definitely didn't want to join the ranks of the Opportunistic and Stupid. Let Kato do that. And Buttafucco.

"You might as well face it," Monte said. "It's time to make your try for the brass ring."

"Why?"

He rolled his eyes as if I were a complete idiot. "For one thing, you owe it to Alison. She's worked harder on your career than you have, Adam. And how long do you think she's going to do that if you don't make an effort? Hmmmm?"

Once again, there was a grain of truth in Monte's analysis. Throughout this trip—except for last night when we made love which was always remarkable—Alison had been annoyed with me. It started with my reluctance to participate in the show at the

Sundog Gallery. I had vacillated like a priest with a hard-on. I couldn't make up my mind about coming.

Gunter pointed to the road. A pair of headlights were weaving along. "Gomez-Gomez," he said.

"Is she tracking us?" I thought of my precipitous exit from the road onto the path that led to this mesa. I must have left drag marks six inches deep with the dragging window bars.

"Not in the dark. My guess," said the highly educated man, "is that she's tanked to the ears."

Though it was hard to judge distances across the sweeping starlit plains, I guessed that the headlights were coming up on the turn. Slowly. Slowly. The tension gathered at the base of my spine. My personal sphincter scale measured a magnitude four point five. I really didn't want to make another run for it. Not in a car with a busted axle.

Gomez-Gomez continued past the turn, and we exhaled a collective sigh of relief.

"Now what?" Monte said.

It was a good question. Should I turn myself in to the state police and hope to find someone who wasn't an asshole looking for the most obvious suspect? Yeah, sure. My odds on that were about as high as shaking hands with a Martian. It wasn't that I thought cops were dumb. After all, I had, at one time, been a cop. But I assumed that the police in New Mexico were as overworked as the police in Portland or Seattle. All cops like a case they can button down fast and tight.

Even with Sheriff Shirley's tequila-soaked incompetence, there was evidence stacked against me. I'd found the body. There was blood on my clothes. And my fingerprints were all over the pickaxe that was probably the murder weapon. Not to mention that I had escaped from jail.

If I'd still been a cop, I would have arrested me. Though I might have a better shot at due process with the state cops than with Gomez-Gomez, the end result might be the same.

I made my decision. I wasn't going to turn myself in until I'd figured out who killed Dental. Then I would produce the killer and hand him over to the cops in a neat package with evidence and exhibits numbered.

Dr. Gunter was the logical place to start. I rolled onto my back and sat up. "When somebody gets murdered, it's usually because the killer wants something that the victim has. So what did Dental have? What would be worth killing him for?"

"The alien."

"I don't want to hear this." With a creaking of joints, I brought myself to a standing posture on the top of the mesa. Overhead, the stars mapped the galaxies, but I was determined to keep my feet planted on earth. "Don't tell me about the fucking space-man."

"I want to hear," Monte said. "Tell me about the alien."

"About eight years ago," Gunter started, "I was in this area, researching Anasazi legends and ancient Pueblo remains. Dental Stoker approached me with his story. It was a legend, passed down through generations of his family who were traders and trappers in the area."

"At the Feed and Seed store?"

"Yes. The date, as far as I can figure, was mid-1860's. And his family told the story of a star that fell from the skies and crashed to earth."

"A spaceship?" Monte asked. He was aquiver with excitement.

"Possibly. In any case, there was a fire, and they found the remains of an odd-shaped metallic object. More importantly, there was a person, described as being a child. The Stoker family, being honest God-fearing folks, buried the remains."

I stared through the starry night at the face of Dr. Gunter, a man who had three doctorates. "Dental told you this fairy tale and you believed him. Why?"

"He had a map."

Now we were getting somewhere. "So you followed the map and found . . . what?"

"Not that easy, Adam. Dental only had a piece of the map. A third of it."

"Who has the other two-thirds?"

"I believe that Rob Crusoe has another third. As for the final piece, I don't know."

"Fabulous," Monte said. "Let's get together with this Crusoe person and find the alien."

"I've tried," Gunter explained. "In spite of the sheet thing, Rob is a fairly reasonable individual. But he steadfastly refuses to cooperate. He and his cult followers want to find the alien and keep him for themselves."

"What about this cult?" I asked, thinking of the unusually obedient teenaged boys. "Are they survivalists?"

"Possibly. They're very secretive. Hence, the No Name designation."

"Must be hell to get mail," I said.

"Indeed. As far as their quest for the alien, it's my opinion that they are experimenting with space travel themselves, and they hope to find answers in this poor, unfortunate victim from another planet."

I dragged Gunter back to the important topic. "Would somebody kill Dental to get his piece of the map?"

"They might if he had carried it upon his person," he said. "But Dental Stoker was no fool. He had hidden his piece of the map, and he wouldn't even tell me where it was. All I have to work with is a copy."

I eyeballed the small Viking suspiciously. It seemed unlikely to me that anybody, especially not an educated guy like Gunter Bjornsen, would devote eight years of his life to chasing a legend from a copy of a piece of a map. "What else did Dental have? What other kind of proof did he offer?"

"Nothing."

He was lying. I hadn't spent fifteen years as a cop without learning the signs. "Come on, Gunter, what did he have?"

"Just the map."

"It must be one excellent map," I said, "to convince you to give up eight years of your life to search. Mind if I have a look at it?"

"Certainly not. It's at my place."

I nursed the car along the road. The frame groaned over every bump, and the alignment was skewed. When I turned the wheels to the right, the rear end would go left.

Once again, the doc had a hiding place. "Pull up here in this grove of cottonwoods and park. We need to be cautious, Adam. The sheriff will surely come here to search for me."

I didn't see any sign of a dwelling, but I followed his instructions. "Where's your house?"

"Oh, I don't live in a house." He pointed through the night. "We can see the outline. It's a teepee."

I could see the silhouette of a cone-shaped object, not unlike a spaceship.

"As in wigwam?" Monte inquired. "A canvas tent?"

"It's quite modern," he assured us. "I suggest we stay here and wait for Shirley to come and go."

"What if she's already been?"

"There hasn't been time," he said. "Do trust me, lad. I know my way around these parts."

And so, we settled back to wait. Even with Monte's picnic blankets wrapped around our shoulders, the high desert night was cold enough to cause my teeth to chatter.

The chill didn't seem to bother Monte who pulled his ten-gallon hat down over his eyes and went to sleep.

Wiggling around in the driver's seat, I envied him. I couldn't get my butt settled comfortably, and when I did, my head rested too close to the knot from yesterday's attack. Maybe I was getting too old for stakeouts. My tired bones and muscles ached, but I decided to ignore them and think about the crime. How did the murder of Dental Stoker tie in with the local alien? It was hard to comprehend. Call me a cynic, but I don't have the proper comic-book mentality to appreciate the whole outer space thing. I have enough trouble with reality, much less science fiction. "Gunter? Supposing this alien exists, is it male or female?"

"That was never mentioned in the legends. The alien was described as a small person, probably a child. Oh, and I should add that the crash took place on Christmas eve—hence, the added significance for Robinson Crusoe's cult."

"How? As a second coming?"

"I'm not a philosopher," he said.

"Neither is Rob Crusoe from what I can tell, but it doesn't seem to slow him down."

We kept our watch.

Ultimately, after about an hour and forty-five minutes, I spotted the sheriff's car as she jostled along the trail. In the glare of her headlights, I got my first clear view of Gunter's teepee, which was over twenty-five feet tall at the peak.

Gomez-Gomez shouted as she circled the teepee, but she didn't go inside which kind of surprised me. I asked Gunter, "Have you got some kind of security?"

"Of course. Inside the teepee is a fairly standard burglar alarm. If anyone enters without deactivating the code, a loud alarm goes off and it rings simultaneously in the home of the nearest farmhouse. I pay the farmer quite well for his assurance that he will respond, shotgun in hand."

Something else was bothering me. "You're rich, aren't you?"

"During my lifetime I have accumulated a respectable amount of cash and possessions. Not to mention the family inheritance."

More of that Viking plunder, no doubt. "So, how come you live on the desert in a teepee?"

"Because I am wealthy enough to have a choice. I do as I please."

I remembered the conversation with Dustin Florence. "Is there a reason why you haven't seen your daughter in several years?"

"Lack of common interest, I suppose. Her mother and I are divorced. They shop, and I pay for it. I dig around in the wilderness, and they reward me with their benign neglect. It's a satisfying relationship."

I could hear the smile in his voice, and I had to agree. It was a pretty nifty divorce arrangement. I could feel myself smiling back at him. I was beginning to like this guy.

After Gomez-Gomez completed her inspection and drove away, we crept forward in the ailing New Yorker which was surely on its last legs. I wondered if my insurance covered damage sustained in a jailbreak.

As soon as we entered the teepee, Gunter punched a series of numbers into a pad. Then he turned on the light and fired up the propane heater.

The teepee was set on a wood floor, about thirty feet in diameter. There were two beds, bookshelves and a mini-kitchen with a dinette. The rest of the space was occupied by high-tech computers, modems, a FAX machine, a copier and a phone.

Monte sashayed from one item to another. "I love it. I really love it."

Gunter sat at his computer and punched up a program. "Get ready. Here's the map."

I stared at the green lines on the screen. There was a straight line with an "X" at the end.

Chapter
Five

"Okay," I said. "Where's the map?"

"This is it. Beautiful in its simplicity." Gunter gazed, mesmerized, at the computer screen. "Is it a river? Is it the shadow of a mesa? Is it the plat line from a map drawn in the 1860's? Fascinating puzzle."

"It's a line," I pointed out.

"But what does it signify? I've cross-referenced all the maps I can find of this area. And still, nothing. There's nothing that will match."

My rear molars ground together, and the ache went from nerve endings of my teeth to a jackhammer in my cerebral cortex. It was a line. A goddamned line with an "X" at the end. And all of the whackos in Morning were trying to follow it.

I wanted to throw something, maybe Gunter, against the walls of his canvas teepee. Any fondness I had for the man was vanishing fast. "You mean to tell me that you've spent eight years following a straight line."

"It's not easy," he said, defensively. "A perfectly straight line is something of an oddity in nature. Dental and I had determined, over the past few months, that the alien was, most likely, buried somewhere on your sister's property."

"On Margot's property?" Monte said. "Isn't that always the way? Margot just sits back, drying her nail polish, and good things come to her. I've never had an alien."

"Shut up, Monte."

"If you boys will excuse me." Monte bounced over to one of the beds, sat on the edge and began pulling at his fancy tooled red boots.

"What are you doing?" I demanded.

"Getting undressed." He wrenched off one boot. "I mean, my pants are almost destroyed, but I really don't want to ruin my shirt as well. This is satin, hand-embroidered." He pulled off the other boot and massaged his foot. "Those pointed toes and heels really hurt. I just don't know how the real cowboys did it. No wonder they were on horseback all the time."

"The bed is mine," I said.

"We can share."

"No." It was a single bed. "I get the bed."

"Why?"

"I'm older, I'm accused of murder and I'll beat the shit out of you if you try to curl up next to me."

"Oh, all right, you big party-poop."

I turned back to Gunter who was looking up at me with a question in his eyes. "Is he—"

"Gay? No." I glared over my shoulder at him. "But he's still not sleeping with me."

"Alrighty, Goldilocks," Monte snipped. "Have your own bed."

I turned back to Gunter. "You're an intelligent man, Doc. You've got more degrees than Arkansas has teeth and you've taught at universities. I can't believe you spent eight years of your life looking at a straight line on a computer screen."

"Of course, not. I did field studies. I corroborated Dental's version of the local legend with several other families, even traveled to Colorado to talk with the last surviving descendant of the famous Henry Humpenhoff who was a trapper almost as renowned as Kit Carson."

"Henry Humpenhoff?" I questioned. My history book had never mentioned a Humpenhoff.

"Yes, indeed. And the elderly Humpenhoff repeated the Stoker family story precisely," Gunter said. "Also, I did earth trajectories for meteorites and discovered that there might be a magnetic pull in this area. There's plenty of reason to keep up the search."

His efforts still sounded scanty to me. Eight years was a long quest with only a straight line on a piece of paper. I had the feeling that Gunter was holding out on me. "Dental must have shown you some kind of tangible proof."

"Not really," he said huffily. "Is there hard evidence of Atlantis? Of the existence of King Arthur and the Round Table? When you get right down to it, is there irrefutable evidence of the existence of Christ?"

I still didn't believe him. "You're talking about faith. But you're looking for an alien. A real being who's buried in the desert."

"Are you sure you're not from the government? You most certainly espouse a government attitude."

"What did Dental have as proof?"

He pointed to the screen. "This map."

"What else? A piece of the space ship?"

He set his little square jaw firmly and folded his arms across his chest.

I guessed again. "Some kind of meteorite or moon rock?"

His lips formed a straight line—similar to his lousy map—in the middle of his white whiskers.

"It has to be an object of value," I speculated. "Something worth killing to get ahold of."

The doc made a harrumphing noise in the back of his throat. "O, ye of little faith."

Obviously, I wasn't going to get anything more from the doc, and so I said good-night.

We were all bedded down. Once the heater had a chance to work, the tent was cosy and warm. The canvas wall shone like a thin membrane between the starlight and the darkness inside. Monte made a whistling snore, and the doc played an alto counterpart. I couldn't sleep.

What was it? The thing. The object. There had to be something that Dental owned and other people wanted.

Tomorrow, I would search at Dental's place.

My wake-up call the next morning was the barrel of a gun aimed at the tip of my nose. I stared down the two black holes, cross-eyed. On the other end of the gun was Gomez-Gomez with black circles under her bloodshot eyes and the lines in her face etched deep.

I smiled up at her. "Rough night?"

"You asshole."

Sitting on the bed right beside me, she matched the barrel of the gun with my nostrils and shoved none too gently. It hurt like hell, but I didn't move.

She snarled, "I ought to break your goddamned nose. Nobody would blame me if I did. You wrecked my jail."

"Just one wall."

"You bastard!" She nudged my nose again. "That was a historic building."

"Oh yeah, I can see why. If there's one thing you need to preserve in New Mexico, it's more fucking adobes."

The butt of her shotgun came around hard, aiming for the bridge of my nose. Luckily, I managed to turn my head fast enough and the blow glanced off my skull just over my ear. There was pain, but nowhere near the blinding agony of a broken nose which is an event I am familiar with, having snapped my septum three times that I'm aware of.

"Bastard!" she repeated.

I could have rejoined with "bitch," but I didn't feel quite that plucky after getting whacked.

"Who helped you break out of jail?" she demanded.

Hadn't Rob and the boys explained? I couldn't see why they wouldn't. And what about the future son-in-law of Dr. Gunter? "Didn't Dustin tell you?"

"They all gave me some bullshit story about a guy in a red satin costume. Bullshit!" she said. "Was it that woman you were with? That Alison Brooks? I'd love to arrest that red-headed little whore."

Now I was pissed. Gomez-Gomez could insult me all she wanted, but nobody—not even a goddamned tin-star sheriff with a gun—insults Alison.

Unfortunately, my arms were pinioned under the blankets. If I could get free, I might be able to knock her gun aside and give her a stiff jab on the chin. Usually, I don't hit women, but Gomez-Gomez had spoken crudely of the woman I love. This time, I'd make an exception.

But she was smarter than I thought. She stepped back a few paces, still holding the gun on me, and ordered, "Get up."

I pulled my arms out from under the covers and folded them loosely across my chest. There might still be a chance. "I'm not dressed," I said.

"Well, excuse me. A thousand pardons." Her sarcasm was unbecoming. When she tossed her head, her long hair escaped from under the Western hat and writhed around her face like snakes. "I've seen it before, McCleet. Now get your skinny ass out of that bed."

As I sat up in the bed, I saw Gunter, already standing near the exit from the tent. His hands were cuffed neatly in front of him. But, apparently, the sheriff hadn't noticed Monte who had, during the night, wriggled across the wood floor and ended up under the computers.

From the corner of my eye, I saw him waken.

Yawning and stretching, I made as much noise as I could to keep her attention focused on me.

I prayed that Monte would be clever, that he'd slyly creep up on the unsuspecting sheriff and disarm her before she could get off a wild shot.

No such luck.

As soon as Monte's eyes opened, he recognized immediately that there was a dangerous situation underway. Throwing off his blankets, he jumped to his feet and said, "Oh, my God!"

Last night before going to sleep, Monte had stripped down to his skivvies. He wore cotton Mighty Morphin Power Ranger briefs. On top, he wore a sleeveless cotton T-shirt with the Pink Ranger performing a karate kick across his chest. I had no idea that there were Power Ranger underwear sets for adult men.

Neither did Gomez-Gomez.

She swung toward Monte. And, for about three seconds, she stared.

That was enough time for me to spring from the bed, shove her gun aside and pop her in the jaw with a hard right.

She went down like a sack of pinto beans.

I wasn't proud of myself. Slugging a woman isn't something that makes a man stand tall. But it had to be done.

I snapped at Monte. "Get dressed."

"Did you kill her?"

"No."

"God, Adam, you're so violent."

Gunter bustled toward me, holding out the cuffs. "She has the key on her belt. Get these off me."

In a matter of minutes, Monte and I had uncuffed him and

had carried the sheriff outside. As far as I could see, there were two choices for escape: We could take the crippled New Yorker or the police squad car. I pointed, "She gets the rental."

We slipped her into the driver's seat. She was just regaining consciousness when I cuffed her left hand to the steering wheel of the New Yorker and plugged the key into the ignition.

Through dazed eyes, she glared at me with an expression of pure venom.

"Be careful with the car," I said. "The axle's going. Just drive real slow, and you'll be all right."

She whimpered. It was a female sound that tore at my heart and made me feel like an asshole of the highest order, but I didn't have time for guilt. Gently, I closed the car door and ran to her Lumina squad car.

Gunter was in the passenger seat, and I slid in behind the wheel just as Monte came hobbling out of the tent, walking carefully in his high-heeled boots. He paused to wave at the sheriff and climbed in back.

I sped away in a cloud of dust.

"Where are we going?" Monte asked. "I'm really hungry. You know that little place next to the jail? There was a sign there for espresso."

"We're on the lam," I informed him. "We're running from the law. Most fugitives don't have time for espresso."

"Well, then, how about a quickie latte?"

"Shut up, Monte." I turned to the doc. "How do we get to Dental's place?"

"Is it safe to go there? Won't the sheriff be looking there?"

"I figure we've got a couple of hours before she nurses that car back to Morning and gets herself out of the cuffs. I'm going to use that time to search. I still don't have a motive for why anyone would kill Dental."

"One thing for sure," Monte said. "In the write-up of this story, for the publicity, you know, we are not going to mention how you punched a lady. Doesn't do a thing for your manly image, Adam."

"No write-up. No publicity."

"I don't think you can avoid it. Back in Taos, some woman already contacted Alison about a story for the *Enquirer*."

"The *Enquirer?*" I said calmly as I guided the sheriff's vehicle across more deserted terrain. "Well, a high-tone publication like that should certainly improve my standing in the artistic community."

"You've got to start somewhere," Monte said. "I mean, Kato Kaelin did okay. And John Wayne Bobbitt."

"Forget it, Monte. I don't do publicity. If somebody wants to buy my sculptures because they like the work, fine. Otherwise, I don't care."

"My, my, well. Aren't we just hoity-toity art for art's sake this morning?"

"Maybe I don't deserve to have an attitude, but I've got one. So, lay off."

Dental Stoker lived in a predictably ramshackle wooden cabin at the end of a road to nowhere. As I got out of the car and slammed the door, I grumbled, "Doesn't anybody around here live in a town?"

"If we yearn for culture," Gunter explained, "there's always Taos or the opera in Santa Fe."

"The opera? Somehow, I don't see Whiney and the Stokers as big fans."

"Actually, Nelda is fond of the opera. She tells me that they've already begun rehearsal for the summer season. They're doing Wagner's *Valkeries*."

In a perverse way, Nelda's interest made sense. I could easily imagine her identifying with an opera where large women dressed in metal breastplates shrieked incessantly. I could even imagine Nelda wearing a similar outfit for a night of kinky stuff with Melvin.

The front door to Dental's place was unlocked and we went inside. The interior was unremarkable, except for a wide-screen television with a cable-control box on top. Gunter and I searched quickly for the map, paying particular attention to books where a sheet of map might be pressed between the pages.

"How big is the map?" I asked.

"About eight by ten, but it could be folded up. It's ragged along two edges where it was torn from the other pieces."

We found nothing of interest except a crate full of vintage _Playboy_ magazines. Apparently, Dental had interests other than Laddie the burro.

Monte had buried himself in the kitchen and I heard the ding of a microwave. He came into the front room, munching on a burrito. "I'm making coffee," he announced.

"We're almost done after we go through these _Playboys_ page at a time." I turned to Gunter. "There's a shack outside. We ought to take a look in there."

"What exactly are we looking for," Monte asked.

"A map." I turned to Gunter. "And maybe something else. Dental must have shown you some other proof, something that proves the existence of a spaceman. What was it?"

"Nothing," Gunter snapped. "There's nothing else."

I could tell that I was wearing him down.

"I'll stay here, and go through the _Playboys,_" Monte offered. He turned on the television. "Oh, look, cable."

I went outside. Around in back of the house, there was a shack, full of prospecting junk. Pickaxes. Lanterns. Saddlebags for the burro. But nothing of value, nothing worth killing for.

Across the yard—if you could call dirt and mesquite a yard—I noticed an odd structure, a piece of wall. Investigating, I found a circular hole, lined with rock. It was about twelve feet across and twenty feet deep. A rough wooden ladder led down one side.

"A kiva," Gunter explained. "These were used by the Pueblo Indians for ceremonies and sacred rituals."

"So," I said. "This is some kind of ancient archeological site."

"No, this was constructed by Dental to resemble an ancient archaeological site. Several years ago, he was trying to sell the property and he thought an Indian ruin might improve the value."

Bizarre logic, I thought, but somehow it was appropriate for Morning, New Mexico. To Gunter, I said, "Doesn't it occur to you that a guy who faked a kiva might also sucker you in with a fake alien?"

"I'm not an idiot, Adam. I did my own investigation, and I am satisfied that Dental Stoker was telling me the truth."

"How much money did you give him to search?"

"Not one red cent. I bought him the television, and I made sure that his needs were taken care of. But Dental wasn't into this quest for the profit."

I didn't push. He was getting that Viking bonfire look in his eyes, again. Instead, I gazed down the stone walls. "Could he have hidden anything down there?"

"It's possible. Sometimes, the Indians would have caches in the rocks for their sacred pipes and tools."

"We're here," I said. "Might as well check it out."

I descended the rickety ladder slowly and carefully, testing each rung before I trusted it to hold my weight. Gunter came after me, moving with equal care. The floor of the kiva was packed dirt. In the exact center, there was a circle of stones for a fireplace.

"You're the expert," I said. "How do we find hidey-holes?"

"Look for oddly jutting rocks or ones that are worn. Feel in the cracks to see if any of them move."

It was slow going. As far as I could tell, all the rocks were irregular in shape and all basically the same reddish-adobe color. Gunter went clockwise, and I went counter, figuring we'd meet in the middle.

This had to be one of the most boring searches I'd ever undertaken. Usually, when you're going through a person's possessions, there are highlights, like the _Playboy_ magazines. But these were just rocks. After about half an hour, the search was beginning to feel futile to me.

Then a rock moved. I jiggled it again. "Gunter. I think I've got something."

Carefully, I wedged the stone from its place in the wall. There was a space behind it, maybe another five or six inches back. I reached my hand inside and pulled out a small book, wrapped in plastic. The leather cover was battered. The gold lettering on the front was almost worn away, but I could still read the words. "My Diary."

I started to unwrap the plastic, but Gunter stopped me. "Please, Adam. We have to be careful with this. It might be from the 1860's, and it's been exposed to this dry desert air. The pages might crumble."

"Is this valuable?" I questioned. "Is this worth killing Dental to obtain?"

"Doubtful."

I tossed the book over to him. "You take care of this, Doc."

His smile was pure delight as he held the book in his hands. "Imagine what this might be. An eye-witness account of the alien landing. A record of daily life in this desolate country during the time of the Indian Wars when the trappers and traders and missionaries roamed this mysterious land."

In spite of my frustration about the lack of progress in my investigation, I was beginning to like Gunter again. You can't help but respect somebody who is so caught up in his work. This wasn't such a bad life, I thought. Wandering around in strange places, exploring like a latter day Viking.

I was so caught up in his excitement that I hadn't heard

someone approach. But someone had. Because, the rickety ladder was suddenly snatched away and pulled up over the edge of the rocks.

"Hey," I shouted. "Is that you, Sheriff?"

"What's going on?" Gunter demanded.

Then there was another sound. A soft thud as a flowered pillowcase was dropped over the edge of the kiva. The pattern reminded me of Rob Crusoe's sheet, and I called out, "Hey, Rob! Is that you, man."

Gunter pointed to the sack. It was moving.

From the mouth of the pillowcase, a very unhappy snake emerged. It was five feet in length with a bony, triangular-shaped head and a diamond pattern on its back. A rattler.

The bag moved again. The first snake had friends.

Chapter
Six

I never was particularly fond of reptiles. During my enforced expeditions in the jungle highlands of Vietnam, I became acquainted with a wide variety of exotic crawling creatures, denizens of earth, air and water, but I never got over that initial shudder of revulsion which was followed by the only sensible reaction for warm-blooded homo sapiens: Kill that fucker.

Perhaps, Gunter didn't have my background and familiarity with the slimier aspects of nature. I doubted that he would have encountered many poisonous reptiles in the ivy-covered halls of academia.

When the snakes crawled out of the bag, he screamed. Not a well-bred, educated, "Eek, a snake." He opened his throat and shrieked at the Norse Gods as if he'd just driven his Volvo into a fjord. Then, he leapt into my arms. Actually, he tried to climb me, using my body as a human ladder to higher ground. I couldn't say that I blamed him. If Gunter had reacted a second slower, or I faster, it might have been me climbing him.

"Stop it!" I tried to disentangle his stocky arms from around my neck as I shuffled from one side of the kiva to the other, keeping as much distance as possible between us and the angry rattlers. But Gunter was possessed of superhuman strength, like those people who can lift semi-trailers in moments of panic.

That's what I was seeing here. Panic. Unadulterated falling-down, throwing-up, soil-your-trousers panic.

Unfortunately, I didn't have time for a counseling session with the good doctor. The snakes appeared to be experiencing their own venomous brand of trauma as they slithered aggressively. That's what snakes do. They're not very clever animals. All they can really do is hiss and stick out their tongues and slither and rattle. And when they're confused and frightened they strike at everything.

The largest of the crew, the granddaddy of the other snakes, had coiled himself into a ball and was shaking his tail.

Now would have been a propitious time for Monte to appear. I stared up at the outer edge of the kiva. But there was no one in sight. Only the round sun showering light, moving inexorably toward high noon.

With Gunter still clinging to my torso like a koala to a eucalyptus tree, I kept an eye on the coiled rattler. I had no weapon, except for the rock I had wedged out of the wall, and the rocks around the center kiva campfire.

The snake made its strike, uncoiling and whizzing through the air like a javelin.

I stepped out of the path of its trajectory, and the big rattler crashed nose first into the wall.

Now, he was extra pissed. His body whipped around like a high-pressure fire hose out of control. His three companions drew into coils of their own. Within the small radius of the kiva, there was no place to stand that wasn't within striking distance of one snake or another.

I stood still as a statue and spoke in the calmest voice I could manage. "Gunter, you've got to get off me."

"No," he said nervously. "I'm fine right here."

"No, you're not. If you don't get off me so I can move around, we're both going to get bit to death."

He trembled uncontrollably. He seemed barely able to find enough wind in his lungs to say, "Please. I can't."

"It'll be okay. As long as you move very slowly and stand perfectly still against the wall, they won't strike at you."

The big snake had coiled again, flicking its tongue and shaking his rattle. Three feet from where I stood, he watched our every move through black, beady eyes.

It took a little more coaxing, but Gunter finally relaxed his grip and lowered his legs toward the ground.

"Slow and easy," I cautioned. "No sudden moves. You'll be just fine."

"If you say so," Gunter whispered nervously.

Killing the biggest snake was easy. As soon as it sunk its fangs into Gunter's calf, I grabbed the reptile by the neck. The snake might have weighed twenty pounds but as it flexed and thrashed and coiled to shake itself free, it felt more like a hundred pounds. At that moment I fully understood the implications of grabbing a tiger by the tail. I held the rattler's head against the kiva wall and smashed it to an unrecognizable pulp with the rock from Dental's stash.

My heart pounded like a pile driver as I flung the twisting corpse to the other side of the circle.

Gunter clutched his chest and slumped to the ground with a prolonged groan. I doubted that the venom had taken affect so quickly. More likely he was having a heart attack. The poor old guy had trusted me and I had gotten him seriously bitten. But it wouldn't be the poison that would kill him. It would be his own heart unless I could get him some help in a hurry.

I tried to go to Gunter's aid, but a second snake, positioned amongst the rocks in the fire pit, rattled nervously. The message was unmistakable. Don't move.

This snake was much smaller than the first, about two feet in length, but I was certain he was no less formidable than his big brother, probably faster and just as poisonous. Though he was a little further away than the first snake, it was still too close for comfort. I stood perfectly still and tried to evaluate my options.

I still held the rock, now shiny with snake goo, but it wasn't heavy enough to do any damage if I threw it. Probably the exercise would only serve to further agitate the snake. But he was coiled amongst the only larger rocks. There was no way he'd let me get close enough to grab him by the neck unless I could get him to bite Gunter's other leg. I toyed with that idea for a moment but I felt far too guilty already.

I didn't necessarily want to kill the snake. I just wanted it to move to the other side of the kiva and let me help Gunter, whose breathing had become shallow and rapid. His chest heaved with each labored gasp. He was hyperventilating, rushing poisoned blood to his heart.

I knew nothing about the boredom quotient of your average reptile but I suspected this was a high point in the life of this particular snake. He probably wouldn't lose interest real soon. I had to make something happen.

Taking care not to telegraph my movement, with a flex of my fingertips, I pushed the small rock toward the rattler. As the rock rolled, the snake struck at it. At that instant, I lunged forward and stomped on its head. The muscular body thrashed and twisted as I picked up the largest stone in the fire pit and raised it above my head. As soon as I removed my foot, I smashed the fifteen-pound rock with all the force I could manage, onto the head of the snake. The body continued to thrash as I raised the stone and smashed it down three more times until the twisting thing fell still. I raised the stone again and prepared to take on the two remaining snakes, but they had coiled themselves in the cool shadow at the opposite side of the kiva, and seemed to have little interest in the demise of their friends.

I turned my attention back to Gunter. "Stay calm," I said, kneeling beside him. "You'll be okay."

"You already said that," he choked, "and now I'm dying."

"I know. And I'm sorry. But I will get you out of here."

The only snake-bite first aid I knew was what I'd seen in cowboy movies, and I remembered hearing that some of that was incorrect but I couldn't remember which part. Gunter had enough to worry about without me telling him that if the venom or his heart didn't kill him, my snakebite treatment might. I yelled for Monte, hoping that the coward who'd thrown the snakes at us had not killed him. In spite of his eccentricities, he was a good friend. The world would be a sadder place without him. Besides, we'd need his help to get out of the pit.

Frequently checking over my shoulder to make sure the other snakes kept to their own side of the kiva, I propped Gunter to a sitting position against the kiva wall. Elevate the heart above the wound. I knew this was correct. Using the pillowcase that had contained the snakes, I tied a tourniquet around his thigh, just above the knee. Not too tight. That sounded familiar. Now came the part that I was mostly unsure of. "Gunter, do you have a knife?"

"In my pocket," he groaned, still clutching his chest.

I yelled for Monte several more times as I searched Gunter's trouser pockets and retrieved a small, stainless-steel key-chain knife with a blunt, single-edged blade, a fingernail file, and a bottle opener with a flat screwdriver tip. Gunter winced as I made a deep cross incision in the center of the inflamed lump on the side of his calf. At this point in the movie, John Wayne would have sucked the poison out, but there seemed to be no need for that. Blood, which had only trickled from two small punctures, now flowed profusely onto the dirt floor of the kiva. I decided to take a pass on the sucking part.

Monte had still not responded to my calls and Gunter was looking worse by the minute. I gathered some of the smaller rocks from the fire pit and laid them beside him. "I'm going to have to climb out on my own. Try to stay calm. Stay conscious and keep an eye on the other snakes. They seem to be content where they are, but if they move closer throw these rocks at them."

Gunter tensed and grabbed my arm. "Please," he moaned, "don't leave me."

"I won't. Not for long. But I need help to get you out of here. I know you're scared. So am I. But I won't let you die." There was no earthly reason why he should trust me, so I added, "We have to find Glows In The Dark."

"Shines At Night," he said, releasing his grip.

"Whatever."

I stood and dug my fingers into a gap in the rocks about two feet above my head. There were enough crevices and edges to grip because this wasn't a professionally mortared job. It was just Dental, trying to make an artifact and doing a crude job of it.

But free-climbing a vertical wall isn't easy.

I tried to visualize myself as one of those weekend adrenalin junkies who conquer sheer cliffs with nothing but the strength of their fingers and toes. Breathing, meditating, concentrating, I advanced my right hand, digging my fingertips into a new crack. Then the left foot, up a few inches. Then the left hand followed by the right foot. Then repeating the process. It was working. I could feel the sweat beading up on my forehead. Each painstaking movement was a new challenge.

"I'm too old for this shit," I muttered.

Not that I was in prime rock-climbing condition at any point in my life. No doubt the only reason I could make any upward progress whatsoever was the strength in my hands and forearms. I'm a sculptor. I chisel and hammer and lift in my daily work. Though I hadn't planned for my art to be conditioning for escape from a snake pit, it made the difference.

The hardest part came when I actually reached the top and

had to haul my entire body up and over. If I fell, at this point, there was a good possibility of broken bones and multiple snake bites.

And where was Monte? I had a bad feeling. Whoever had trapped us in the kiva and dropped the snakes must have discovered Monte in Dental's cabin. I felt a chill as I tried to come to grips with the possibility that he might be dead or seriously injured.

I had my shoulders over the edge. Using my toes, poking in the rocks for footholds, I forced myself higher until I was up and out of the kiva.

For about half a minute, I just lay there gasping, like a beached seacow, too weary to move back into the safety of the surf.

Then, I dragged myself upright, got the ladder and lowered it back into the hole. I was soaked with sweat, out of breath and exhausted when I reached the bottom.

Gunter had remained conscious and the snakes had stayed in their shady resting place. I wasted no time in hoisting Gunter over my shoulders for the final ascent.

My legs trembled and the weathered rungs of the ladder creaked and popped under our combined weight, but everything held. And in a few minutes we were out for good.

In the sunlight, Gunter didn't look as bad as he had in the shadows of the kiva, surrounded by poisonous reptiles. I laid him down in the dirt so I could catch my breath and I could see the sincere gratitude in his eyes. "You saved me, Adam."

I'd also been the one to suggest he stand very still so the big rattler couldn't possibly miss. But I didn't remind him of this fact. With great confidence, I said, "You're going to make it. You'll be all right."

"I owe you the greatest debt. I owe you my life."

"Forget it."

"I've not been forthcoming with you." He shuddered but

seemed determined to continue. "You were right when you said Dental must have owned something worth killing for. He did. It was something that convinced me there really was a spaceman."

"What was it?"

He exhaled a deep breath. "A screw."

"No, really. I deserve to know, after what we've been through together."

"A screw. From another planet," he said.

"Okay." I wasn't going to push; Gunter was probably delirious. "Rest here for a minute while I find Monte."

The exterior of the house didn't look good. There was no sign of movement, and the television was playing loud. Too loud, I thought.

Cautiously, I pushed open the door. A blast of music, MTV, assaulted me. "Monte?" I yelled.

A trilling voice responded, "In here, Adam."

He was sitting in a La-Z-Boy recliner with his red boots up, flipping through *Playboy* and watching a music video at full volume. He pointed the remote at the big screen television and turned down the sound. "How about that Madonna?"

"That's all you have to say for yourself?"

I had just faced venomous death from four rattlesnakes and had been through a twenty-foot, knuckle-scraping climb from a kiva. And all that time, my sterling cohort, the man who had promised to be Sundance to my Butch Cassidy, was sitting here a couple of hundred feet away, ogling rock video sluts on the tube. "Fuck Madonna!"

"Wouldn't I just love to! Truth or dare."

One thing was certain, one-hundred-percent certain, if I was to continue this investigation—and there didn't seem to be much alternative—I wasn't dragging Monte along with me. "Of all the worthless—"

"God, you're a mess, Adam. You've got some kind of soot and gunk all over your face. You know there's a shower here."

Before he launched into a lecture on my hygiene, I said, "Gunter's been bitten by a rattlesnake. We need to get him to a doctor."

"A snake?" Monte plunked his red boots on the floor. "I know all about snakebite. Where's Gunter?"

I led him outside, noticing that he had subtly tucked one of the _Playboys_ into the waistband of his tight, white, filthy pants. "How do you know about snakes?"

"I dated a herpetologist. She liked to play snakebite and have me suck poison out of her body. Of course, that's not really how you do it."

"Of course not," I said. "Maybe that's how John Wayne would do it, but I know better."

Monte would have made a good nurse. He knelt down beside Gunter, soothed his brow and made cooing noises. After he took a look at my loose tourniquet and the ragged slash, he looked up at me and nodded. "Good job, Adam. Very professional. I don't suppose you ever dated a herpetologist."

"What do we do next?"

"Now, we need to get Gunter to a doctor."

"No doctor," Gunter moaned. "Take me to _la curandera_. She lives in Pig Eye."

"Where?"

"Pig Eye. Back to the main road. A mile over the ridge."

Monte patted his arm. "What's a _la curandera?_ "

"I've heard of them," I said. "It's a healer of some sort. Gunter, has she got a name?"

"Ask anybody in Pig Eye."

I hoisted Gunter under his armpits and Monte took his feet. With a minimum of difficulty, we loaded him into the back seat of the police coupe. I was about to leap into the driver's seat and burn rubber when Monte pointed out the obvious, "Adam, you can't go anywhere like that?"

"We're not going to a fiesta, Monte."

"You have blood all over. I imagine that, even in Pig Eye, New Mexico, you're going to frighten the local residents. Not to mention the local police, and I don't think—"

"All right." I went back into the house, rummaged in Dental's closet and found one of his woolen jackets with a lining. Once it had been red and black, now it was faded to a worn blur. But it would keep me warm in the night and would cover the blood on my own clothes. Dental's penchant for overlarge clothes served me well; the jacket only pinched slightly in the shoulders. I stuck one of his beat-up, sloppy-brim cowboy hats on my head for good measure.

Even if I had time for a shower, I wouldn't have taken one. I wanted to look as mean and dirty as Clint Eastwood in the early spaghetti Westerns. When some unknown person dumped those snakes into the kiva, this fight became more personal. I was no longer battling to save my good name, but my ass as well. Threat of bodily harm tends to affect me that way. I get cranky.

I returned to the car where Monte was leaning over the passenger seat, showing Gunter pictures in *Playboy*.

"God, Adam, that's awful. You have no fashion sense."

"Good," I said. "I want to blend in."

I started the car.

"You're mad," Monte said. "I can tell you're mad."

"Shut up, Monte."

"I have good news." He held up a yellowed scrap of paper, about eight by ten with ragged edges on two sides. "I found the map. It was tucked in the centerfold for Miss July of 1982. Her name is Sahara Sonora. She likes her martinis dry and her men wet."

"Give me that."

I studied the map. It was, as Gunter had insisted, a single straight line with an "X" at the end. From the ragged edges I could see that this was the upper left portion. The paper was old and weathered, but it had been thoughtfully laminated to preserve it. I wondered if that was Dental's idea or Gunter's.

Gunter made a loud groaning noise from the back seat and I handed the map to him.

He accepted it reverently. "Nice work, Monte."

"Well, it really was tedious, reading all those magazines, you know. But somebody had to do it."

When I thought of him ogling vintage _Playboys_ with the MTV blaring, I could have killed him with my bare hands. But then that would be murder, and the charges against me would be justified, and I wouldn't give Gomez-Gomez the satisfaction of being right.

I drove to a mesa overlooking a ribbon of paved highway that almost resembled a main road. Though it was unmarked, I could see actual traffic—two trucks—rumbling along at the lazy mañana pace that seemed to be the norm in Rio Arriba county, New Mexico.

Since the police car was not a subtle means of transportation, especially not if Gomez-Gomez had reported it missing, I waited until the trucks were out of sight. Once on the road, I floored it. In the wink of a pig's eye, we were there. I knew it was Pig Eye because there was a huge sign that said: Elk Snort Cafe, Home of the Pig Eye Fry.

I rolled down the window of the car and asked a local resident who was carrying a paper bag by the throat, "Excuse me, do you know where I can find _la curandera?_"

He pointed to a dirt road and upended his bag.

Gunter was lying real quiet in the back seat, and I knew I needed to hurry.

I swerved. The road meandered past a couple of pitiful, adobe houses. These were hovels with sticks and clumps of sod for roofs on unmarked streets where the only color was chipped paint on the doorways. I'd heard that _curanderas_ believed they got their power from God, so I guessed I'd found the place when

I saw a life-sized nativity scene in the yard of a three- or four-room adobe house with a blanket for a door.

A huge sow wallowed in the pathway that led to the house, and I couldn't help but wonder about the sanitary conditions. I turned around in the seat. "Gunter, are you sure you want to go here?"

"Really," Monte said. "I mean, I'm all in favor of alternative medicine, but this is so primitive."

A little boy with brown eyes like a Keene painting appeared in the doorway. He darted up to the car. "My grandmother says you should bring Gunter inside."

Here is where things get even weirder, I thought. But Gunter was trying to open the back door of the car himself. Here was where he wanted to be.

Chapter Seven

Monte and I carried Gunter into the home of *la curand-era*. On the other side of the blanket was an open door. The little boy closed it behind us and said, "My grand-mother says you must wait here."

I wasn't surprised. All medical professionals have waiting rooms, even *la curandera*. I looked at the boy. "So, where are the insurance forms?"

He pointed at the ceiling. "God don't take Blue Cross. My grandmother prepares. She will be with you soon."

Monte and I lowered Gunter onto a dusty sofa under a black velvet painting of Jesus wearing a crown of huge, barbed-wire type thorns with rivulets of bright red blood pouring from the wounds. The eyes of the painting were haunting, and they seemed to follow my every move. As if I didn't already feel guilty enough about Gunter's snakebite, now I was being watched by Jesus.

Monte stuck his hands on his hips and stared at the painting. "Well, glory hallelujah! So, Adam, what do we do next?"

"*We* don't do anything. *You* go back to Taos." I knelt down beside Gunter who seemed to be breathing more easily. "How are you doing?" I asked him.

"Been better."

"We're here at *la curandera*'s place," I told him. "This is where you wanted to be. Right?"

"Yes." He smiled weakly and closed his eyes.

Monte pouted. "I don't know why you want to get rid of me, Adam. Butch would never do this to Sundance."

"You want to play Butch and Sundance?" As I stood, I could feel the small vein in my temple begin to throb. "Remember how they ended up? The Federales blew numerous large holes in them, Monte. You want to become a human pegboard?"

"All right, Adam. Point made. Jesus!" He glanced at the painting. "Sorry."

"As soon as humanly possible, Monte, you go to the Sundog Gallery. Sell some of my sculptures for a lot of money, just in case this doesn't work out and I need to hire a squad of expensive attorneys."

"I'll set up publicity," he said. "There was that possible interview with the tabloids. And, of course, I need to tell everybody about the whole alien thing."

Gunter made a coughing noise in the back of his throat. "No. Don't tell anyone about the alien. Not until . . ." He wheezed. "Not until I find it."

I agreed with him. But not for the same reason. I didn't want to talk about Yada Yada Hokey Dokey because mention of the alien seemed to bring out the weird in people, Gunter included.

Though I hated to think that Dental was murdered because of the alien, the map, and the space screw, that was probably close to the truth. And there was, very likely, some alien-hunting reason why someone had dumped the snakes into the kiva, but the logic escaped me. Why would anybody want to kill me and Gunter? Who would want to kill us? If I'd been a betting man, I would have laid odds on Rob Crusoe. The pillowcase with the flowered sheet pattern was something of a calling card for his cult.

I was about to settle back into serious contemplation of the crime when an old woman, no more than five feet tall, appeared from behind a ragged curtain on the far side of the room. Her skin was a dark brown with deep creases that followed the contours of her face like a topographic map. A cascade of silver-gray hair draped her shoulders and extended nearly to the floor. A full, long sleeved dress of wrinkled black linen covered her delicate frame from neck to toe. She was ancient—older than Gunter—older than anyone I'd ever seen before. But her dark eyes were bright and innocent like the eyes of a child, at the same time wise, all-knowing. They were the same eyes as in the Jesus painting over the sofa. Around her neck she wore an ornate rosary with an enormous silver crucifix that might have been more appropriate for the archway of the Sistine Chapel. In her bony hands she cradled a shallow wooden bowl containing a clear liquid. No introduction was required. She was _la curandera_.

As she crossed the room, she didn't shuffle or hobble or even walk. She just crossed the room.

I looked at Monte who stared, mouth agape, transfixed. For the first time since I'd known him, he was speechless.

I was about to tell her that Gunter had been snake bit about an hour and a half ago. But the old woman held up a hand to silence me before I could make a sound. It was almost as if she'd heard the words when they formed in my mind.

Standing at Gunter's side, _la curandera_ mumbled something in Spanish, a prayer, barely audible as she dipped the tip of her index finger into the bowl and traced a cross on his forehead.

Gunter gasped and began to tremble violently. For a moment I thought he would pass out, but then his eyes opened wide and his breathing eased. The woman took his hand and he stood, slowly, as if in a trance. They crossed the room together and disappeared behind the ragged curtain.

For several minutes neither Monte or I spoke. We just stood there trying to fathom what we had just seen. Then the boy came with beans and tortillas and a pitcher of water.

We ate and drank in silence, listening to the singsong chant emanating from behind the curtain. At first the words were Spanish, but then I started to recognize other languages mixing into the chant. Japanese, Yiddish, Arabic, Russian. After a while the language seemed to change with each word. I fell asleep listening to the old woman's song.

I slept deep and solid without dreams or interruption until I felt a hand on my shoulder. My eyes opened slowly and focused on the boy standing over me.

It took a moment to realize where I was. The only window in the room transmitted golden, half-light rays of afternoon. I'd been sleeping for hours, sitting upright on the lumpy sofa. But I felt no stiffness in my neck, no fuzz in my head. For that matter, I couldn't feel the nagging ache at the back of my skull where I'd been wacked by Dental Stoker's murderer. Monte sat at the other end of the sofa, still asleep.

I turned back to the boy. "Is Gunter—"

"My grandmother is finished," the boy said. "Your friend is well. He would like to see you."

I stood, expecting pain in my lower back from sleeping in a sitting position, but there was none. "Monte," I said, giving his shoulder a shake.

He woke the same way I had, first looking around the room and then realizing where he was. He checked his wrist watch. "I don't believe it. It's almost five o'clock. I've been asleep for hours."

"We both have. How do you feel?"

Monte stood and placed his hands at the small of his back. He stretched and twisted his neck from side to side. "I feel great. I haven't felt this fabulous since I was sixteen."

Neither had I. This was truly a magical place. "Let's see how Gunter is doing."

The boy led us through the ragged curtain then retreated. The small square room had no windows. At least a hundred candles burned on tables and chairs and shelves surrounding the narrow bed where Gunter sat, propped upright against the wall, his legs covered by a brightly colored patchwork quilt. The scent of paraffin and herbs permeated the air. A crucifix, even larger than the one the old woman wore around her neck, and another Jesus painting hung on the wall above Gunter's head.

On the other side of the room, opposite the bed, another painting, hung by thumbtacks—a beautiful unframed watercolor of a dahlia in pastels of pink and purple and lavender. It was an original work. Not a print. I recognized the artist's signature. So did Monte. He went straight for it.

Reverently, he whispered, "Oh my God. Adam, this is a Georgia O'Keeffe."

"I know." I was as astounded as he was. But now, everything about this humble little dwelling and the woman who lived here astounded me. I turned my attention to Gunter. Taking into account that everyone looks better by candlelight, he looked healthier than I could have imagined possible.

"How do you feel, Gunter?"

He smiled serenely. "I can't remember a time when I've felt stronger. I spoke to the Gods."

"I'm sure you did. There was a lot of praying going on in here."

"No, Adam. I didn't just pray. I saw the Gods, and I spoke to them."

"You mean like Norse Gods? In a dream." Monte questioned.

Gunter laughed heartily. "No, young man. I mean like Jesus and Buddha and Allah and Krishna. And many more. I spoke to them all at once." He was animated. "They were here. In this room. All of them. I was wide awake and they spoke to me with one great, heavenly voice."

"Really?" Monte asked. "So? What did you talk about?"

Gunter scrunched up his bushy gray eyebrows and thought for a moment. "I can't remember. But it was wonderful. Magical. Truly magical."

Neither Monte or I commented. I think we both sensed that this was not the place to question miracles. Now, if I could only get *la curandera* to figure out who killed Dental, life would be truly perfect.

The boy poked his head into the room. "Señor Adam, I think you should come with me."

I followed him to the waiting room. He pointed toward the window. "Look."

I had a real nasty premonition about what might be outside. It wasn't likely that the boy had called me out here to see the New Mexico version of the Good Humor man, selling chili-flavored ice cream on a stick. Whatever was outside was unpleasant, and I didn't want to look. Just for a few minutes, I wanted to prolong my sense of rightness with the universe.

"Look," the boy repeated.

I peeked around the edge of the window frame. Outside, at the end of the worn path leading to *la curandera*'s door was Shirley Gomez-Gomez. Even from this distance, she looked meaner than hell and more pissed off than a pillowcase full of rattlesnakes. Her jaw, where I'd popped her, was swollen and discolored. Her hat was off and she'd tied a red bandana around her matted black hair. Sneering like vengeance, she propped her hip against the leather seat of a Japanese-brand motorcycle with knobby dirt-bike tires.

"What's she doing now," I muttered. I asked the boy, "Why hasn't she come in here to arrest me?"

"Respect for _la curandera,_" said the boy. "In here, the sick and troubled find sanctuary."

Sanctuary was a plus, but I suspected that our continued safety was tenuous, especially when Shirley ripped the poptop off a beer can with her teeth and downed the contents in three glugs. She crumpled the can in her bare hand and flung it down in the dirt. I couldn't believe she'd be patient for much longer. I didn't much trust her sense of logic, either. For some reason, the feminist sheriff from Morning was still playing Lone Ranger. She hadn't called in the state cops. Why?

I turned to the kid. "How can we get away from here without being seen?"

He shrugged his skinny shoulders. "Wait until dark."

I didn't think we had that much time. My sense of urgency elevated when I heard Shirley bellow. Her voice sounded raw as a prolonged belch.

"I know you're in there, McCleet. Get out here so I can lock up your fucking gringo ass."

Since the Morning jail was demolished, I wondered where she kept her alternative lock-up. The trunk of her car? A deep kiva with more snakes?

"I have an idea," the boy said. "Wait here."

His offer was an affront to my manhood and my intelligence. This was a ten-year-old kid who probably knew more about the Mighty Morphin Power Rangers than escaping from the law. We didn't need to rely on a kid to plan our escape. I squared my shoulders. "Okay," I said.

Back in the sick room, Gunter was recovering nicely. He and Monte were chatting calmly about the murder and the suspects.

"Don't forget Dustin Florence," Gunter said.

"Who?" Monte questioned.

I explained. "Dustin is a preppie who's about to become Gunter's son-in-law."

"Not if I have anything to say about it," Gunter snapped with renewed vigor. "I didn't like him."

I liked him fine as a suspect for murder. Dustin was just the sort of individual who begs for a major slap in the face, and it doesn't get more major than Murder One. "Unfortunately," I pointed out. "Dustin couldn't have killed Dental because he didn't show up until the day after the murder."

"He's after something," Gunter said.

"Your daughter?"

"My Freya," Gunter said. "She's a beautiful woman. Blond and healthy. Wide hips. That's good for child-bearing. Ah yes, she's a fine catch, but I think her fiancé is after something else." Darkly, he whispered, "The alien."

Not the alien, again. Before we got off into wild speculation, I updated them on current events, including the arrival of Shirley Gomez-Gomez.

Gunter's smile didn't falter. "You know, Adam, whoever finds the alien will be wealthy beyond their dreams."

"I don't care."

"I do," Monte said. "How much?"

"The certified body of an alien would command a tremendous price in legitimate markets, including the United States government. And suppose the finder wanted to sell to a tabloid or private individual with a yen for interplanetary objects. I'm sure you are aware of the princely sum paid for the bones of the Elephant Man."

"Millions," Monte said wistfully.

I still didn't care. My only concerns were to find the murderer, to get Gomez-Gomez off my butt, and to return to my formerly contented life as a semipopular artist.

I heard Shirley yelling from the front yard. "McCleet! Hey, you asshole! Why aren't you coming out? Hey, chicken shit."

"It could be us," Gunter continued. "We could find the alien. Monte, give me the map and I'll show you."

He spread the laminated piece of paper on the bed quilt. "It's a straight line, true. But look over here at this edge. There's just enough of a trace there to make out the beginnings of letters. After careful study, Dental and I had deduced that the letters were 'S' and 'F.' "

"Seed and Feed?" Monte guessed.

"It stands for Stoker Farm, which is what Morning once was. Now, I postulate that those letters indicated the Stoker Farm as a landmark. Then, there is this straight horizontal line pointing in a direction that I hope is northwest."

"Leading to Margot's hacienda," I concluded. "But, you know, Gunter, I still don't give a shit. Okay? I don't care about any Yada Yada Glow in the Dark. I don't even believe in it."

"What about the space screw?"

"A screw?" Monte said delightedly. "Oh my god, a real screw from outer space. This is so exciting. Gunter, you've got to tell me all about it."

"Slightly over three inches long." Gunter held up his thumb and forefinger as a caliper. "Flat head, Phillips style. The threads go all the way up. And it does have luminescent properties. It glows in the dark."

"Fancy that," Monte said. "Spacemen got Phillips screwdrivers."

"Though Dental never allowed me to take the screw from him, he accompanied me while I ran tests, using the most sophisticated facilities at Los Alamos labs. And I had to pull some high-ranking strings to gain unquestioned access."

I could believe it. Los Alamos was, of course, the facility where the atom bomb was developed. Though it went against my better judgment to encourage him, I asked, "What did you find?"

"This screw was made from a metal unknown on this planet. It is indestructible."

"That must be a pretty valuable find," I said.

"Absolutely."

"Valuable enough that Dental might have been murdered by somebody who wanted the screw."

Quietly, Gunter nodded.

"Which means," I deduced, "that some person or persons unknown might have killed Dental Stoker to gain possession of the space screw."

Monte gloated. "You see, Adam. It's all about the alien, after all."

"No, Monte. This is about greed, the most common of human motives. Dental was unlucky enough to have possession of a thing, a glow-in-the-dark screw, that the killer wanted."

From the front of the house, I heard Shirley squawking about something. I went to the waiting room, looked out the window and watched as the kid with the plan led a procession of three people on horseback up to the door.

Shirley paced at the perimeter of the property. "Don't try anything," she yelled. "I'm warning you."

"Horses," the boy said as he reentered the room. "You can go now."

"Great! What do we owe you?" I asked as I felt for my wallet and remembered that the sheriff had confiscated everything in my pockets. "Monte, do you have any money?"

Monte produced a calfskin wallet from his hip pocket and extracted a wad of crisp bills.

The boy plucked out three twenties and paid the people, two men and a woman, who had been on horseback.

"That's not enough," I said. "Not for the horses."

"The horses belong to my grandmother, and *la curandera* cannot take your money. She works for God."

Monte started to put his money away.

"But," the boy added, "I can."

"How much?" Monte asked.

The boy concentrated for a moment and sequentially

touched all the fingers on both his hands, as if tabulating the accumulated expenses. Then he looked up to Monte and said, "All you have."

Without so much as a whimper, which was highly uncharacteristic for Monte, he emptied his wallet and handed the boy about three hundred dollars and change.

"When you are finished with the horses," the boy instructed, "let them free. They will come home."

From the front yard, Shirley screeched, "McCleet!"

With _la curandera's_ horses, I felt a little more optimistic about our chances for escape. Never mind the fact that I hadn't been on horseback for approximately fifteen years and my equestrian skills were on a par with my knowledge of snakebite treatment, meaning that I had, at one time in my life, watched a lot of cowboy movies.

Disguising ourselves as the people who had ridden up to the door, Gunter and I wrapped blankets around our heads in a style that was combination Bedouin and Pueblo Indian. Monte, of course, took the more exotic disguise of the woman. He slipped into the long turquoise skirt, flung the shawl over his head and posed. "Slap my face and call me Priscilla, Queen of the Desert."

"Let's go, Priscilla. I'll slap you later."

"Do you think I should ride sidesaddle or is that too showy?"

"This isn't a performance, Monte. Okay? Gomez-Gomez isn't going to applaud no matter how you ride the damned horse. We'll be lucky if she doesn't draw her pistola and blast our sorry butts into kingdom come."

"Don't you worry about me, Adam. I once dated a jockey." He snickered. "She was really fast."

"Shut up, Monte."

We shuffled outside, mounted our horses and rode forward slowly, with our heads down, toward Gomez-Gomez. I fought an urge to look at her so I could gauge her reaction to our escape party. So far, so good. We were almost even with her dirt bike.

I figured she had to be pretty well drunk to not recognize us right away.

She stepped into my path, blocking the way. "Hold it, you assholes."

I peeked out from under the blanket headdress, wishing my eyes were a nondescript brown instead of blue. I hoped *la curandera*'s magic was still protecting us.

"Dismount," Gomez-Gomez yelled.

Monte guided his horse up beside mine. When Gomez-Gomez reached for his reins, he dug in his heels and his horse reared.

She backed off a few paces. "I said for you people to dismount. I want to frisk you."

Monte reared his horse again. "In your dreams, sweetie."

He took off. Gunter and I were right behind him. As we charged into the open country, it was obvious that both Monte and Gunter were better horsemen than I was.

Monte's turquoise skirt flared out behind him. He leaned forward, streamlining himself and becoming part of the horse.

Beside him, Gunter rode hard, his short legs gripped the flanks of the horse. If I hadn't been there myself, I wouldn't have believed that a scant few hours ago the old Viking had nearly died.

I was third in line. Completely out of sync with the rise and fall of the horses back, my ass crashed against the saddle like a paddleball. The more I resisted, the harder I bounced.

We charged off the road and into the mesquite desert. The hot wind kicked up around us. The hooves of the horses pounded and stirred a cloud of red dust. Though I've never been an animal person, and don't own a dog or a cat or even a goldfish, I liked this horse. His gallop had an easy rhythm and he didn't seem to mind that I was a hopeless tenderfoot. After a few hundred yards, I caught the tempo and relaxed a little. Only occasionally did I flail my arms and make whooping-crane noises.

I was almost enjoying myself when I heard the blast from Gomez-Gomez's pistola. Glancing back over my shoulder, I saw that she was following us, probably twenty yards behind. Her ride on the dirt bike was more difficult because she had to dodge the mesquite bushes and rocks.

But she wasn't stopping. I knew she wasn't going to quit.

Riding hard, I pulled between Monte and Gunter. "We need to split up."

"Oh, my God," Monte said. "It's Butch and Sundance time, again."

"You go to Taos," I said, ignoring any scenario he might have in mind about leaping from hundred-foot cliffs into raging rivers. "Take Gunter."

"I'm going to Santa Fe," Gunter said. "I have a friend there, and I need to study the diary we found at Dental's place."

I'd forgotten all about the diary. "Keep in touch," I ordered him. "Sundog Gallery."

"Right."

Monte called out, "Good luck, Adam. Break a leg but not really."

We were coming up to a mesa. "Split," I ordered.

Our separation was a precision move, worthy of trick riders in a rodeo. Monte's skirts billowed in Priscilla-like splendor. Gunter exploded with a Viking bellow of farewell. "In Valhalla, Adam. See you in Valhalla."

I really hoped not. If my recollection of Norse mythology was accurate, I seemed to recall that Valhalla was where warriors go when they die. Though it sounded like heaps of fun to be carried off by large Nordic maidens, Valkyries, in breastplates and helmets with horns, I wasn't ready.

I leaned forward on my galloping steed, my charger, my mount. The longer I rode, the more I was geting into this. Even though I had no clue of where I was or where I was headed, I felt purposeful. In my head, I was John Wayne, Clint Eastwood and Eddie Arcaro rolled into one.

Predictably, Shirley Gomez-Gomez had chosen to follow me. When I glanced over my shoulder, she seemed to be gaining.

There were a number of mesas I could have climbed, but I would have made an easy target while the horse toiled up the hills. I stayed in the open country, away from box canyons and unpredictable dead ends. I was coming up to a small arroyo that led into a creek bed. Tugging at the reins, I indicated a turn, but *la curandera's* horse had a different idea. It kept going straight, running hard. Then, it leapt.

I had never made a jump on horseback before. People who do this kind of thing say that it's exhilarating. I had a different word: insane.

Everything went into slow motion. My brain told me this leaping stuff would never work. The combined weight of me and my horse was too heavy to get off the ground. And if we did get airborne, we were looking forward to a crash landing.

But we were flying. Without wings, without a net, we soared across the arroyo. I closed my eyes and held on tight.

La curandera's horse must have been equipped with landing gear because I barely felt a jolt on the other side of the arroyo.

Crossing this natural obstacle was going to leave Shirley farther behind, but I didn't make the mistake of thinking I'd made a clean getaway.

I tried to get the horse to veer right, but he pulled in the opposite direction, and I gave him his head. Obviously, the horse knew the terrain far better than I did. He charged down a narrow canyon that was getting tighter and tighter. It occurred to me that I was putting a great deal of blind faith in an animal that had a brain the size of a peanut.

At the end of the canyon, I heard the engine of the dirt bike echoing off the walls. Occasionally, the whine was punctuated by Shirley, yelling obscenities.

We were in an open-ceiling tunnel, a chute. It was as if this land had been sculpted by a playful god constructing a complex maze. Though I didn't see any light at the end, the horse seemed to know exactly where it was going. When it looked like we were out of space, the steed dodged along a tight trail. For a moment, we were out of Shirley's sight.

We burst across an open stretch. In front of us were the entrances to three canyons.

The horse selected door number one, the farthest on the right. Then, he stopped dead in his tracks.

"Come on, boy," I whispered. "Doing good. Keep it up."

La curandera's steed bent his head down and nibbled the yellow flowers off a shrub.

I dug in my heels. "Let's go, boy."

He wasn't moving.

I heard the dirt bike pull up. Shirley yelled, "I'll get you, McCleet. If it's the fucking last thing I do, I'll get you."

That was reassuring.

I heard the dirt bike plunge into another of the canyons.

Immediately, my alert steed galloped out and backtracked toward Pig Eye.

After following half a dozen twists and turns, I was completely lost, but the horse seemed to have a clear sense of direction. And, more importantly, we had lost Gomez-Gomez.

We climbed to a ridge, overlooking miles of terrain. There were no signs of human habitation, but the sun was setting behind me, so I was pretty sure of my directions. Alison wouldn't have believed me. She would have insisted that I needed a map.

Thinking of her, I smiled. She was at the Sundog Gallery. To the south. To the north, I guessed was Morning.

My horse stomped impatiently, and I turned toward the north, toward Morning. Until I solved Dental's murder, I would have no peace. So, what did I hope to find in Morning? I wasn't sure, but the major suspects seemed to be clustered in that general vicinity. Rob Crusoe and his gang of cult. Whiney, the caretaker. Consuela, the jailhouse photographer. Nelda and Melvin.

Not Melvin. I really didn't believe that Melvin killed his own father for a space screw or for any other reason. Even if there was an inheritance involved and Melvin really wanted that big-screen television, he didn't strike me as being a murderer. In my past life when I was a cop, I had developed a sense about these things. By no means was it an infallible sense, but I tended to trust my gut feelings. I sensed that I might have an ally in Melvin Stoker. Not only did the big guy have a vested interest in finding the person who murdered his father, but he was also a Viet Nam vet which made us part of a loose brotherhood.

After a lot of circling around and backtracking on *la curandera's* horse, I wound up on a ridge overlooking Morning and dismounted. Two things happened when my feet touched the hard-packed New Mexico soil. First, my legs turned to rubber. I sat down hard on the ground, but that was okay because my butt was so numb from riding that I hardly felt the impact. Then, the horse gave me a friendly nicker, turned its head and took off in a southerly direction.

"Hasta la vista," I said, waving good-bye to my stalwart steed. As he galloped off, I realized that the horse was no beauty. Though he rode like Trigger or Champion or any of those other movie horses, he looked more like a low-budget Mr. Ed. In moments, he was gone, heading back to his home with *la curandera*.

I lay down flat on the mesa top and surveyed Morning. The plan would be to wait until dark, then to approach Melvin Stoker and try to nudge him into more than five syllables.

The night chill was gathering fast, and I was glad that I'd taken Dental's jacket. I took his battered hat from my pocket and stuck it onto my head.

A half-hour's surveillance of Morning produced negligible results, except to note that the New Yorker and the cop coupe had made it back here. Two people in the sheet garb of Crusoe's cult entered the Cafe-Tavern and Jail. I caught a glimpse of large Nelda as she followed a customer onto the porch and babbled at him. But I didn't see Melvin at all.

The sun was almost gone, sliding below the mesa horizon, when Melvin Stoker came out on the porch of the Feed and Seed. He stretched and yawned and scratched his belly. After locking the doors on the Feed and Seed store, he sat down on the porch steps and pulled out his whittling. Not a murderer, I thought. He was too calm, too collected. But I could be dead wrong.

If ever my instincts had played against me, now was not the time.

As night settled, there was still no sign of Shirley Gomez-Gomez and her dirt bike. Perfect, I thought. At least, she wouldn't be waiting for me. Another car parked in front of the Cafe-Tavern and people went inside. I spotted Whiney, shuffling along the road from Margot's place, probably worried about the possible tumor and/or callus on his heel.

I crept down from the mesa and walked toward Melvin who was still sitting on the porch whittling.

He spied me well before I got there. He stood and stared through the night, watching me intently. When I got within fifty feet, I heard him whisper one syllable, "Dad?"

Chapter
Eight

My first mistake was strolling out of the dusk wearing Dental's old clothes. It truly had never occurred to me that I could be mistaken for Dental Stoker. He was shorter than me and ancient. Though I'm no spring chicken, I'm not Gabby Hayes, either.

My second mistake was not immediately correcting Melvin's impression that I was the ghost of Dental past.

Big Melvin Stoker took one step off the porch, then another and another. He started to run at me in a clumsy, loping gait.

Instinctively, I retreated. Being much faster than Melvin, I gained a few yards before he stopped running and shouted, "Wait."

I halted.

He stood very still. His big hands stretched out toward me. His rough fingers grasping through the twilight like a kid reaching for forbidden candy. Then he curled his fingers into fists and dropped them to his sides as if despairing of ever touching his father again.

Then he started to talk. His voice was low and hoarse, rusty from disuse after a lifetime with Nelda and her mind-numbing chatter. "I'm sorry, Dad. I didn't mean for it to turn out like this. I sure as hell didn't mean for you to up and get yourself killed. But I had to do what was in my heart. You know that, Dad. I couldn't let you or anybody else find that little guy and dig him up. That's not right. He was buried with honor and dignity, and I don't hold with turning him into a carnival-show exhibit."

He took another step toward me.

Just as quick, I backed up. What little guy? He had to be talking about the alien.

"Nelda wanted to go along with you." Melvin shook his head slowly from side to side. "You and her never much agreed about nothing. But you were both foursquare against me on this one. She said we'd make a lot of money if we dug up the alien, and then we could get the hell out of Morning and buy ourselves a condo in Santa Fe. But I couldn't do it, Dad. It just wasn't right. I couldn't give you my piece of the map."

He came forward two more strides.

This time, I backed up fast. My brain was telling me to run. I'd just gotten a useful bit of information. Melvin Stoker had the third piece of the map. One belonged to Dental. The second to his son. And the third, according to the doc, was in the possession of Rob Crusoe.

There was a catch in Melvin's voice. He cried out, "Don't run away from me, Dad. I miss you."

His anguish was real, and I felt like the lowest of the low for toying with a man's grief for his recently murdered father. I shouldn't have been there. I shouldn't have been playing this game, no matter how accidentally I had fallen into it.

"You know, Dad, I keep thinking that the little guy might have been a soldier . . . like I was. He might have had a family of his own someplace. And your great-great-grandpaw did the right thing in burying him, leaving his remains to rest in peace. It's not up to us to disturb him."

I hadn't thought that I could feel any more guilty, but I did.

"I'm sorry for what happened, Dad. Can you ever forgive me?" He got down on his knees. "Please, Dad, give me a sign. Tell me it's all right."

I really wanted to give him what he wanted, but I knew that as soon as I opened my mouth and spoke up, Melvin would realize that he'd just spilled his guts to an impostor ghost.

"Please, Dad."

I had to tell him who I was. Gently, I said, "Listen, Melvin. There's been a misunderstanding here."

He jumped, going from a kneeling position to upright in a second. He backed up.

"Melvin," I said, "I'm sorry, man. I didn't mean—"

"Keep away from me! You're not my daddy."

"That's what I was trying to tell you. It's me, Melvin. You know me. I'm—"

"You're Satan!"

He held up his fingers in a cross. His mouth hung open, slack-jawed. His eyes popped open so wide that, even in the dark, I could see the whites around the pupils. Perhaps, I thought, Melvin was experiencing a PTSD episode, delayed shock about the death of his father who was, as far as I knew, still lying in state in Consuela's freezer, a corpse-sicle. On the other hand, it was just possible that Melvin Stoker was crazier than a shithouse rat.

I tried again to explain. "It's me. Adam McCleet. Come on, Melvin, you know me. You took me to Margot's hacienda."

He waved his hands furiously and clapped the palms over his ears. "I won't listen to you. Don't tempt me."

"I don't want to tempt you, man." I wanted to slap him up side his big, stupid head. Melvin was my best source of inside information in Morning, and he was acting like he was a couple pecans short of a banana nut cake.

Hesitantly, I took another step toward him. For good measure, I removed Dental's battered hat. In a soothing voice, I said, "See. I'm Adam. It's okay."

He nodded blankly, then pivoted and began running back toward the Seed and Feed. He yelled, "Nelda, get my shotgun!"

I'd be damned if I was going to embark on another chase across the desert with one of the inhospitable inhabitants of Morning on my ass with a loaded weapon. I raced after Melvin.

All I really had to do was show myself. Even if Melvin was seeing demons, Nelda would recognize me. She wouldn't let her husband shoot me once they knew who I was.

I followed Melvin as he circled the Feed and Seed Store. He wasn't a runner. I could have overtaken him, but I didn't want to provoke the big guy. I kept a safe distance, trailing him around the school bus with the word "Espresso" spray-painted in green on the side.

Melvin was still running, headed toward a trailer house parked at the edge of a cottonwood grove.

"Nelda," he bellowed. "My shotgun. Get my gun."

I stayed back by the Seed and Feed Store. There was no sense in making myself an easy target. I saw big Nelda's body silhouetted in the light from the trailer. As soon as she spotted her husband, she started talking, "Melvin Stoker, what are you doing, running like that? You're going to have a heart attack if you don't blah-blah-blah."

"My gun, woman. Get my damn gun."

Though Nelda was incapable of giving a simple response, I heard the words "okay" and "I'll get it."

Obviously, I needed to make myself disappear. But I wasn't David Copperfield. I wasn't Sigfried or Roy. If I'd been one of them, I could have turned myself into a Siberian tiger and ended all my problems with one slash of my claws. I wasn't a tiger. And I wasn't Satan, either.

Thinking I might hide out in the Feed and Seed Store, I ran to the back. The heavy door was locked up tighter than a poor man's Fort Knox. Without anything as sophisticated as a dead-bolt, there were five Yale locks fastened on latches. If I'd been equipped with a screwdriver and an abundance of patience, I could have undone all the catches. But I'd left my Phillips head on my spaceship.

From the trailer, I heard Nelda say, "Here's your stupid old blah-diddy-blah gun, Melvin."

Maybe I could get into the store through the school bus. It was flush with the building, attached as neatly as an addition on a house, but there were a lot of windows on the bus. I picked up a rock to break one when I heard Melvin charging toward me, outraged as a bull elephant. I slid under the bus and waited.

Melvin stormed right on by. I heard the blast of his shotgun as he undoubtedly blew away a clump of mesquite. Then another blast from farther away. Just when I was thinking it might be safe to come out from under the bus, Nelda thundered past.

I settled down quietly to wait. The encounter with Melvin hadn't gone well. True, I'd gotten a good piece of information about the map. But I had some new questions as well. Why had Melvin begged the ghost of his father for forgiveness? The ragged depth of his sorrow worried me. Did Melvin and Dental have one last fight about revealing the location of the burial site? Did Melvin become enraged? Had he taken the pickaxe and whacked his own father?

I heard another distant rifle blast and a shriek from Nelda.

What the hell should I do now? I could continue to hang out in Morning, hoping that the murderer would reveal him or herself. However, this seemed highly hazardous, and I was making no headway in my attempts at crime-solving. Given enough

time, it seemed like I could probably offend the entire population, inciting them to organize a posse or lynch mob.

I heard someone else approach the bus where I was hiding.
I tensed, ready for what kind of action, I didn't know. There
wasn't a lot of maneuvering room under here.

In the back of my head, I knew what I wanted to do. I wanted
to find Alison and curl up next to her and have her tell me that
everything was going to be all right. She was good at comforting
gestures.

In the moonlight, I saw a pair of miserable-looking moccasins. The feet that were wearing them weaved in a drunken
dance, and the voice that accompanied them chanted an indefin-
able tune. It had to be Whiney.

He dropped to his knees and peered right in my face. "Hiya,
Adam."

"How'd you know I was here?"

"Footprints in the dirt. I tracked you," he said triumphantly.
"I am a full-blooded Pueblo Indian, you know."

I skittered out from under the bus. "I need a little help,
Whiney."

"Why ask me? It's not my problem. Why does everybody try
to take advantage of me?"

"You owe me," I said. Much as I hated to exploit my connection to Margot, I added, "My sister pays your salary for caretak-
ing."

"I know." He frowned deeply. "But she never comes to visit.
I wanna meet her."

No, you don't, I thought. Coming face to face with Margot
was an experience roughly equivalent to staring into the one
burning eye of Cyclops. But I wasn't going to tell him that. "She'd
want you to help me, Margot would. Can you tell me how I could
get to Taos?"

"We could drive," he said brightly.

"Have you got a car?"

"Nope." He shook his head loosely. Then he dug around in his pockets and produced a shiny car key. "But Margot does. I'm not supposed to take it out of the garage. Sheriff told me that if she finds me driving again, she'll lock me up until doomsday. But I do it anyhow. It's parked over the ridge so the sheriff can't see it."

"Perfect."

Moving in a direction opposite Melvin and Nelda and their intermittent shotgun blasts, I allowed him to lead me to a turn off the road where a 1982 Cadillac sedan gleamed in the moonlight. The body was in mint condition. When I keyed the ignition, the engine fired on all eight powerful cylinders.

Whiney carefully belted himself into the passenger seat. "Where are we going?"

"Taos."

I wanted hot food and a bath. I wanted to see Alison.

"Okay-dokey," Whiney said. Then, he passed out.

I eased carefully along the side roads, leading away from Morning. As soon as I found something resembling a paved highway, I floored it.

The nice thing about desolate New Mexico is that there's virtually no traffic. And the roads, when they're paved, shoot straight as an arrow from one destination to another. I thought of Gunter's map. He must have gone crazy trying to decide which stretch of road to follow.

Within half an hour, I was approaching Taos. Though I didn't know where Alison was staying, I knew how to find the Sundog Gallery. I drove into the town square where there was, apparently, some kind of fiesta underway with people dancing, mariachi music playing, and fireworks. Despite all the adventures of the day, it was only nine o'clock.

Miraculously, I found a parking place only a block away from the gallery. I turned off the car and sat there, regretting my decision to go for the mean and dirty look.

Here I was, showing up for the grand opening of an art display that could launch me toward international acclaim, and I looked like shit cubed. Too late to worry about it now. Maybe I could pass myself off as eccentric. Or maybe I could get in and out of there without anybody knowing my name.

I skulked up to the plate-glass window display at the front of the gallery where a thirty-by-forty-inch painting by Pena occupied the position of honor. Farther back in the store, beyond the elegant crowd, I could see the head and shoulders of a mermaid balanced on the outstretched tentacle of an octopus. That was one of mine, an original McCleet in aggregate. Though there weren't too many people standing and admiring my mermaid, they weren't spitting on it, either. From this distance, I couldn't see if the card describing the mermaid had been marked "Sold."

In contrast to the fiesta in the town square, the interior of the gallery was cool and serene, very high-class and suitable for the famous and international clientele. Seldom had I seen such an impressive arena for showing art. The lighting was subtle, but perfect for each piece. I was humbled by the front display of one of my marble pieces. It was an unusual green marble, like jade, depicting a sea nymphet who looked a lot like Alison.

The real woman materialized beside the sculpture. I felt the familiar rush of longing and excitement, accompanied by a determination not to be incarcerated for murder. I doubted that any penitentiary facilities came equipped with Alison. More likely, there'd be a big guy named Butch.

She turned her head, catching the light on her perfect cheekbones, and smiled up at her companion, the swarthy Frenchman named Jacques LaFraque.

He leaned close to her ear and whispered something, probably something pretentious, and Alison laughed. Then, he rested his hand at her waist. It didn't appear that she was trying too hard to stave off his advances.

My heart sank into the pit of my stomach. She didn't actually like this guy, did she? Then I reminded myself that Alison's business was dealing art. She had a high tolerance for creeps who ogled her while they signed checks for thousands and thousands of dollars. Probably, she was simply being polite with Jacques.

She laughed again, tossing her auburn hair. That was a flirtatious gesture if I'd ever seen one. Now, I was seriously annoyed. What did Jacques LaFraque have that I didn't? Besides a bath, a shave, and clean clothes?

Before leaping to any conclusions and throttling Jacques on the spot, I decided to creep into the gallery, mingling subtly with the well-heeled lookie-loos. I whipped off Dental's jacket, beat the dust off my Levi's and strolled inside.

The door closed silently behind me, blanking out the raucous mariachi music and fireworks from the street feista. In here, soft, melodious, New Age music played. I saw Yanni sitting in the back corner behind a synthesizer.

Almost everybody was dressed in black. Those who weren't, were dressed in white.

I angled my way through the gallery, trying to get close enough to hear Alison's conversation but not for her to see me. I found myself in the back, near Yanni. An evil-looking character, all in black and looking a lot like Dennis Hopper, asked the New Age musician if he knew any Steppenwolf.

I overheard Jacques describing a bronze sculpture by Tommy Hicks. "Zis piece, eet eez sexual, no?"

"Not really," Alison responded.

I glanced at the piece. It looked like a curly French fry to me.

"Zis reminds me of zee delicate crease between zee back of a woman's leg and zee buttocks."

His hand on Alison's back crept lower. If he touched her delicate buttocks, I would have to kill him.

"Hello, Adam," came a voice from behind me.

Distracted, I turned my head and muttered, "I'm not Adam."

"But of course you are." It was Dustin Florence, the prepster who wanted to marry Gunter's daughter. "I've been looking all over this godforsaken country for my future father-in-law."

"Okay," I said, keeping my eyes trained on Jacques's wandering hand. "Great."

"Is Gunter okay?" Dustin asked.

"Yeah, fine. Had a little snakebite, but he's okay."

"Snakebite?"

I tore my gaze from Alison as she and Jacques moved to another part of the gallery. "What are you doing here, Dustin?"

He gestured at the crowd as if it were obvious. He was here because anybody who was anybody in Taos was here. "Where else would I be? Look around you, Adam. That's Yanni playing the music. There's Pena. And movie stars. See the guy in all white? That's William Shatner."

"How appropriate." I wondered what would happen if I told the former captain of the *Enterprise* that I was on the trail of a real alien.

"I bought one of your sculptures," Dustin said.

I was torn by this piece of information, and I pondered it as I moved parallel with Alison and Jacques. If Dustin had the good taste to purchase one of my sculptures, he couldn't be all bad. "Which one?"

"The three-thousand-dollar one. A cute little thing. Actually, I bought it for Freya. She likes that kind of stuff."

The implication was that he, Dustin, had better taste, and I didn't ask for his opinion. It was kind of a compliment in reverse. I didn't care if people like Dustin were unimpressed by my work.

I sneaked closed to Jacques and Alison, hiding myself behind a nude sculpture near the ladies' restroom.

Jacques pointed to a still-life watercolor of a zucchini and two avocados spilling from a horn of plenty. "But, of course, thees eez a two-dimensional representation of zee primal lust, no?"

"I don't quite see it," Alison said.

"You must look deeply," he said, raising his hand to her shoulder and pulling her close. "You see? You can feel zee arousal, no?"

Alison turned her head toward him. Their noses were only inches apart. "Perhaps," she said.

What was wrong with her? Couldn't she see through this quiche-eating bag of frog snot?

William Shatner approached Dustin and me. He nodded and gestured to the door behind me. "Excuse me, gentlemen, I need to get in there."

"There?" Dustin questioned. "But that's the ladies' restroom."

"Oh my god, I was about to go where no man has gone before."

Embarrassed, he turned and strode away. Boldly.

I looked back at Jacques and Alison, who stood in front of another painting. This one was rolling hills and lightning. I didn't even have to eavesdrop to know that he was describing breasts to Alison.

Dustin was still beside me. "What did you mean when you said that Gunter was snakebit? Where is he, anyway? In a hospital?"

Quite honestly, I said, "The last time I saw him, he was riding into the sunset."

"Do you mean that literally or figuratively? He's really okay, isn't he?"

"He's okay."

I wanted this prepster to leave me alone so I could get back to obsessing about my girlfriend and her French appendage. I was really close to them, hiding myself behind a mobile of atomic art by Tony Price.

"Isn't this excellent," Dustin said. "Did you know Price uses discarded hardware from Los Alamos to make these sculptures?"

"Uh-huh." I knew that.

Once again, William Shatner came toward us. He was still carrying his wineglass and still looking. I turned to him and pointed. "It's over there!"

Unfortunately, my emphatic directions resulted in a slight bump against the mobile of atomic art. The shiny metal pieces went into frantic motion, clanking and chiming so loudly that Yanni stopped playing.

Everyone in the gallery stared at me. I could only hope that they'd think I was somebody else.

No such luck.

Jacques announced, "Ah ha! Eet eez Adam McCleet." Just in case people didn't associate the name, he added, "Zee sculptor from O—ray-gone. Le Portland."

Alison came at me. I could tell from the quicksilver expression in her eyes that she was vacillating between punching me in the nose and kissing me on the lips. She opted for a middle course, taking me by the arm and leading me toward the exit.

"We need to talk, Adam, and . . ." She sniffed the air, "Do you have any idea how wretched you smell?"

"Like two days in the desert and a life-and-death battle with a rattlesnake?"

"Monte told me all about it. You're all right, aren't you?"

"Fine," I lied.

"What's all this business about a screw from outer space?"

Before I could explain, Whiney staggered through the door, a bottle of tequila dangling loosely from his unwashed hand. He draped an arm around my shoulder and offered me a swig.

I declined and turned to Alison. "You remember Whines for No Reason, don't you?"

"Yes," she said with a strained smile. "Whiney is the Indian primitive artist who did those paintings at Margot's place."

Primitive? Yes. Indian? Yes. But the jury was still out on whether Whiney did those paintings. As I recalled, he was too concerned about tumors and split ends to tell us.

Alison focused her attention on him. "You did those paintings, didn't you?"

He moved away from me. He held up his bottle and raised his eyebrows.

"Whiney?" Alison said. "You're an artist, aren't you?"

He stumbled forward a few steps, then back. Then, he did a half-gainer that Greg Lougainis would have been proud of, into a potted plant beside the door.

Yanni stopped playing again. We were undoubtedly upsetting his vibes.

As if we hadn't caused enough of a disturbance at the Sundog Gallery, the door crashed open. The woman who entered was dressed for a fiesta, with a blood red hibiscus pinned in her coal black hair. It was my sister, Margot.

From behind us, I heard Jacques exclaim, "Sacré blue!"

In her beautifully manicured hand, she held a tabloid newspaper which was not the *Enquirer;* that would have been far too classy. This was a tabloid rip-off of a tabloid. There was a photograph of me, peering out from behind the bars of the Morning jail. The headline screamed: Artist Arrested for Murder.

The first words Margot said to me were, "Screwed up again, didn't you?"

Chapter
Nine

Heeding the frantic encouragement of the gallery's owner, Dustin and I extracted Whiney from the potted plants, and Alison ushered our group outside onto the street where the fiesta was lively, the night air was cool and Margot was, as always, snarling. She wasted no time in boosting my confidence. "You're pathetic, Adam. How could you get your face plastered all over some cheesy tabloid? Do you realize how embarrassing this is for *me?*"

"That's why I did the whole thing," I said. "Yes, that's it. I said to myself: how can I really annoy Margot? I know! I'll arrange to be found standing over a dead man with a bloody pickaxe in my fist."

"I don't doubt it. If I didn't have to spend all my time worrying about my family, I could have a brilliant career."

This was a new note in her limited egomaniacal repertoire. Margot's usual goal in life had nothing to do with a career. She only wanted to find a shiny new husband with a pot of money. There had been five so far. Maybe she was wealthy enough to quit.

"Really," Dustin said, innocently. "And what is your career?"

She glared at him, then at me. "Who's this twerp?"

"His name is Dustin Florence. He's a friend of a friend."

"Well, Dustin Florence, I've decided to be a novelist," she announced. "Based on my own true-life experiences, I could write a best seller. I think of myself as a modern-day Scarlett O'Hara."

I couldn't pass this up. I looked my sister straight in the eye and said, "Frankly, my dear, I don't give a damn."

"Of course, you wouldn't, Adam. You don't even know how to be famous. Getting your picture in this ghastly paper is too typical. It's not even the *Enquirer.*"

"Much as I'd like to debate this with you, we need to decide the basics. Like where's everybody going to sleep tonight?"

"Absolutely," Dustin concurred. "There are no decent rooms left in Taos."

Curious, I glanced at him. Why was Dustin so anxious to become part of our merry band? Except for Alison, we weren't particularly attractive. Except for Margot, we weren't rich. Why would we appeal to a status-seeking preppy?

"Excuse me," Margot said to him. "Do you own a hotel?"

"No," he said guardedly.

"Then, why the hell should you be concerned with our accomodations?" She fluttered her hand at him. "Move along, sonny."

I was surprised by her cavalier attitude toward a man who gave the appearance of having money. Had Margot undergone some sort of psychological face-lift? A greed-ectomy?

As if accustomed to being insulted, Dustin maintained an air of snobbery as he said his good-byes and returned to the Sundog Gallery. Margot tossed her head and sneered, "Nouveau riche! I despise wannabes."

Margot might be first-generation wealthy, but if you counted the combined heritage of all her husbands, she probably had royal ex-in-laws on three continents. She'd alimonied her way into enough old family money to consider herself an aristocrat.

"Dustin's okay," I said with a shrug. "After all, he did purchase one of my sculptures."

"Actually," Alison said, "he bought it for Freya. And paid with her credit card which I thought was a little on the tacky side."

"So, I was right." Margot underlined her words. "He's not rich, but he wants to be. I can always tell."

Not wanting to compare notes with her on the subject of humankind, I turned to Alison. "Are you staying with Monte?"

"And his flamenco stripper?" She shuddered. "I really didn't have the castanets for that."

"So, where were you planning to stay?" I asked.

As usual, Margot took control. "This is insane! I have a perfectly lovely hacienda within a few miles of here. We can all go there." She glared at me. "I still do have a lovely hacienda, don't I? You haven't burned it to the ground or anything?"

I decided to hold off on telling her about the excavation project in her backyard. No sense pouring kerosene on a raging bonfire. "As far as I know, it's still standing."

"Then, this is settled. We'll all stay there. Now, I'm going back inside to say hi to Yanni. The poor man is besotted with me. He keeps turning up everywhere I am."

She barged back into the gallery, shoving William Shatner out of her way. I was left on the street with Alison and an unconscious Whiney.

"So, Alison . . ." I wanted desperately to ask this question, but I didn't want to sound possessive.

"Yes, Adam?" She looked up at me with her trusting green eyes.

Last night, I had shared sleeping accommodations with Gunter and Monte after he broke me out of jail in the rented New Yorker. Which meant that Alison had driven to Taos and given him the car. Which meant that she didn't stay at Margot's hacienda last night. And if there had been any spare rooms in Taos we would never have gone to Margot's hacienda in the first place. "So, Alison . . ."

"What is it, Adam?"

I didn't want to come off acting like a jealous moron. Though I tried to be subtle, suave and cool, I couldn't help myself. I blurted out, "Who'd you sleep with last night?"

"I'm going to pretend you didn't say that, Adam." Her voice was low and dangerous. "You've obviously had a rough day and you don't mean to sound like an overbearing jerk."

Or maybe I did.

"I slept in a bed. By myself. It was quiet. It was peaceful. Nobody got murdered, bitten by a rattlesnake or beaten up. Can you say the same?"

"And where was this bed?"

"In Jacques's suite."

Alison was an understanding woman . . . to a point, and that point had been reached. Her eyes flashed the message: Don't push this, Adam. Then, she glanced down at Whiney and frowned. "I wonder if he really is the artist?"

"Check under his fingernails," I said. *Jacques's suite?* Did she really think I'd believe that she was in that sleazoid's suite and nothing happened? Even if Alison was the soul of chastity, he would have been panting over her.

"Why should I look under his fingernails?"

Patiently, I said, "If he's the one who was doing those paintings, he's probably got paint under his nails. It doesn't look like strict personal hygiene is one of his attributes."

She picked up Whiney's limp hand and studied it. "You're brilliant, Adam. There's paint. He's the one." She dropped his hand back on his chest. "And he's all mine. I can make some bucks with a talent like him."

"And what am I? Refried beans?"

_____

"No, darling." She smiled. "You, Adam McCleet, are almost internationally famous."

"If I'm such a hot shot, how come you couldn't spring me from the Morning Cafe and Jail?"

"Maybe you're just a few minutes shy of your fame. But soon, Adam, I promise."

I didn't want to belabor a sore subject, but I needed to know. "So, where were you planning to sleep tonight?"

"I ought to stay here in town, making you famous in spite of the brilliant first impression you made tonight by crashing into the art. And Jacques was nice enough to—"

"I'll bet he was." Churlishly, I imitated, "Zee reum, mademoiselle. Eet eez sexual, no?"

"Adam, don't."

"What is it with you and him?"

"He's very charming once you get past the accent and the pose. I think he only acts that way because he's insecure."

There was nothing insecure about Jacques LaFraque. He was going straight for Alison like a piss ant to sugar. I hated this. She was making excuses for that escargot-sucking dog. Alison wasn't usually this gullible. I wanted to tell her that he wasn't worthy, and I wanted to point out that I was far more charming than Jacques, but I couldn't say a thing. That's the worst part about being jealous. I wanted to say crappy things about the competition, but if I did, I'd come off sounding as childish as Whines For No Reason. "Fine," I said in a mature, adult voice. "Stay with him."

"You're angry."

"No, I'm not angry." The inside of my head erupted like Mount St. Helen's. "Of course not, Alison. If you want to spend the night with . . ." Some ridiculous, perverted, sex-crazed French fornicator. ". . . with Jacques, then I can understand."

"Try to be grown-up about this, Adam. It's not like I'm sleeping in the same room with him. He has a suite."

I held up my hand. "No need to explain." Just keep an eye on your panties, I wanted to say, or he'll be wearing them over his head before you know it.

Seeking a more fun topic, Alison said, "Monte tells me that you think Rob Crusoe and his no-name cult were responsible for the snake attack and, possibly, the murder."

"The rattlesnakes came wrapped in a flowered pillowcase which seems to implicate the cult. It's worth looking into. But I can't think of a single reason why Rob would want to kill me and Gunter."

"The alien," she suggested.

"Highly probable, but what about the alien? If he thinks we've dug something up, why kill us?"

"Maybe he's got the alien and he doesn't want you to find out." She shook her head. "I don't know."

"What I'd like to do is infiltrate their compound and get some inside information. Unfortunately, Rob knows me."

"He's met me and Monte, too," Alison said. Then she brightened. "But there is somebody he isn't familiar with."

"Not Margot?"

At the sound of his mistress's name, Whiney rolled over on the sidewalk and farted loudly. I echoed his opinion.

"Why not?" Alison demanded.

"She's a monster." That seemed like a succinct and rational reason to me. "Why is she here, anyway?"

"I was looking for a lawyer," Alison explained. "With all her divorces and legal actions, Margot has had more lawyers than O. J. Simpson. I thought she could help you."

"Margot? Help me?" The concept was more alien than the indestructible screw from outer space.

"I didn't expect her to come down here," Alison said.

Margot made her exit from the gallery, holding the door wide and waving. "Bye-bye, Yanni. Ta-ta, Dennis. You, too, Bill. Sorry

I didn't recognize you out of uniform." She held up both hands, giving the Vulcan sign of good will. "Live long and prosper."

She allowed the door to close and turned to us. "What a bunch of putzes!"

Alison took this moment to explain our predicament to Margot, ending with, "So, people in the cult know me and Adam, but they don't know you. Do you think you could—"

"Spy on a bunch of weirdos? Gain their confidence, then screw them over?" Margot nodded. "Sure, why not?"

Alison smiled. "I thought you'd be good at this."

"I'd be great. Let's go, Adam."

I pointed down the street. "We're parked down there."

"How nice for you, but we're taking my car. It's right here." She strode through a crowd that had gathered around the double-parked vehicle. "Step aside, peons."

Margot's car was a long, low, crimson, jet-type thing of undetermined make and model. Something like a Stealth Viper 6000. She must have rented it from NASA.

"Get in," she ordered, climbing behind the wheel.

I slung Whiney over my shoulder and gave the keys to the Cadillac to Alison. "It's right down the street. A great, huge, lime green thing."

She touched my arm gently. "Adam, I'm worried about you. Please don't antagonize the sheriff. Don't take any chances."

Margot leaned on the horn, which sounded like an air raid siren. "I'm ready!"

"I've got to go. Margot's ready to launch." I took Alison's hand in mine. Juggling Whiney's butt over my shoulder, peeking around the dusty seat of his pants, I said, "I love you, Alison."

It was a tender moment, one I would not soon forget.

"I love you, too."

Margot yelled, "Yeah, yeah. You love her. She loves you. I'm getting bored here, people. Let's go."

I dumped Whiney in the small space behind the bucket seats,

climbed into the passenger side and fastened my shoulder harness. The dashboard of the car looked like Darth Vader's wet dream. "How many G's you get in this thing?"

She punched a button and a row of lights flipped up on the aerodynamic hood. "Don't piss me off, Adam. I can push the ejector-seat button any time."

She dropped the transmission into warp drive, and we burned rubber for half a block until she slammed on the brake. Traffic in Taos is too congested for fancy driving, but outside the town, we ate up the highway toward Morning. Not a long drive, but it seemed interminable as Margot detailed her plans to become a best-selling novelist.

"Have you got a plot?" I asked.

"I told you already. The book would be loosely based on me. What could be more interesting? I'd start with my first boyfriend." Though it was unnecessary for her to recite her entire life story—I had been there for many of the more gruesome events—she started in. "His name was Danny or Lanny or something like that. And I was eight."

I recalled that incident very well. Defending my younger sister's honor was the first time I'd had my nose broken.

After a few dozen miles, we were well into husband number two with Margot spilling details of their sex life that made my stomach turn. I wished I could turn off my ears and stop listening, and I feared that I might go deaf if I heard too much of this horror story.

"Yeah, Margot, you could give Stephen King a run for his money."

"Damn right, I could. There's only one burning question in my mind. Should I write my story as a novel? Or should I just do a biography and call it *Margot?*"

"Hell, why stop with a biography? Why not a mini-series."

There was a terrifying thought: Margot: *the Mini-Series.*

She pulled the car over to the side of the road and stared at me in shock. "Great idea, Adam!"

I thought she was smiling, but with Margot it's hard to tell. She always bares her teeth before going for the jugular.

"My life!" She extolled. "On television. Mini-series, hell. I deserve a whole year. A series! Not a sit-com, either. But a high-drama series, starting with 'Margot: The Early Years.' "

"Maybe you could do it husband by husband."

My sarcasm was totally wasted on her. She was off and running. "But there are a couple of husbands who deserve more than one episode. I could spread them out and devote some shows to my lovers. Ha! That should easily take up a whole season of hour-long shows." She cast a baleful eye in my direction. "I can't believe you thought of this, Adam. You're usually such a worthless slug."

She grabbed her purse from under my seat and dug around inside. "I'd better write this down before I forget."

I watched with fascination, unable to believe that Margot was actually carrying writing supplies, preparatory to her brand-new brilliant career.

She whipped around, miniature tape recorder in hand. Breathlessly, she pushed the "on" switch. "I'm in New Mexico. I've had an inspiration. My life as a television series. But who should play me?"

I knew. Margot very much resembled Angelica Huston in her Morticia make-up. I suggested the name, and she made a face. "She's way too old. What a stupid suggestion! Sometimes, Adam, you are positively tasteless."

Ms. Huston was surely younger than Margot and extremely fashionable to boot, but I didn't correct her. It wasn't worth the battle.

"I need someone young and vibrant and, of course, astoundingly beautiful. All these young actresses are so plain. I know! I could play myself." Into the tape recorder, she said, "Tomorrow morning, first thing, go to Hollywood."

"Wait, Margot, first thing tomorrow you're going to infiltrate the no-name cult and get some information so I can prove I didn't kill Dental Stoker."

She glared at me. "You're so selfish. All you ever think about is yourself."

"Believe me, Harpy Queen, if I could do this myself, I would. But they know me and Alison and Monte." Though I doubted she could find out anything of value, because Margot was always too busy thinking about Margot, I didn't have a choice.

"And you expect me to put my life on hold to help you? After you went and got your picture in that tabloid rag? Honestly, Adam, I have things to do. The networks are waiting."

I had only one alternative to convince her to help me out. I had to lie. "This actually might be a break for you."

"How so?"

"The leader of this cult goes under the alias of Robinson Crusoe, but he's really a Hollywood producer." He looked like Hollywood, I thought, with his mane of sun-streaked blond hair and his Malibu tan. Plus, he was from southern California. "He'd come out here to rest and got caught up in this search for the alien."

"Really?" Her eyes narrowed. "If you're lying to me, Adam, I'll tear out your fingernails one by one and use them to slit your miserable throat."

I gulped. Margot didn't make idle threats. "No lie."

"Well, all righty. I'll go to this encampment and look for your stupid map. But I'm not staying longer than a day."

"Fine."

"Besides, it could be a new episode in my life. *Margot Goes Undercover. Margot, the New Age Mata Hari.*"

She slammed the car into gear again, and we took off. If I had been smart I would have stayed in the desert and slept with the snakes.

It was bright and early the next morning . . . around noon. Margot had finally completed her makeup and wardrobe, and we were on our way to Morning. Half a dozen times, I repeated the simple instructions to my sister: "If you hear anything pertaining to the murder of Dental Stoker, remember it. Try to make a search for the map to the body of the alien."

"Sure, Adam. Are you sure this guy is a producer? Why would he call himself Robinson Crusoe?"

"You know those Hollywood people," I said. "Always kidding around."

"And what's my cover story again?"

I tried to stick to the truth. "You've just been through a painful divorce and you need time to contemplate. Your name isn't Margot. It's Margaret."

"I don't like Margaret. It's boring."

"But it sounds like Margot, so you should be able to remember it. Okay?"

She sat quietly for a few minutes, then said, "Do you think this will be dangerous? I mean some of those cults are pretty wild. Do you think they'll tie me up and ravish my body?" She sounded hopeful. "Do you?"

"If there is the slightest sign of danger, get out of there. Do you understand that? I'll be nearby. As close as I can get, and I'll be listening. But it is entirely possible that someone in the cult is a murderer."

I left her in her rental car about a mile from the gated entrance to the no-name encampment. My instructions to her were to wait for about half an hour so I had time to sneak closer and hide.

Of course, she came swooping up to the entry gate in fifteen minutes. I ducked behind an outcropping of rock, just within earshot.

The young man at the gate, wearing a designer sheet of pumpkin orange stopped her. "Excuse me, ma'am but this is private property."

"Yes, I know. I've come to join up."

"Are you expected?"

"No, but I'm sure you'll all be glad that I'm here. You see, I'm a famous novelist and I'm simply burned out after my last great masterwork. I need time for rejuvenation and relaxation. Um, contemplation, too."

The young man mumbled unintelligibly into a walkie-talkie, then turned back to Margot. "How did you hear of our encampment?"

"Everybody at the Betty Ford Clinic speaks very highly of you."

I ducked lower behind the rocks and groaned quietly. The Betty Ford Clinic?

I took solace in the fact that for this trip into the desert, I was semi-prepared for action. My luggage was still at the hacienda, so I had changed into comfortable desert boots, Levi's and a long-sleeved flannel shirt. Margot's ex was apparently an avid outdoorsman who had vacated the premises in a hurry. In a large storage closet in the back of the garage, I found a ton of camping and survival equipment. I grabbed a fisherman's vest with dozens of pockets. In these pockets, I carried a heap-o-supplies: a canteen, freeze-dried food like the astronauts ate, sun block, leather gloves, a length of cord, two different knives, a compass and a really nifty Pez dispenser that looked like a hand grenade. The grenade was mine, a gift from a couple of my Viet Nam vet buddies who now owned a novelty store.

The youthful-looking guard at the gateway turned back to Margot and asked, "What's your name, ma'am?"

"Uma," she said.

What? I almost jumped out from behind my rock and called an end to this charade before it got any worse. Uma?

"Uma Basinger," she said.

The young man grinned. "Go right on in, Uma. Our leader, Rob, will meet you outside the main house."

As usual, Margot tore down the road like Mario Andretti, kicking up a tornado of dust.

Since nobody had given me directions to the inside of the compound, I was operating without any knowledge of my surroundings. Keeping low and moving fast, I crossed the outer boundary and kept running through a vast acreage of sandy soil and mesquite. The noontime sun beat down hard, and I was sweating under my vest. This wasn't the first time I'd been assigned to reconnaissance and surveillance, but the other occasion was in the jungle of Viet Nam. I missed the high grass. I missed the back-up of other Marines. Most of all, I missed my youth when I could run for hours without getting winded.

I was panting like a Chinese tailor when I finally came in sight of the main house and dropped to my belly to observe.

The backdrop was a spectacular view of Taos Mountain. In the foreground was a huge adobe-style lodge with several smaller adobe houses surrounding. The whole thing was a soft, reddish clay color with graceful, natural curves and window awnings in bright turquoise. The lodge was three stories tall and looked like an Indian pueblo, but with one major difference. There were no dirt-poor Indians living in this abode. The cars parked in front were a variety of Broncos, Pathfinders, Le Barons and a Jaguar.

I found the collapsible binoculars in one pocket of my fishing jacket and peered through them. On the porch, Margo and Rob were chatting and laughing uproariously. I resented that she was having fun. This was my life we were playing with here, my freedom from murder charges. And Margot, alias Uma, had turned it into a garden party.

Margot had that familiar predatory glint in her eye. Usually, she didn't bother digging her claws into men who weren't Fortune 500 material, but she was definitely on the make for Rob Crusoe. I almost felt sorry for the guy. But if he'd been the one who killed Dental Stoker and threw the rattlesnakes into the kiva, he deserved the horrible fate that awaited Margot's prey.

I lay there and watched for a while, then decided that this was doing me no good whatsoever. I needed to hear the conversation. Stealthily, moving in shadows, I crept closer. At the edge of the big house, I thought a sheet might come in real handy right now as a disguise, but I had not had that kind of foresight when I loaded the fishing vest with survival gear. I took my chances, darting from shrub to shrub until I was able to slide under a Jeep parked beside the house and low-crawl from there to under the front porch of the headquarters building.

Above me, I heard Rob and Margot swapping stories about Hollywood. I knew that Margot's stories were total lies, fabricated on the spot, and I had the strong feeling that Rob was operating at the same level of deceit. Maybe they deserved each other.

"So," she said, "what's with the cult, Robby darling? You're not radicals, are you?"

"Absolutely not. We're all Republicans. We have a kind of survivalist theory. When the big quake comes and drops the Pacific coast into the ocean, this will be beach-front property, and we're not letting anybody in."

"Very exclusive. I just adore it! Religion?"

"Some. But low-key." I could almost hear his jaws stretching in a toothy smile. "Our main thing is a communal investment fund, managed by Dean Witter. And we're working on something big, a major find."

"Which is?"

"We have a lead on the location of a buried alien from outer space. It landed in a spaceship on Christmas Eve, with the exact date being twelve, twenty-four, eighteen sixty-three. Which, numerically indicates a power of nine. A highly mystic number. I'm a nine, as well."

The word bullshit danced on the tip of my tongue. I bit my lower lip to preserve my silence. After my experience the day before at the unassuming home of _la curandera,_ Crusoe's new age claptrap was exceedingly difficult to swallow.

"I've always thought of myself as a ten," Margot said.

"That you are, lady."

As I lay in the dirt under the porch, I prayed fervently that she wouldn't let go of this opportunity to talk about the alien. Please, Margot, keep on the topic.

"About my series," she said. "I really do need to cast a male lead. Have you ever acted?"

"Don't you want to hear about my alien?"

Great, I thought, Rob was as self-centered as she was.

"I suppose," Margot said. "How are you going to find it? Do you have a map?"

"A piece of one. Bona fide and certified as authentic. You want to see it? We've got it framed and hanging in the front hall."

Eureka! I'd hit pay dirt. The front hall had to be inside the front door. If I could slip in there, steal the map and take off, this portion of the investigation would be concluded. Except for figuring out if Rob was desperate enough to kill for a space screw. With the map in my possession, I could negotiate.

There was a squeal of tires and a spray of fine gravelly dirt, indicating the arrival of a new player.

Rob, from his position on the porch, muttered, "Shit."

The car door slammed and I heard the snarling voice of Shirley Gomez-Gomez. _"Buenos días."_

"Sheriff Shirley Gomez-Gomez, I'm glad to see you."

"Oh?" Her tone indicated disbelief. "And who is this?"

"She's come to join us. Probably only for a few weeks."

The porch above me creaked as Margot stood. "Pleased to

meet you, Shirl. I'm the famous novelist and screenwriter, Uma Bacall."

"I thought it was Basinger," Rob said.

"Well, Bacall is my middle name. After my auntie Lauren. Yes, that's it. Uma Bacall Basinger."

"Have you found McCleet?" Rob asked.

"No. I almost had him near Pig Eye, but the sonofabitch got away on horseback. So, Uma, you are famous? Why have I never heard of you?"

"Well, I don't think we travel in the same circles, dear. No offense, but what happened to your jaw? It's all swollen and awful."

"I was doing my job as sheriff."

"Well, carry on."

"I think, Uma, that I would like to ask you some questions. Would you come with me, please?"

"Excuse me," Margot said. "I must not have heard you correctly. It sounds like you're arresting me."

"That's exactly what I'm doing."

"I think not, Shirley. And don't you dare wave that gun at me. You have no just provocation, no possible reason except that you're jealous of the attention Rob is paying me, and I consider this to be harassment of the highest order. Take me into your slimy little jailhouse, and I promise that I'll not only have your badge, but I'll slap you with the fattest lawsuit you've ever seen." She paused for breath. "You can't arrest me for no reason. This is America, after all."

"*Sí,* this is America. And I am the law."

"You're pathetic. Get a life."

I heard her turn and march into the big house. Right over my head, Margot pivoted and volleyed one parting shot. "While you're at it, do something about your hair, Shirl."

Margot's footsteps disappeared into the house. She hadn't even stayed around to hear the patented Gomez-Gomez string of Hispanic cursing that ended with "Goddamned bitch. I'll be back here, Rob, with reinforcements. So, you tell Miss Uma that she's gone too far."

When the sheriff drove away, I decided that it was no longer necessary for Margot to play spy. On the other hand, it wouldn't hurt my sister one bit to be arrested by the local sheriff. A little time in a jail cell . . . I mused on the pleasant possibility of having Margot locked away.

I hung around for a while longer, biding my time until I could sneak inside and snatch the map. It seemed pretty quiet, and I scrambled out from under the porch. Dodging out of sight from a wholesome young couple in sheets, I circled the house, peering in windows. I spied Margot in the dining area.

"Margot," I called.

She looked around, vaguely startled.

"Over here, by the window."

She came and stood beside me. "This is really quite posh, Adam. Like a spa but without all the fat people. And, oh, that Rob!"

"Yeah, swell. Listen, you can leave now. I'm going to swipe the map, and you get out of there."

"But I'm enjoying myself. Don't you want me to have any fun?"

"It's not going to be fun if the sheriff arrests you. Now, I'm leaving. I won't be here to protect you if something goes wrong."

"Ooooh, I'm shaking in my boots."

Somebody else entered the room. "Uma?"

"Hi, Rob." She slammed the window on my fingers. "What's going on?"

"Volleyball," he said.

"Gosh, I'd love to, Rob. But I left my string bikini in my other bag."

"That's okay, Uma. We play in the nude."

"I'm there."

"Ten minutes. The net is set up behind the big house."

I managed to hold to a low whimper my expression of pain from having the tips of my fingers traumatized, as I tore my hand from beneath the windowsill. I'd done my bit and warned her. If Margot wanted to take her chances with Rob and the no-names and the wrath of Gomez-Gomez, then it was her problem. As far as I was concerned, she could get outer-space, glow-in-the-dark, metallically screwed.

I lurked around until the un-sheeted crew made their mass exodus to the volleyball court, then I sneaked inside the house. Front hall. There was the map, neatly framed and ripe for the picking.

A little voice in the back of my head warned me that this was too easy, but I didn't listen.

The frame was fastened to the adobe by a dry-wall screw at each of the four corners. I pulled a utility knife from my fishing vest and extended the screwdriver blade. The first screw was exceedingly long and several minutes passed as I clumsily backed it out with my unbruised left hand. I didn't feel like I could spare the time to remove the remaining screws, but the frame was now loose enough to work my fingers behind and pull. As I tore the map off the wall a screaming banshee siren began to wail.

Chapter
Ten

"**S**hit!"

I stashed the framed map under my arm and bolted from the house. From the backyard volleyball court, a horde of no-name cult members followed me in hot pursuit. A glance over my shoulder told me that every one of them was bare-ass naked.

From history classes, I remembered learning that the first Olympic games were conducted in the nude, in order to celebrate the perfection of the physical form. That had sounded pristine and noble and even a little heroic.

This marathon was nothing like that. Most of these people weren't Olympic athletes. They were average people—Republicans, according to Rob. Naked with golf tans, most of them were saggy in the butt, pot-bellied, floppy-breasted, flaccid Republicans. The experience of being chased by this crew was unsettling on several different levels.

Since I was fully clad with a good pair of boots, I felt pretty smug. Out-distancing the nudie no-names would be no problem.

I took another peek backwards. After a couple of hundred yards, most of the women had already dropped out, having been thoroughly pummeled by their own breasts. Some of the younger men, including Rob and the teenagers from the jail, still charged after me. But I wasn't too worried about them catching up. They were either barefoot or in sloppy sandals. I had boots and a decent head start. Plus, I felt superior because they looked silly. No matter how well developed a body is, jiggling genitalia are always funny.

My biggest problem would be to keep from breaking into laughter.

That's what I thought. But I'd forgotten about the vehicles parked in front of the house. The first four-wheel-drive, off-the-road Jeep came roaring across the sandy mesquite terrain.

"Shit!"

I stepped up my pace. My stride was hampered by the framed map I still clutched. But I was moving fast, lots faster than I would have guessed I was capable of moving. No time to think. Now wasn't the time to have an angst attack about being middle-aged.

I could see my escape, my safety. Straight ahead of me was an arroyo, a narrow ravine that marked the landscape like déjà vu. When I'd been riding *la curandera's* magical steed, the horse had fearlessly taken the jump and we'd flown. I could do it! I'd launch into space like a human cannonball, leaving the vehicles behind.

Coming up on the narrow ravine, I dug in my toe and threw myself into the air with a magnificent broad jump. The earth fell away. I was airborne. I was flying. I was about two feet short.

I crashed into the sandy edge of the ravine which was, fortunately, fairly shallow. All the breath whooshed out of my lungs, and when I tried to inhale, I sucked up a mouthful of grit.

Now might have been a good time to quit. I might as well

accept the fact that I was in okay shape for a guy in his forties, but I was no Olympic athlete.

"Bullshit!"

What I lacked in speed and stamina, I made up for in determination. This wasn't just a piece of the map I was stealing, it was—hopefully—my ticket out of the murder charges. This was my fucking escape from Morning. Besides, I had a grudge. It was almost certain that one or more of these naked no-names had dumped a bagful of rattlesnakes into the kiva, causing poor old Gunter to be bitten and scaring him so badly that he nearly had a heart attack.

Staggering, I was on my feet and raggedly running again.

I heard a crash as the pursuing Jeep fell into the deceptively wide ravine that had nearly been my undoing.

But there were other off-the-road vehicles. I glanced back and saw a Pathfinder and a white Bronco. As if that wasn't bad enough, the naked cult-sters were gaining on me.

The Bronco pulled up beside me. Hanging out the window, the bare-chested, gray-haired driver laughed maniacally. He yelled something at me, but all I heard was the Texas accent. Something about "whupping my ass."

Using the Bronco, he cut off my forward momentum, edged me to the left, herding me like a lone dogie on the range.

But I've always liked to think I was smarter than the average long-horned steer. I stopped dead. He kept going. And I was headed straight again.

In the distance I could see a mesa. If I could climb to the top of the damned thing, I might have a chance. It was too steep for any of these urban four-wheelers.

Then I saw the Hummer, the vehicle that had been used in Desert Storm. Ugly as a camel with acne, but this thing could go anywhere, anytime. I've heard tell that Arnold Schwarzenegger drives one in case he encounters rugged road on his way to the opening of the next Planet Hollywood.

The Bronco, the Hummer and the Pathfinder began to circle me. The first time, I managed to dart out of the circle and break for the mesa. The second time, I had to dive behind a rock to avoid being run over by the Bronco whose driver was now yelling, "Yee-hah!"

The third time they trapped me, I was ready to give up. I stopped running and stood there, bent over and panting like a son of a bitch. I was drenched with sweat. My lungs felt like they were about to explode.

Their circle got tighter and tighter. The teenagers were spacing themselves around the outer perimeter. I hoped that their punishment for spies was a good swift dunk in the hot tub, but I didn't think so. These people looked like they were out for blood—my blood.

And then my salvation appeared in a most unusual guise. I saw Margot in her sleek, cherry red, car rocket.

Though her vehicle wasn't a four-wheel drive and wasn't made for going off the road, she was racing across the landscape, probably destroying the undercarriage and axle as she shot over mesquite, rock and ravine.

With the aggression of a demolition-derby driver, she intimidated the Hummer and drove right next to me.

I leaped into the passenger side of the car, gasping and grateful.

She snarled, "You owe me for this, Adam. You owe me big!"

Using that same genteel charm, she bashed away from the other cars and aimed for the road.

I struggled to fasten my shoulder harness, then lay back, listening to the pounding of my heart as Margot careened along the graded road.

This was one hell of an automobile. The rear end barely fishtailed as we took curves at top speed. The shock absorbers must have been ultra-heavy duty because the ride was smooth as silk, and the air-conditioned interior of the car was a cool sixty-eight degrees.

Approaching the exit to the compound, Margot slammed on the brakes and muttered, "Son of a bitch."

The young man she'd spoken to earlier stood in the center of the wooden gate guarding the exit.

She buzzed down her window and shouted at him. "Move it or lose it."

He braced himself. I could have told him not to play chicken with Margot.

Window up, she revved the powerful engine, and threw the car into reverse. Then she went into forward gear, aiming for the exit gate and the man standing there. She didn't slacken her speed one bit, and he dove out of the way just in time.

"Jesus, Margot!"

"Don't give me grief. I saved your sorry butt."

"Thank you," I said humbly. "And might I also add that I'm grateful you stopped to put on your clothes."

"Well, I wasn't going to leave my things there. I had to pack."

I kept my silence. Though she'd been in her room, calmly packing her underwear and makeup, while I was facing certain death by Bronco, she had rescued me from the naked clutches of the no-name cult.

Once we were out of the compound, she tore away from the pack at breakneck speed. Most people, even when in pursuit, have some regard for vehicular safety. Not so with Margot.

She skidded around curves and flew over the ruts and pot-holes like a skier jumping moguls.

Nearing Morning, she slowed to a relatively sedate pace, and we drove to the road that led to her hacienda.

"There's something bothering me, Margot. Why?"

"Because I'm a good sister."

"Really, why? I'm curious."

"Well, we were out there, playing naked volleyball, and Rob

had these sexy little bimbos hanging all over him. Margot Stang doesn't compete. I don't need to."

"Uh-huh." And what did this have to do with rescuing me?

"I thought if I made a dramatic exit," she said, "that if I left Rob with his dick hanging out, he'd realize what he's missing."

"You know, Margot, it's just possible that you could be a mini-series. On the Fox channel."

"Thank you, Adam."

We were greeted at the hacienda by a conscious and some-what sober Whiney, who was anxious to give Margot a tour of her house.

The night before she had been so preoccupied with the pros-pect of her mini-series that she hadn't bothered to look at much more than her bedroom and the bathroom where she'd done her all-morning-long makeup. Though Whiney had attempted to show her around the next morning, she dismissed him because she was too busy selecting just the right outfit for infiltrating a New Age survivalist compound.

I sympathized with Whiney's frustration. Invariably, no mat-ter what anybody wanted her to do, she always had a different agenda. And to Margot, the only agenda that mattered was her own.

She flung herself down on the pillowy sofa in the front area.

"Please, Miss Margot," Whiney started. "I want to show you the house by daylight."

"Not now. Can't you see that I'm exhausted? I've had a tiring day." She frowned slightly. "And I think I might be in love again. Wouldn't that be just perfect, Adam? If I've fallen in love with a Hollywood movie producer."

"Rob?"

"Of course, Rob. Not only is he a good connection, but he has great hair."

"Please," Whiney said.

"Give the guy a chance," I said, interceding on his behalf.

"He's not going to leave you alone until he's shown you the damned house."

"Oh, all right."

When she finally gave in, Margot was appropriately impressed with the style and decor. I was appropriately nauseated with Whiney's obsequious manner as he escorted her from room to room.

"For many years," he said, "I have waited—"

"Is this the guest bathroom?" She charged inside. "Very nice. Pink marble."

"Yes, the bathroom." Whiney took a deep breath and started again, "For many years—"

"How many bedrooms?" she interrupted.

"Five. And a den."

"Five? This is an excellent piece of real estate. I never knew my ex-husband had such good taste."

"For many years—"

"But he must have had good taste." She cackled. "After all, he married me."

In the bedrooms, she was not impressed with Whiney's artwork until I told her that Alison thought it was valuable. "Really? It's not my kind of thing, but I do trust Alison's expertise. How valuable?"

"I'm not sure."

Whiney started again, "For many years—"

"What's in the kitchen? Is it stocked with food?"

In the living room, I placed my hand on her forearm. "Margot, would you be kind enough to listen to this guy. He's trying to make a speech for you."

"Oh, all right." She sat in one of the front room chairs, like a queen receiving one of her subjects. "Go ahead, Wino. I'm waiting."

"For many years, I have waited for your coming. I dusted and swept and kept the vandals away from this land as best I could."

"Yes, yes." Margot flicked her hand dismissively. "Thanks a lot."

"In return, you have been my benefactor. You have paid for my room and board and, with your financial support, I have been able to live well."

"Nice. Are you finished now?"

"I wish for you to have this."

He held out his fist and slowly opened it. Inside was a twisted up piece of aluminum foil. Whiney unwrapped it. There, resting in the center of the foil, was a three-inch-long Phillips-head screw.

I was holding my breath. Was this the screw from another planet? Had this alcoholic whiner just entrusted a gift that men were killed for to my sister?

"A screw?" Her eyebrows lowered. "Is this supposed to be some kind of suggestive hint, Whiney? Because I don't want you to get any ideas."

"Where did you get this?" I asked.

"I found it," he said defensively. "Finders keepers."

"Where and when?"

"Late one night, a couple of months ago. It was the time when everybody started digging holes in the yard and I had taken to sitting outside, keeping watch over the lands of my benefactress. I had fallen asleep, and when I wakened, there were more holes, and I cursed the sleep that had covered my eyelids."

This was a fairly poetic speech from Whiney. I wondered if he had practiced it.

"Then I walked about," he said. "I twisted my ankle really bad, and it took days and days to heal. I think it's still a little swollen."

He sat on the floor and started to take off his moccasin. "Want to see?"

Margot and I chorused, "No."

"All right, back to my story. When I was walking around I saw a glow, like blue neon. A star that had fallen from the skies. And I went toward it. That's when I saw this. The first thing I thought of was the venerable legend of Tonna-Hokay-Pokay-Lawnchair-Yada-Yada."

"Of course," I said.

"The legend of what?" Margot demanded.

"He Who Glows In The Dark," I explained.

"Shines at Night," Whiney corrected. "Then, I feared the screw might be radioactive. Since there were all these holes, anyway, I got a tin can, dropped it in and buried it."

I flopped down in a chair opposite Margot. Whiney's gift blew my theory of Dental's murder all to hell. He couldn't have been murdered for the screw because he didn't have the screw. And Whiney couldn't have killed him because Whiney was in jail on the night of the murder.

What about the map? But Dental wasn't carrying the map. He'd left the thing back at his house, tucked into the folds of Miss July of 1982. So, why was the old geezer murdered?

There were the other top favorite motives: Revenge, hate, and lust. But I always favored greed. Greed should have applied in this situation. Except for one thing, Dental didn't have anything worth stealing on his person.

Whiney's voice took on that scratchy, plaintive sound. "You don't think it really is radioactive, do you? I mean, I've been careful not to touch it, but the glow might have something in it."

"Give it to me," I said. "I'm going to take this thing and hide it, and I'm not going to tell you where. But it will be safe." I grabbed it and put it in my pocket.

"Get a grip," Margot advised. "It's only a screw."

"And that's all you need to worry about. I'm also taking this map. If Rob and his boys show up, tell them I promised to bring it back."

Figuring that Rob and his no-names would soon figure out

Margot's connection, I had to move fairly quickly. I took Margot's Stealth Viper 6000 and headed out to Gunter's place to make a copy of the map, several copies in fact. I could have cared less about the historic value of the original.

Amazingly, I was not accosted en route. Now that various no-names and Gomez-Gomez were after me, I had to watch every corner. But I found Gunter's teepee without much problem. There was the problem of the motion detector, but he'd told me the code. One-two-two-four-six-three. The date that the alien had landed. The power of nine.

There was another car parked in front. A Cutlass, and I prepared myself to do battle. But it was only Dustin.

"Dusty, old bean!" I clapped him on the shoulder. "How's tricks?"

"Where's Papa Gunter?"

He was looking a little frayed around his prepster edges, and that pleased me. At least, I wasn't the only one suffering in the desert. "Don't know," I said. "He took off on some technical project and I don't know when he'll be back. What's the matter, Dustin from Boston? Freya won't let you off the hook?"

"I don't expect you or any of the other heathens in this godforsaken land to understand." His upper-crust accent grated on my nerves and made me want to smack him. He continued to drone, "But there are proper etiquette procedures to be followed in a wedding. All I need to know is if Freya's papa intends to walk her down the aisle and give her away or not. A simple yes or no. Is that too much to ask?"

"Couldn't you just lie to her?" I suggested.

"No!" He was clearly appalled that I would even suggest such a maneuver, which was probably why me and the other heathens didn't get it. "I need the answer from him. From his very lips."

I opened the teepee, rushed inside and punched in the code.

Dustin followed. His blue eyes widened as he surveyed the array of computer equipment and office machines.

"Pretty nifty stuff, huh?" I turned on the copy machine and waited for it to warm up.

"Why in a teepee? Papa Gunter is wealthy. Why would he choose to live like this?"

"It's right for him."

I knew Dustin wouldn't understand about how a man's got to do what a man's got to do. Dustin was a guy who knew the rules, and one of the rules was that rich people, like Gunter the Viking, don't live in teepees. "I just don't understand you people. Living in tents. Digging for spacemen. Talking to animals. Wearing rags. I just don't understand."

And he probably never would, so I switched subjects. "Hey," I said, "I don't think I properly thanked you for buying that sculpture of mine. Thanks."

"I found it quite lovely. Reminded me of Freya, actually." He grinned in a manner that women would find boyish and charming. "She's quite a gal, my Freya."

"Is that why you used her credit card to pay for it?"

"This whole trip was her idea, and she offered to pay for everything," he explained. "Perhaps, I have been a spendthrift. But that will surely teach her a lesson, won't it?"

I looked him straight in the eye. Good old preppy Dustin was a bit of a cad. I knew that the sculpture, a small piece, had sold for three thousand scoots. "Kind of an expensive lesson."

"You underestimate yourself, Adam. I see real promise in your work. Someday, that sculpture will be worth five, nay, ten times more than what I paid."

"So, you're an art expert?"

"I studied art for two years in college."

"I thought you were in law," I said.

"Law. Art. And dentistry. Do you have any idea how much orthodontists make?"

Indeed, I díd. Margot's last ex-husband, Phil Stang, was an orthodontist. But I wondered why Dustin from Boston cared about how much money was to be made in honest professions. He acted like a rich boy who had been coddled since birth.

"A professional student," I said. I disliked people like him, from the depths of my blue-collar roots.

"I've attended school for many years," he admitted. "By the by, are you still wanted for murder?"

"Why? Are you considering a career as a bounty hunter? I'm real sure it doesn't pay well."

"Just curious."

I kept watching him, keeping him under my eagle eye surveillance. Something was going on with this guy. Was he after the alien, too? Not averting my gaze, I lifted the framed piece of the map and smashed the glass against the edge of Gunter's desk.

He flinched, a natural reaction, but he didn't protest or shriek. His blue eyes were cool as he watched me. He wasn't scared.

"Copy machine's warmed up," I said by way of explanation.

I plucked the map from the remaining shards of glass and placed it flat on the copier. I set the counter for twenty and waited.

As I left the teepee, I handed a copy to Dustin. "Here you go. Hang onto it. Might be worth something, someday."

"I'll treasure it always." His preppy good manners slipped along with his upper-crust accent. He crumpled the paper and threw it on the ground. "Like hell I will. If you see Gunter, tell him I'm looking for him. All I want is a simple yes or no."

I doubted that he'd get it. Unless he could pull off some noble and heroic stunt to win Gunter's approval, his was a quest that was surely doomed to failure.

I bade farewell to Dustin and zipped back to Margot's hacienda, encountering only one brief chase with a no-name vehicle, but they were seriously overmatched by the red jet car.

I handed the original of the map to Margot. "Rob is going to be coming after this," I said. "You can give it to him or not, as you see fit."

"I'll make him beg," she promised.

My next step was to devalue the map, just in case someone decided that it too was worth killing for. This was fairly easy. The map started loosing value as soon as I made the copies. Giving Dustin, Margot and Whiney each a commemorative copy made it worth that much less. I kept a copy for myself and addressed a batch of them to people I knew, including my best buddy on the Portland Police Department, Nick Gabreski, who was home with his wife, awaiting the birth of their eighth child and planning a sailboat trip up the coast to Alaska. I left the innocent-looking white envelopes with Whiney to mail for me. "Be sure to tell Rob Crusoe, when he shows up, that I've mailed copies of his precious map all over the country."

And I knew what I should do with the screw. Since it wasn't much good as evidence, this reputed piece of a spaceship should go to Melvin. As far as I knew, the space screw had originally belonged to Dental. As Dental's heir, Melvin was the rightful owner.

After his speech to me in the desert and his subsequent flip out, it was the least I could do.

I struck out on foot and found my favorite hiding place overlooking Morning about an hour later. I was waiting for the sun to go down, lying on my back behind a grouping of large boulders, letting my thoughts meander, when a human form blocked the sun. It was a woman.

"We need to talk," she said.

Chapter Eleven

I squinted at her silhouette outlined against the setting sun, and for a minute, I thought she was a fantasy woman who had materialized from mesquite and air, like something Carlos Castaneda would see on a peyote dream. Maybe it was the combined insanity of this situation, maybe exhaustion, maybe the weird vibes from the space screw were getting to me, but I imagined this dream lady would soothe my fevered brow and tell me I was strong and brave and heroic. If I was lucky, she'd even compliment me on how well I was doing with this investigation.

That was the job I had hoped Alison would do, and I mentally superimposed her features and form on the mystery woman. I was kidding myself because I knew Alison was miles away, hanging out at the Sundog Gallery with Jacques LaFraque or some other pretentious weiner dog. That was her job, I told myself. I had no right to be jealous. But I was.

"Hello, Adam."

The mystery woman spoke in melodious alto tones, and a big, stupid grin stretched across my face. She was lovely.

But the very fact that I was fantasizing like a long-term psychiatric patient was not a good sign. I dredged my brain back to reality. Who was she? Too soft to be Margot, too gentle to be Gomez-Gomez. And she was much too small to be Nelda or even Nelda's left breast.

"Consuela," I said. "Taken any good pictures lately?"

"No," she said. She knelt beside me, and the folds of her cotton skirt flared out around her knees.

"I don't suppose you have any idea how that photo you took in jail ended up on the front page of a tabloid."

"I might."

Gracefully, she reached up and adjusted her off-the-shoulder peasant blouse. She wasn't wearing a bra.

Though I was pretty certain that the adorable Consuela had sold me out to the ghastly publication, it didn't seem all that important. According to Monte, I ought to be thanking her. Instead, I asked, "Have you brought me burritos?"

"No, Mr. McCleet, I have no food."

"Call me Adam." Everyone else does, that is, everyone who doesn't call me asshole. I dug into a pocket of my fishing jacket, pulled out a freeze-dried package and read the label. "Would you like some lasagna like the astronauts eat? It comes in a bar."

"No, thank you."

Biting down hard, I tore off a chunk. It stuck to the roof of my mouth. "You don't know what you're missing, Consuela. The texture is . . ." I remembered Alison's friend at the gallery, Jacques LaFraque. ". . . eet ees très magnifique. Eh! No! Oui?"

Consuela looked me straight in the eye and said, "I'm very worried about the sheriff."

"Eet ees the Gomez-Gomez? Oui?"

"*Sí.* Oh, Adam, this has been so hard on her. She tries so hard."

I shrugged, not willing to waste a lot of sympathy on the woman who whacked me with her gun and pursued me on her dirt bike. "She can quit investigating anytime. Why doesn't she call in the state police?"

"They will laugh. _Comprende?_ Shirley has too much machismo."

I didn't argue.

Prettily, Consuela continued. "I don't know what to do. Dental is still in the freezer on the porch right on top of the salsa I froze last sumer. And then, there are repairs we need to make at the jail." She cast an accusing eye in my direction. "That's your fault."

"Uh-huh," I said sagely. I wasn't sure what she was after, but I could tell right away that she wasn't planning to offer comfort, solace and praise. "Why are you here, Consuela?"

"Maybe you can help me." She batted her thick black eyelashes and smiled. It was the kind of smile that women use when they want men to do something ridiculous and dangerous like go to their mother-in-law's house for dinner. "Will you help me, Adam?"

"Okey-dokey." I was hooked.

Her dark eyes flashed with a beguiling light. "Tell me about yourself, Adam."

Was she coming on to me? Was this young, dusky New Mexico enchantress making the moves on me? Though I don't consider myself to be overly modest, I couldn't believe Consuela was honestly attracted to me. I was probably old enough to be her father, and my performance in New Mexico hadn't exactly been dashing. On the other hand—given the male population of Morning—I might be the best thing to come along in years. "What do you want to know?"

She added a light musical giggle to her repertoire of charms. "When did you become a sculptor?"

"This is my third career. First, I was a jarhead in Viet Nam. Then, a cop in Portland. Now, I make things with clay and chisel, wood, steel, bronze. Whatever medium I feel like working in."

"What do you make?"

"Mostly women," I said. "Beautiful women like yourself."

I wasn't sure why I'd said that. Even if Consuela was coming on to me, I hadn't intended to flirt back. I was devoted to Alison. For the past two years, we've had this kind of unspoken commitment. But there was this whole Jacques thing. It seemed like Alison had been testing the waters with him. Maybe it was time for me to do a little testing of my own.

"I wish to see your sculptures," Consuela said.

"Then, you're in luck. There's that display at the Sundog."

"Take me," she said. Her voice was breathy.

Take me? Did she actually say: Take me? I was so unaccustomed to the male-female mating dance that I said, "Where?"

She laughed again. "What did you have in mind, Adam?"

Duh, I thought. "You tell me."

"Take me to Taos."

Now, there was a spectacularly dumb idea. If I strolled into the Sundog Gallery with Consuela hanging on my arms, gazing up at me with dark longing, Alison would not be pleased. As a rule, Alison wasn't a jealous woman. She didn't need to be. She was beautiful and intelligent and confident. But she would definitely be irate if I drooled on a lovely young lady in her presence.

On the other hand, an appearance with Consuela—that might be just what Alison needed to appreciate me again. But that would be a head game. Alison and I were, or at least I thought we were, above that. I remembered us agreeing not to play such games. We were too old for that.

I swabbed at the corners of my mouth and decided it was time to set things straight. "Level with me, Consuela. Just tell me what you want, and we can cut the seduction scene."

"You think I'm a seductress?" She leaned forward and her blouse gaped enough to offer a glimpse of golden brown, silky smooth cleavage.

"You're a very pretty young woman. And I'm a very tired old man who's accused of murder."

She frowned delicately. "I understand. You prefer Miss Brooks to me. She's wealthy. She owns a gallery in Portland."

Quietly, I asked, "How did you know that?"

"Shirley Gomez-Gomez has run background checks on all of you."

"So, you really didn't need to ask me about my history."

"I wanted to hear from your own lips." She reached forward and touched my chin. Her thumb ran across the surface of my mouth, and she took her hand away. "About you and Alison? You have been friends for many years?"

"More than friends," I said.

"But you don't love her. If you loved her, you would marry her."

"I would, if she wanted to." I was surprised when those words came out of my mouth. I had always sidestepped the issue of marriage. Then, on the few occasions when I had the balls to mention the "M" word, Alison had danced away. The last time I mentioned wedding bells, she suggested that we go steady. "If she'd consent to marry me," I said, "I'd do it in a minute."

"She would be very pretty in a white gown," Consuela said.

"She's very beautiful in anything." Or in nothing at all. Which made me wonder why I was out here in the high desert at sunset talking to another woman. "Listen, Consuela, you're a vision, a beauty, a wonder of the world. But I still don't know why we're having this conversation. Is it about the alien?"

"Shines At Night." She nodded slowly and sighed. "Have you found him?"

Now, finally, we were getting somewhere. "Even if he does exist, and I'm beginning to believe that he does, I don't have a clue about where to look."

"_Qué?_ Why not?"

"There are three pieces to a map. One of which belonged to

Dental Stoker. I have two of the pieces, and I'm pretty sure of where I can find the third."

"A map?"

"Yeah, I guess it was put together on Christmas Eve of 1863 when the forefathers of the Stokers saw a flaming UFO fall from the skies and crash somewhere around here." Her former softness had been replaced by an intelligent interest that I much preferred. "Now, it's your turn to tell me something."

"What would you like to know?"

"You said the sheriff has run background checks on all the suspects. Correct?"

"*Sí,* the FAX machine has been busy. She was very disappointed to find out that you have an honorable background."

"I'll bet she was. What about Robinson Crusoe?"

"This is an alias," she said, unnecessarily. "He is really Robinson Jackson, a former rock-and-roll singer who was arrested many times for drug possession. Since he changed his name, however, he has been very clean."

"What about the rest of the suspects? Gunter and the Stokers and Dustin from Boston and Whiney?"

"First, tell me why you began to believe in the alien?"

I mentioned the diary that Gunter and I had located in the kiva. After a quick mental debate of the pros and cons of spilling my guts, I also said there was a screw from the spaceship, and it glowed in the dark. I did not tell her that I had the screw in my pocket at this very minute. "Your turn, Consuela. Give me a recap of the suspects' backgrounds."

"The local people, the Stokers and Whiney, have no secrets. They have always been here, except for when Melvin was in the war."

"What about Nelda?" I asked. "Is she from around here?"

"No, she is from Denver. But Melvin married her when he was in the service. They have two children. Both are grown and they live in big cities."

I wondered if they would return home for the burial of their grandfather. It pleased me to think that Melvin had some other family, even if it was only kids who had moved away.

"And Gunter?"

"He is very rich," she said.

"And Dustin Florence? Is he rich, too?"

"Not so much as Dr. Gunter, but he must also be wealthy for he has never worked at a job. He has been divorced and widowed. And he has been to many colleges in the East."

"Harvard?" I guessed.

"I do not think so."

Consuela rose gracefully from the dirt and gestured toward the west. "It is almost night. Good luck, Adam."

"Where are you going?" I imagined her hard at work in the Cafe-Tavern and Jail, making tortillas from scratch and burning bacon. "Do you have to make dinner?"

"I'm not a very good cook." But she smiled, and I forgave her.

"Then what?" I wanted to ask her why a charming individual such as herself was doing tucked away in Morning. What's a nice girl like you doing in a place like this?

"I have work to do." She backed away from me, and I distinctly heard the words "FAX machine."

Then, she vanished as quickly as she had appeared. I rolled over to my belly and kept my eye on the Feed and Seed. Once again, Melvin was out on the porch, whittling.

In order to avoid a repeat of the prior ghostly appearance of his father, I took a more circuitous route through the brush. The escape from the naked no-names had taken its toll on my leg muscles. I munched on a freeze-dried chocolate mousse to keep my strength up.

I came around from the cottonwood grove near the trailers and approached the porch. "Hi, Melvin."

He looked up at me and grunted once, before returning to his whittling. His lack of interest was good, I thought. At least, he wasn't accusing me of satanic intent.

"Mind if we go inside?" I asked. "The sheriff is still after me."

He nodded and hoisted his large body to an upright position. He was a big one, all right. Probably six feet, six inches tall and well over two hundred pounds. He fiddled with the multitude of locks on the door and ushered me inside. Then, he turned and nodded at me. "I'm listening."

"It's about this alien, Melvin."

He strolled over to the display of kachinas that all looked like Nelda. "Yeah?"

"Until the alien gets found, everything in Morning is going to be all screwed up."

He frowned. Still, not saying anything.

"Melvin," I said gently. "I've got two pieces of the map. I know you've got the final piece. Let's put it together. Let's find whatever there is to find, and we can end this."

"No," he said.

I didn't have any reason to expect otherwise. After all, Melvin had held out on his own father. Why should he give the map to me? I turned to leave.

"I expected you to understand," he said. "You and me, Adam. We're Vietnam vets. We know what it was like to leave men behind."

"I remember." It wasn't something I'd ever forget.

"The alien is like that," he said. "This little guy got stranded here on earth. It's not right for people to be digging him up and desecrating his remains."

"Okay, buddy." I reached up and patted him on the shoulder. "Okay."

I understood where he was coming from. Though I didn't entirely agree with the idea that a long-dead alien from a space-ship was the same as leaving a fallen comrade in a jungle hell, I understood. Melvin Stoker had been through a lot, and the poor guy had just lost his father. I wasn't about to pressure him so that Gunter could do his experiments or Rob Crusoe could lead his whacked-out nudist no-names into the New Age.

Somehow, it was right that Melvin should be the guardian of civilized behavior in Morning. I stuck my hand into my pocket and pulled out copies of the two pieces of the map which I spread on the countertop in front of him. "With your piece, you've got the whole map. I'll leave the decision up to you."

He nodded again. His forehead scrunched, and his heavy lower lip trembled. I thought maybe he was going to break down and cry. Or start babbling about Satan again. "Dad wanted to dig him up."

"I know."

Time for me to take off . . . before Melvin started weeping. I was never good with tears, especially not with tears from large ex-Marines.

I headed toward the door, then remembered why I'd come here in the first place. Fumbling through my multitude of pockets, I found the space screw and set it in the middle of the map pieces. The light in the Feed and Seed Store was dim, and the screw took on a slight radiance. "I guess the screw was important to your dad," I said. "Thought you might want to have it."

"You son of a bitch."

He whirled on me and swung his giant arm in an arc. His fist was like a wrecking ball on the end of a chain.

I ducked fast and felt air whistle over the top of my head. "What the hell—"

Melvin lowered his head and charged like a bulldozer. Luckily for me, he was just about as agile as a Sherman Tank, and I was able to step out of his way. He stumbled and crashed into the shelves full of candy. Ancient Milky Ways and Mr. Goodbars clattered to the floor like hard tile.

The big guy wasn't stunned by the impact. He doggedly got

to his feet and came at me again. This time, he moved slowly, cutting off my escape routes with his bulk.

There was one thing for sure, I didn't want him to connect with any part of my body. I tried to reason with him. "Melvin," I yelled. "What's wrong?"

He grunted and dove at me.

I dodged, but my legs were clumsy and I fell into a comic-book rack, spilling yellowed *Supermans*.

Melvin's large body flung across the countertop, overturning several display cases.

I staggered to my feet. "Why are you doing this?"

"You killed him," Melvin said. "You killed my father."

"Hell, no."

"That's the only way you could have gotten that screw." He took another ferocious swing, missing me by half a yard. "You killed him for the screw."

"Yeah?" I stuck my jaw out. "Then, why am I giving it to you? Huh? If I wanted the goddamned screw so bad, why would I give it to you?"

He paused. For a moment, he puzzled over my statement. I was beginning to think that I was safe when he reared back and ran at me. "Fuck you, McCleet."

I didn't have anyplace to run. Though I managed to deflect the main force of his charge by shoving him sideways, we were too close for me to manage an escape. In order to flee like the reasonable human being I was trying to be, I turned my back on him.

This was a big mistake.

Melvin grabbed my shoulder. His arms closed around my torso in a bearhug. He began to squeeze. I tried to get in a punch, but I had no leverage and I was facing the wrong way. My feet left the floor. My ribs began to crack. I couldn't breathe. In what might be my last gasps, I smelled Melvin's odor and his breathe. I didn't want that stink to be my last earthly sensation.

_____

I threw my weight forward, and Melvin stumbled a few steps in that direction. Close to the counter, I braced my legs against the wooden top and pushed off as hard as I could.

We went flying, falling backwards in a disorienting arch, free falling. I landed hard on top of Melvin. I could feel the breath go out of his lungs, but I didn't make the mistake of believing I could beat him.

With the last bit of strength in my legs, I bounced off his belly and staggered toward the door.

"Wait," he choked out.

"Why? So you can kill me?"

"Sorry," he said.

"Great." I had my hand on the doorknob. "That makes it all better. You're sorry? That's just fucking great."

"You wouldn't give me the screw." He forced himself to inhale like a giant bellows. "If you killed Dad."

"That's what I said!"

Wary of a trap, I edged closer to him.

"How'd you get it?" he asked.

"Somebody found it," I told him. "Out near Margot's place."

"Who?"

I thought of Whiney the Indian. There was no way he could withstand an assault from Melvin. "Trust me on this. Nobody stole the screw from Dental."

Melvin pushed himself to a sitting position and held out his hand. "Help me up."

There were two choices here. I could tuck my tail between my legs and run like a dog—a dog who would live to see another day. Or I could take the big man's hand and run the risk of bodily dismemberment. If I thought about caution being the better part of valor, my actions would be canine. But I've never been good at logic.

I took his hand, helped him to his feet and braced myself for the next assault.

Melvin smiled warmly at me. "Thanks. You keep the screw."
I pocketed it again.

"My father and I fought about it all the time," Melvin explained. "About the alien. I can't think of anything that would make me change my mind, Adam. My forefathers buried him with dignity, and I think he ought to stay buried."

I left the Feed and Seed Store by the back way and headed toward Margot's hacienda. This afternoon had been less than productive, and I was looking forward to a night's sleep in an actual bed, even if it meant Gomez-Gomez would find and arrest me before dawn.

Nightfall descended as I walked, fairly slow along the dirt road. Though I heard the horse coming and had plenty of time to get out of the way, I was too tired to care.

Rob Crusoe brushed past me, then whirled around. His palomino stallion reared up on its hind legs. With his flowing blond hair and sheet, he looked like Lawrence of Arabia. "McCleet?"

"What?" I wasn't in the mood for bullshit.

"Margot called me from her cellular phone," he said. "Does she really have the map?"

"That's right."

"You really fucked up, Adam. Why did you steal it?"

"I wanted to give all your Land Rovers a workout."

"You could have been killed, you know." For a moment, he pondered the weight of the universe. "My people would do anything for me."

"Witness the nude volleyball game."

"I need that map. It's a symbol."

"Of what? Gullible assholes with too much disposable income who come to seek enlightenment through divesting themselves of all common sense?" As long as I wasn't being tactful, I pressed forward, asking the big question, "Did you kill him, Rob? Did you kill Dental Stoker?"

"Why would I?"

"The alien."

"Dental wasn't going to find the alien. No way. If anybody could locate the being, it would be Gunter."

This should have been the moment when I cleverly tricked him into admitting that he'd dropped the rattlesnakes into the kiva to kill Gunter. But I wasn't up to clever, I was barely up to conscious. "You want to see Gunter dead."

He spread his hands and gazed up at the cosmos as if seeking comprehension, then he looked back at me. "You make too much of this, Adam. Death is not to be feared. Life is but temporal."

"Nice theory, but when it's my life being temporal, I get testy. How do you feel about snakes?"

He shrugged. Trying to read his reaction was nearly impossible. This guy was a trained con man.

"Snakes," I repeated. "Rattlesnakes in a flowered pillowcase."

"Traditionally, the snake symbolizes wisdom, sometimes forbidden wisdom. Someone who knows too much might be bitten."

He nudged the flanks of his stallion and rode off, leaving me to contemplate his words. Was that a threat? An admission of guilt? Or merely New Age bullshit?

Unenlightened, I continued to slog along the path.

Within half an hour, Rob was charging back at me. He pulled up to a walk. "She wouldn't let me have the map."

"Margot's like that." Like a snapping turtle that grabbed onto something and wouldn't let go. I didn't bother explaining that this was one of her more endearing traits.

"She wouldn't even talk to me about it," Rob said. "She told me I'd have to change clothes and lose the sheet before she could be bothered to engage in a discussion."

"You know what they say. Clothes make the man." If that

were true, Rob Crusoe was a man made by Wamsutta or Canon. "Margot's big on appearances."

"Maybe she's right," he said. "Her words were profound."

"Are we talking about the same Margot?" I was shocked. Margot hadn't had a deep insight since she discovered the Wonderbra. Was Rob Crusoe, the Casanova of Rio Arriba county, falling for the fatal charms of my sister? Had I liked Rob, I might have warned him.

"Appearance," he said, "can be the ultimate illusion."

"As in, being shallow means you're deep?"

"Exactly. Being superficial enough to worry about what you're wearing really means you're deep enough to care what you look like."

"Profound," I said. He and Margot deserved each other.

"Adios, Adam." He galloped off.

When I finally got to the hacienda, I was greeted at the door by Whiney who was dressed in a clean white shirt, pressed denim jeans and a pair of loafers that looked suspiciously like they had once belonged to me.

Margot had not, however, completely reformed him. Whiney was drunk as the proverbial skunk, clinging to the doorframe to keep from falling. Beside him, equally plastered, was Monte.

As they showed me inside, they announced the occasion with a rousing medley of show tunes, starting with "Hello, Dolly" and ending with "Give My Regards to . . . Margot."

Margot strode into the front room. She was dressed all in red, screaming loud red. Her silk tunic and wide pants swirled around her like a dragon's tail as she crossed her arms beneath her breasts, stared at me, then looked away as she studied her cuticles. "Oh, Adam. It's only you."

"Who were you expecting, Dragon Lady?"

Her eyes narrowed to slits. "Dinner," she said.

"Carry-out?"

"No, this is a live rat with long blond hair. I might have to tear his head off before I fry him."

Whiney was clearly captivated by his new mistress. He gazed at her longingly. "She's so pretty."

"Margot?" Monte slapped his arm. "What about me?" He threw back his head and sang "I Feel Pretty."

I seriously considered going back outside and sleeping with the scorpions when I heard a calm voice speak my name.

Joining Margot and over-matching her in sheer feminine power was the most beautiful woman I've ever known. Alison Brooks. She was pure class, always chic, but her clothes weren't important. It was the aura that seemed to surround her, a soft light that danced in her shining auburn hair and glowed from her eyes.

Without talking and asking a billion unanswerable questions, she saw that I was tired. She came to me. "Rough day, hon?"

I could have told her about being chased by naked no-names, flirting with the sultry Consuela and being pummeled by a Melvin, extra-large. Instead, I said, "Yup."

She took me by the hand and led me into the kitchen, talking as we went. "First, I'm going to feed you. Then, a massage. Or maybe a geisha shower—"

"You be the geisha," I said.

"Naturally. And then, we might just—"

"Humpenhoff," Monte said, poking his head around the corner of the kitchen entryway.

Behind him was Whiney, who echoed, "Humpenhoff. That's right. Humpenhoff."

"I beg your pardon," Alison said archly.

The musical twosome harmonized on a strange rendition of "Oh, What a Beautiful . . . Humpenhoff."

"Must be a code," I said. I knew I'd heard the word before. "Henry Humpenhoff?"

"How would I know?" Whiney stopped his singing to whine. "Nobody ever tells me anything important."

"I don't know why not," Monte said, flinging his arm around his new best buddy. "It's not like you'd remember or anything."

I turned to Alison. "Henry Humpenhoff was a trapper—like Kit Carson—who settled around here."

"Fascinating." She looked up from the sandwich she was preparing for me. "And when did you become an expert on the life and lore of New Mexico?"

"Gunter told me," I explained, then I looked back at the Three Stooges Less One. "So? What about Humpenhoff?"

"Gunter called me at the gallery," Monte said. "He said to tell you that the book is a Humpenhoff."

The diary, I presumed. "Anything else?"

"Gunter is coming back tomorrow," Monte said.

"And he wants to talk to you," Whiney added.

"Okay," I said. "Is there anything else?"

Monte and Whiney searched each other's faces, then turned to me. "No," they said in chorus.

"Thanks, guys. Now, why don't you go terrorize Margot for a while."

"Aye, aye," Monte said. He attempted a salute, but accidentally slugged Whiney, who yelped and stomped on Monte's toe with his brand-new loafers which had to be mine.

Alison presented me with a ham sandwich and an ice-cold beer. "I think we should go to our room," she said.

I agreed.

As soon as the door closed behind us, I set down the food and pulled her into my arms. Thinking of my weird conversation with Consuela, I almost asked her if Jacques was still trying to get into her pants. Instead, I said, "How's the art show?"

"You are selling very well, thank you. I hate to admit it, but Monte was right about that stupid tabloid publicity. Everybody knows who you are."

"Everybody thinks I'm a mad dog killer?"

She shrugged. "It seems to sell art."

Her warm, firm, resilient breasts rubbed up against my chest. Again, the word "marriage" was in the back of my throat. What came through my lips was, "I want to make love to you."

She stepped out of my embrace. Lightly, she unbuttoned the front of her blouse and stretched out on the bed. "Take me."

For the first time in days, I knew exactly what to do next.

Chapter
Twelve

Throughout the night, I heard comings and goings. There seemed to be a number of loud altercations which didn't surprise me in the least. With Margot in residence, tension was a certainty. At one point, Monte and Whiney got stuck on "There's No Business Like Show Business," and belted it until they were both hoarse.

I kept waiting for the scream of a police siren, but it never came, and none of the other noises distracted me. I had locked the door to our bedroom. Alison and I made love first in the bedroom, then in the shower, then back in the bed, all nice and clean. When she woke me in the morning by nibbling on my earlobe, I started to protest, but she convinced me that once more for the road was good luck. It didn't take much to change my mind. Besides, I figured we were going to need all the luck we could get.

I leaned back on the pillows and watched her getting dressed after she came out of the shower. It was a ritual I always enjoyed. First, she smoothed her already perfect skin with a lotion that smelled like spice and flowers. Her hands massaged the curves of her heel and calf.

She glanced over at me. Even without makeup, Alison was sophisticated. "I can't believe that the sheriff hasn't dropped by to arrest you."

"Maybe she did stop by last night and Margot ate her."

"Always a possibility," Alison said. "There are certain advantages to having a carnivorous sister."

"Blood-sucking," I said. "But did I tell you how she saved my butt from those naked no-names?"

"Yes, you did." She pulled the towel off her head and shook her wet hair. "You see, Adam. Margot really isn't as awful as you make her out to be."

"Sure, she is. She only takes an occasional and infrequent dip into the milk of human kindness when it suits her purposes. Obviously, in this instance, she's getting ready to sink her claws into Rob Crusoe. The poor sucker."

"Rob? I have a hard time feeling sympathy for him," Alison said. "From what you've said, the guy seems like a major manipulator who is bilking all those cult people."

"Only those who want to be bilked," I said. "Plus there are benefits, like nude volleyball."

She looked me in the eye. "Do you think Rob killed Dental?"

Ah, yes, that was the big question. Who had murdered the old prospector? Which one of them? "Much as I hate to admit it," I said, "Shirley Gomez-Gomez might have been onto something when she arrested the entire town. Somebody who was in that jail cell killed Dental."

"Who?"

"Might be better to ask why."

Alison retreated into the bathroom, and I heard the blow dryer start up. I wished I could simply enjoy the fact that she was lovely, and obviously—after last night's mutually brilliant sexual gymnastics—she loved me and not some pretentious Frenchman. I wished I could settle back and enjoy the gallery showing that might lead to international success. But I had these pesky murder charges hanging over my head. So, I kept thinking. Why? Why kill Dental?

Until now, I had been operating under the theory that Dental had something of value, and one of these people had bumped him off in order to get their hands on it. But the only valuable items were the piece of the map and the space screw, both of which we'd found.

Alison returned to the bedroom. Her auburn hair shimmered in loose waves to her shoulders. Though she was breathtaking, I forced my brain back to the topic at hand. "Dental didn't have anything worth stealing."

"Probably not," Alison agreed. She glided the towel off her body. Un-self-consciously, she dabbed perfume behind her knees and in the crook of her arm. "From what I've seen, Dental wasn't anything more than a local character. Like part of the landscape. A scenic old prospector."

The vision of naked Alison blanked everything else from my mind. It wasn't until she'd slid her crimson lace panties on and fastened her red satin bra that I was able to breathe normally.

"Maybe Dental knew something," she suggested. "He could have been blackmailing someone."

I shook my head without taking my eyes off her. "Nobody around here has any kind of ambitions. How could they be blackmailed?"

She glanced over her shoulder, and her back arched just enough to form a delectable curve. "What about Rob and his boys? From what you told me, he's got quite an expensive operation out there on the No-Name compound. Maybe he's got something to hide."

"True." According to the adorable Consuela, Rob had been arrested on drug charges and was once a rock star. Neither occupation would go down well with followers seeking the pure life . . . if that was what the No-Names were after.

"And why does he wear a gun strapped to his hip if he's not expecting to use it?"

"Rattlesnakes?" And that reminded me of the flowered pillowcase and the snakes in the kiva. All things considered, Rob Crusoe looked like the best suspect.

"Probably something to do with the alien. Also," she reminded me. "Shirley Gomez-Gomez is dating Rob. If he did it, she'd want to cover up."

She slipped a silky red blouse over her satin bra, and I gave a small whimper of protest. Though I wasn't really desirous of more sex, I enjoyed watching her. I could have stayed in bed all day, studying Alison in various stages of dress, or undress.

But she had a different idea. "You need to get dressed, Adam. Every one at Sundog—except perhaps Jacques—wants to chat with you and then to spend huge sums of money on your sculptures."

"Sure, Alison. You know how much I love hanging out in galleries." Just about as much as I enjoyed taking a swan dive into boiling acid. "But there's that little detail: I'm wanted for murder."

"Oh, that." She slithered a pair of black Levi's up her legs and buttoned them. "Don't you think we could talk with the real police, the state police, and get that all straightened out?"

"Maybe. But there are additional complications. Escape from custody, resisting arrest, assaulting an officer, theft of a police vehicle. Cops really have no sense of humor about that stuff."

"Well, what do you suggest, Adam? Spend the rest of our lives sneaking around unincorporated Rio Arriba county?"

"Solve it."

Alison groaned as she sank down on the bed beside me. "All right, Adam. What do we do next?"

"Gunter left that Humpenhoff message. Maybe he's got a

lead." I took another long, appreciative look at Alison. "It's hard to think about anything else when you're around."

"Why's that?" she teased.

I reached for the top button on her silky blouse to show her, but she slapped my hand away. "Not now, Adam. We have artworks to sell."

"They can wait," I growled.

"You get dressed. I'll call Gunter on Margot's cell phone and arrange to meet him."

With that, she bounced out of the bedroom and left me to dress myself.

My morning ritual took far less time than Alison's. I took a quick slosh in the shower, ran a razor across my chin and covered my bruised and battered body with clothes. I inventoried my pains: The knot on the back of my head from getting whacked. The bruise on my cheekbone from where Shirley clubbed me with her gun. My butt was sore from the horseback ride. My rib cage ached from yesterday's battle with Melvin. Oh yeah, I thought, Melvin. Had he killed his own father? I thought about the possibility. Melvin, when he thought I was Dental's ghost, had shown an inordinate amount of remorse. But then, he'd bashed me around the Feed and Seed like a sack of oats when he assumed I'd killed Dental. Was Melvin smart enough to fake his rage? On the other hand, he might have gotten enraged with Dental, whacked him and then erased the murder from his consciousness in a post-traumatic stress disorder kind of thing. Yeah, sure.

Alison would like the complicated psychology of that theory. She was into that kind of stuff, and I decided to tell her about it in the hope that she'd think I was sensitive.

I marched into the kitchen of the hacienda and confronted a homey scene. Alison sat at the table, sipping her coffee. Whiney slumped in the corner like a deflated balloon. And Monte—who was already dressed in a fancy white shirt and snug black pants tucked into high boots—sipped at a disgusting-looking brew from a crystal goblet.

"What's that?" I asked him."

"Hangover remedy. Never fails."

"Okay. And who are you dressed as today?"

"What do you mean, Adam?" His hangover made him surly.

"Well, you don't look like Roy Rogers. Or the Sundance Kid."

"I'm bored with the Old West," he said. "So now I'm Señor Monte Zorro, the gay caballero."

"Olé," Alison said, precluding any smart comments from me. "I talked to Gunter, and he's fine. Said he would meet us at his wigwam in forty-five minutes."

This meant I had time for a cup of coffee, then we hit the road. I took the giant Caddy that came with the hacienda, and eased cautiously past the Cafe-Tavern and Jail in Morning. There was no sign of Shirley Gomez-Gomez's police car.

I only followed one wrong turn before we meandered our way to Gunter's place. Unfortunately, we were not the first to arrive.

Sheriff Shirley was there before us. With her pistola drawn, she approached the car. "Don't try to get away, McCleet."

With total disregard for her order, I slammed the big car into reverse and tried to turn. My escape route was blocked by a giant blob of mesquite and another cop car. State police. Finally, Shirley had gotten wise.

She was laughing when she came to the driver's side door and yanked it open. "Get out. You heard me, get out of the damned car."

At that moment, Gunter drove over the hilltop in a funky gray Volvo.

As Shirley stood watching, the state cops took the stocky little man into custody. She turned to me. Her expression showed total satisfaction. She gloated, "Gotcha, McCleet. Not so smart now, are you?"

"How'd you know where to find us?"

"I've been monitoring your sister's cell phone."

That was so simple. "Oh," I said.

"She's some piece of work, that sister of yours. A real bitch."

I wanted to say that it took one to know one, but thought better of it.

"You know, McCleet," Shirley said quietly. "I figured it out. I figured the whole damned thing out."

"Is that so?"

"Yeah." She looked like hell. Her hair had gone beyond greasy to strands of matted slime. Her jaw was swollen black and blue where I hit her. And her eyes were red-rimmed and kind of wild. She said, "You didn't kill Dental."

I brightened. "So, you're not arresting me?"

"Hell, yes, I'm arresting you. You destroyed my jail, resisted arrest and assaulted me. Make no mistake, gringo, you are in deep shit."

"But I didn't kill Dental," I reminded her.

"No, you did not."

"Who did?"

"That, McCleet, is none of your fucking business."

She swaggered over to the two state cops and began giving orders. "We're going to take the whole bunch of them in. We'll book them, then sort out the mess on who gets charged with what."

The other two officers nodded respectfully. "Whatever you say, Shirley."

"One minute," Gunter said. He pointed at the entrance to his teepee. "Look at that! It's standing open. Somebody broke into my place."

"So?" Shirley raised her eyebrows.

"At least let me close it up and set the alarm. I have a lot of sophisticated equipment in there."

A state cop frowned. "In a teepee?"

"Please," Gunter begged. "It'll only take a minute."

Shirley and the other cops exchanged a glance. She said, "I'm not letting any of these people out of my sight. They appear to be harmless, but they're tricky as hell."

On behalf of the entire group, I said, "Thank you."

She rolled her eyes and started toward the teepee. "I'll take care of it. How do I set the alarm?"

As Gunter started to reply, Shirley Gomez-Gomez stumbled over something in the entryway to the teepee. Before she could react, the explosion hit. Red fire flared in a tight ball. Inferno heat blasted at us with enough power to knock me and one of the cops off our feet. From the force of the blast, I imagined about a half pound of TNT, roughly equivalent to a hand grenade. Enough to cause a respectable explosion, more than enough to cause serious physical harm to Shirley Gomez-Gomez.

Her body lay facedown, five feet from the entrance to Gunter's teepee, which was burning. Her hat was still stuck on her head. Her arm and the back of her shirt were aflame.

I got to my feet and started toward her, holding up my hand and arm as if I could stop the waves of radiant heat that crashed against me.

"Get back," Gunter yelled. "I've got propane tanks in there."

I kept charging forward. It wasn't heroism that compelled me, but stubbornness. Booby traps were a coward's device. The same kind of brainless destructive crap that would be used by somebody who would kill an unarmed prospector, who would whack me on the back of the head, who would throw rattle-snakes in a pit. I wasn't going to let the bastard win.

I grabbed Shirley's feet and pulled her away from the flames. Ten feet back, I turned her over. Her face was gone. Flesh hung in ragged shreds from a gaping hole in the center of her chest.

Still, I dragged her farther away from the potential explosion. There was enough left of Shirley Gomez-Gomez to bury, and I intended to keep it that way.

Near Shirley's car, one of the cops grabbed my shoulder. He threw a blanket over her body. "Get the hell out of here, man."

I turned back, gauging the distance from the teepee to the cars. How many tanks of propane did Gunter have in there? Two? Three?

I wrapped Shirley's body in the blanket and carried her away from the cars.

"Put her down," the cop ordered. "Can't you see she's dead?"

But I wasn't going to leave her behind. I was halfway up the side of the gravelly gully wall, carrying my limp bundle, when the first propane tank exploded.

The impact knocked me down, but I got up again. Just a little bit farther. Twenty feet.

I was on the flat top of the low hill when the second propane tank went off and the flames spurted higher, like a volcanic geyser.

Gently, I placed the remains of Sheriff Gomez-Gomez on the hot flat earth. Then, I collapsed beside her, lying on my back. I closed my eyes against the light of the sun. "Shit," I muttered.

When my eyelids opened, only a minute later, Alison was hovering over me. She was shivering. Her complexion was waxy. "Are you all right?" she asked.

I nodded.

"My god, Adam, what the hell were you doing? You could have been killed."

But I felt okay inside. I hadn't left Shirley there to be burned and charred. "Maybe I have more in common with Melvin than I'd like to admit."

She stroked my cheek. Her touch was cool, and I felt a sudden dampness. A teardrop. Alison was crying. "You asshole. You absolute asshole."

I propped myself up on an elbow. "I'm okay. Not hurt."

"Fuck you, Adam." Her beautiful face streaked with tears. "Just fuck you."

Below us, I saw one of the cops run to their vehicle and radio for help.

They were going to need a hell of a lot of back-up. The fire spread quickly across the arid landscape of dried wood and mesquite. Aided by the wind, the brushfire reached out with long hot fingers across the plains. Closer to us, the fire jumped to Gunter's Volvo.

The cops moved their vehicle. And Monte, shrieking with every step, got into the Caddy and backed away from the fire.

I could hear wailing fire engines approaching. We were going to be all right. All of us, except the sheriff. Shirley Gomez-Gomez had known the identity of the killer. Now, Shirley was dead.

At least with this murder, I had an idea of why.

The ensuing conversations with cops and firefighters meandered on a lengthy and confused path. Alison was the only one among us who kept returning us to the straight and narrow. After we were finally introduced to the main cop, a lieutenant named Honorio Snead, she repeated the single question she'd asked of just about everyone. "So, Lieutenant, are we under arrest?"

"Do you want to be?"

"No."

"What would you expect me to charge you with?"

"Nothing," I said before Alison could run through our criminal potential. "We're just down here for the Art Festival in Taos, and accidentally got tied up with the rest of this stuff."

He stared at the smouldering remains of Gunter's teepee. When he looked back at me, his gaze was hard. "Are you the one who pulled her out of there?"

I nodded.

"Let me ask you a few questions."

I filled in whatever blanks I could without implicating myself or Alison or Monte. My only stumbling block was talking about Tonna-Hokay-Pokay-Lawnchair-Yada-Yada.

"An alien?" Snead wrinkled his face in distaste.

"He supposedly glows in the dark."

I considered showing him the magical screw that I was still carrying in my pocket, then thought better of it. Snead was a professional, a deviation from the standard operating lunacy of Morning. I didn't want to go all weird on him.

After I finished, Snead indicated that he was pretty much unconcerned with the murder of Dental Stoker. That case was nothing but dead trails because Shirley hadn't seen fit to confide her final suspicions in anyone.

"She didn't tell you the identity of the murderer?" he questioned.

"No."

"We'll find him." His voice was calm, dead calm. "Nobody gets away with killing a cop."

No matter how annoying and weird she'd been, Shirley was one of them, and Snead didn't take the murder of a comrade lightly. When I suggested that the two deaths could be connected, they thanked me for my opinion and told me to shut up and get the hell out of there. "You're not under arrest. None of you. But don't leave the area."

"Yes, sir." I didn't need to be told twice.

We loaded into the big Caddy. Some damage had been sustained in the explosion. The windshield was cracked, and there was a crater in the hood. It was a shame, I thought. After Whiney had taken such good care of it for years, we'd trashed the car in a matter of hours.

I was driving. Alison sat beside me. In the back seat were Monte and Gunter.

"Would you look at this shirt," Monte said. "It's filthy. I have ruined more clothes on this trip than I do in a year at home."

"That's what happens in the Wild West," I informed him.

He looked to Gunter. "I don't suppose you'd happen to know of any really good dry-cleaning establishment. Normally, I wouldn't worry, but this is rayon and—"

"No," Gunter said. He leaned forward so his head was right behind my ear. "The diary, Adam. It was written by Amelia Humpenhoff. She describes the whole thing. The falling star. The crash. An authentic record."

"Swell," I said.

"It's proof," Gunter said. "The diary is proof."

I drove to the intersection of two roads. To the right was Taos. If I turned to the left, we'd be on our way back to Morning.

"Go right," Alison said firmly.

"But I can't go to Taos looking like this," Monte complained. "We need to go back to Margot's and change."

"I'll buy you a new outfit," Alison said. She stared hard at me. "Turn right, Adam."

"Left," Gunter said. "We can put the map together. We have all the pieces."

"No," I corrected him. "We know where the pieces are. But we don't have them."

Still, my inclination was to turn left. Shirley had said that she knew the identity of the killer, and I hoped that she'd left a clue at the Cafe-Tavern and Jail. If we didn't get there before the cops descended, I would never know who killed Dental.

Alison seemed to read my mind. "Leave it. This isn't your problem. Let the state police handle this. Lieutenant Snead seemed very capable."

I took her hand in mine. We'd been down this road before. Many times before, Alison and I had clashed on our definitions of what was intelligent and prudent versus what was the Right Thing To Do. I looked into her deep green eyes. "You know I can't walk away."

"I know." She sighed. "It's your most annoying characteristic, Adam, this questing thing."

At the risk of provoking an outburst of fury from her, I said, "It's the Right Thing To Do."

"You and your ridiculous moral compass," she muttered. "This may come as a shock, Adam, but every murder that occurs is not a personal affront to you."

"Maybe not."

"Dammit, Adam." She squeezed my hand. "Go ahead. Turn left. But if you get yourself killed, I'm never going to forgive you."

At the Cafe-Tavern and Jail, there was a "Closed" sign in the window. But that really wasn't much of a deterrent since the jailbreak had left a giant hole in the back.

While Gunter and Monte trotted next door to the Feed and Seed, Alison and I picked our way through the rubble.

"Nice job," she said. "Monte missed his true calling. He should have been a wrecking crew."

"He'd never last," I predicted. "Overalls and a hardhat are too drab for him."

Inside the building, we were in luck. The door to the jail cell was unlocked, as was the door leading into the kitchen.

Though I'd never had a chance to explore back here, it wasn't hard to figure out where the office was. There was a closed door with a sign that said: Office.

The knob twisted easily in my hand, and Alison and I stepped inside. The interior wasn't as high-tech as Gunter's teepee, but there was a computer, a printer, a copy machine, a police radio and a FAX machine. In the center of the plain oak desk was an unopened bottle of tequila and a manila folder. The tab on the side said: Dental Stoker.

I fanned through the pages quickly. These were typical police-blotter records that contained a few quick facts on all the suspects. I was looking mostly for notes that Shirley had made to herself. But there was nothing.

"Maybe she hadn't figured it out," I said. "Maybe she just thought she did."

"Nice decor," Alison commented as she eyed a series of black and white lithographs depicting some kind of fiesta celebration. "This New Mexico lifestyle is beginning to grow on me. I've never seen so much art, so casually tossed around."

I returned the folder to its place on the desk. A quick search of the drawers turned up another tequila bottle and my wallet, which I immediately reclaimed and stuck in my back pocket. The file cabinets were packed with police reports and records that I didn't even begin to search through. I turned back to Alison. "Okay, let's go."

She trailed behind me. "Dare I hope that you're now finished investigating?"

"Not quite yet. I'd like to ask Rob Crusoe a couple of questions. That booby-trap explosive makes me think of him. His group of no-names might be into survivalist militia techniques."

"Just the sort of people I'd love to be acquainted with," Alison said.

As we circled around to the front of the Cafe-Tavern and Jail, approaching the Feed and Seed, I considered Melvin as a suspect again. The booby trap had also reminded me of Vietnam. No doubt Melvin knew how to set explosives. "But how would he know to put it there?" I said.

Alison frowned up at me. "Beg your pardon?"

"How would the murderer know that Shirley was going to be there at the right time?"

The first thing I saw at the front of the Feed and Seed was Laddie, Dental's burro. His lead rope was wrapped casually around the rusting metal of a bicycle rack. Beside the animal stood Gunter. From the back, in his battered hat and flannel shirt, Gunter resembled Dental.

All of a sudden, a light went on in my brain. The pieces fell into place.

And I heard the crack of a high-powered rifle.

Chapter Thirteen

I didn't need to worry about protecting Alison. All by herself, without prompting, she hit the dirt and covered her head as automatically as a schoolkid doing a bomb drill. Her immediate reaction to gunfire made me think we might be spending too much time together. And I might be spending too much time being chased, shot at, and whacked over the head. Exactly what kind of relationship were we developing here?

"Get behind the jail," I told her.

She was up and running.

I sprinted toward Gunter who must have heard the shot but had not registered its significance. Innocent and stupid as a newborn, he blithely patted Laddie on the nose and looked up in the sky, as if the gunfire had been a sonic boom.

I dove toward him, knocking him off his feet.

An instant later, there was another gunshot and the wooden post behind Gunter splintered.

"Adam, what's going on?"

I pulled Gunter upright, then half pushed, half dragged him

up the porch steps and into the Feed and Seed, slamming the door as two more gunshots rang out. "Melvin," I yelled.

Nelda poked her head out from the Espresso bus. "Oh, it's you, Adam. And Doctor Gunter. How nice to blah-blah-blah. Can I interest you in a friendly cup of cappuccino?"

"Interest me in a gun," I said.

"We have firearms," she said, sauntering toward the back of the store. She was so wide that the swaying of her body completely filled the aisle. "Melvin usually handles these sales. He's the expert what with his military background and blah-diddity-blah. But he's not here right now."

She stood in front of a locked glass case where several rifles were displayed. Her fists were planted on her ample hips and she shook her head. "Isn't this always the blah-blah. Don't have the key. I'll have to take a look around for it."

Rather than taking the time and effort to explain to Nelda that we were under siege, I grabbed a poker from a dusty display of fireplace implements and pulled her out of the way.

"Listen here, Adam, what do you think you're doing?"

I smashed the glass front of the case and reached inside. I grabbed a 30-30 Winchester hunting rifle with lever action. Using the butt of the rifle, I smashed another glass case to get to the ammo.

While I loaded the rifle, Nelda waddled to the front doorway. "I'm calling Melvin. That's what I'm going to do. Blah-blah. You're going to be sorry, Adam McCleet. You can't come in here and blah-blah-ditty-blah-busting things up. We're blah—"

As soon as she opened the front door, a shot rang out.

"Yikes!" Nelda slammed the door and widened her piggy little eyes to the size of ball bearings. "Somebody took a shot at me."

I really doubted that. If a sniper had intended to hit Nelda, it would be hard to miss. She was as big as the proverbial side of a barn.

"They're after Gunter," I said.

The rear door of the Feed and Seed creaked open and I heard Alison call out, "Adam? Are you all right?"

"In here."

She strode through the ramshackle store with an amazing display of confidence and grace. She wasn't cowering like a woman who had just been shot at. Her silky red blouse was sooty from the explosions and fires. Her snug black jeans were torn at one knee. And she had a large smear of dirt across her left cheekbone. She would have been adorably cute if her green eyes had not been hard as emeralds. "Now, I'm pissed," she announced. "What the hell is going on here?"

For once, I had an answer for her, but I didn't have time to tell her. "In a minute, hon."

Using the barrel of the rifle, I knocked out a pane of glass in the front window, poked the rifle through it and fired off three shots to let the sniper know we were armed.

I stepped aside and waited for a returning volley, but none came.

Alison was right behind me. "Do you have any idea what you're shooting at?"

"Not a clue," I said. "But they fired the first round."

Alison turned to Nelda. "Do you have binoculars?"

"Well, of course, I do. Would you rather have the high-power or the opera-glasses type? Blah-blah—"

"Get them," Alison ordered. "The best you have."

We took turns using the high-powered binoculars, scanning the landscape from horizon to horizon until I was completely sure that our sniper had taken a powder.

I handed the binoculars back to Nelda who examined them carefully.

"Look here," she said. "There's a scratch on these. I can't sell them to anybody else. You know the rules, Adam. You break it, you bought it. Blah! Blah! Pay me for the ammo and the gun and the cases and the—"

"Stop," I said, digging in my pocket for my wallet. I counted out two hundred dollars in cash and placed it on the countertop in front of her. "That's all I've got on me. You can have the gun and the binoculars back."

"I don't want them back, and it's not enough. I'm telling Melvin."

"Go right ahead. Where is Melvin, anyway? You don't suppose he was the one out there shooting, do you?"

The thought must have also occurred to her because her eyes shifted nervously and a couple of her chins disappeared when she stuck out her jowls. "Certainly not," she said vehemently. Then, her lower lips quivered. There was a catch in her voice when she said, "Melvin would never shoot at me."

Alison dashed forward to comfort her. "I'm sure he wouldn't." She glared at me. "How could you suggest such a thing, Adam."

"Well, somebody was out there shooting at us."

I walked away from the women and strolled through the shelves of merchandise, still not locating a single sack of Feed or Seed, until I found Gunter, sitting cross-legged on the floor as if he were meditating. We hadn't had much conversation since he'd been out of the hospital, and I wondered if the physical strain of all this was getting to him. I squatted beside him. "How are you holding up?"

He stared at the floor. "What did you mean, Adam, when you said they were shooting at me?"

Alison and Nelda had moved close enough to hear, and I explained to all of them. "Something that has bothered me from the very beginning of this whole mess. Why? Why kill Dental Stoker? He didn't own anything of value. He might have been obnoxious, but not enough so that you'd want to kill the guy."

"He wasn't obnoxious," Nelda said. "How dare you speak ill of the dead. If Melvin—"

"Shut up," Alison said sweetly. "Continue, Adam."

"A little while ago, when I walked up to the front of the Seed and Feed, I saw Gunter standing there beside the burro, and—for a second—I thought he was the ghost of Dental. Old men in flannel shirts and jeans and battered hats look pretty much alike, even in daylight. Dental was killed at night. In the dark."

Gunter shuddered. "Are you saying that the killer was after me?"

"Afraid so. Take a look at the subsequent events. Somebody threw those rattlesnakes down the pit, trying to kill you. The booby trap was rigged at your place. Logically, you should have been the one who tripped it. It was just bad luck Sheriff Gomez-Gomez went first."

"What happened to Shirley?" Nelda asked. "Is she—"

"She's dead," I said abruptly and turned back to Gunter. "Now, somebody's taking potshots. And I'll bet they're aiming at you."

His round little face compacted in a frown. "Dental died in my place. He died for me."

"Now, don't start with that Viking shit." I had no idea what Norsemen did when they felt guilty, but I didn't want to find out. I paraphrased the NRA slogan. "You didn't kill Dental. A murderer killed Dental."

"There's still the problem of motive," Alison pointed out. "Why would somebody want to kill Gunter?"

I looked at him. "Maybe he can tell us."

"Oh, I have enemies," he said. "But I can think of no one who would wish to kill me. That's rather extreme."

"Maybe someone thought you were getting too close to finding the alien using scientific methods instead of the Dental Stoker random digging approach. And, you're a wealthy man, Gunter. Money affects people strangely."

"That's right," Nelda said. "Lots of people talk about that, you know. What they're going to inherit when you die." She had the grace to look slightly embarrassed. "Well, you own half of Rio Arriba county, Gunter, and that's a fact."

While she rattled off all her other knowledge about Gunter Bjornson's possessions, Alison sidled up to me. "That was brilliant detective work, Adam."

"Thank you, my love."

"Very intelligent," she said. Lest I got too carried away with her compliments, she added, "It's nice to see you using your head for something other than a punching bag."

"I think so."

"Well, I think we have this pretty well wrapped up," she continued. "Let's pass on this insight to Lieutenant Honorio Snead and leave the investigating to the state troopers. In the meantime, Gunter, you should lay low. Maybe go back east for a while until they apprehend the murderer."

"Excellent advice," I said. "Nelda, would you let Gunter use your telephone to call Santa Fe and make plane reservations? Go stay with your daughter, Freya. If she's managed to get herself hooked up with a creep like Dustin from Boston, she might be interested in some fatherly advice."

Dustin from Boston had just moved up on my list of suspects to the number one position. If Gunter were dead and Dustin married Freya, he would probably inherit big time. Unfortunately, there were a few problems with this scenario. Like Dustin hadn't arrived until after Dental's death. And Dustin appeared to be wealthy in his own right.

I placed a consoling hand on Gunter's shoulder. "Let's get you out of town, man."

Gunter stood and threw back his shoulders. "Would Eric the Red run from danger?"

"Hell, yes," I said. "A good Viking knows when to retreat so he can come back and fight another day."

"I can't leave. I won't. I'm too close."

"Too close to what?" Nelda demanded. Her strident twangy voice was louder and more insistent than usual. "What happened to Shirley? What kind of booby trap are you—"

The front door to the Feed and Seed swung wide and Melvin tromped inside. His gaze went immediately to the broken pane of glass, then to me. "Busting up my place again, Adam?"

"Melvin!" Nelda floated toward him. Due to her bulk, I wouldn't say that she flew on gossamer wings. She'd require the aerodynamics of a 747 to get her bulk aloft. In any case, she was in his arms. "I'm so glad you're here. People were shooting at us. Have you heard about Shirley Gomez-Gomez?"

"I was over there. Damn shame."

"Well, you've got to tell me all about it," Nelda demanded. "And we had some excitement over here and blah-de-blah with shooting at Gunter."

"Melvin!" Gunter hastened toward the big man with an eager gait, stopped right in front of Melvin and his wife and beamed up at the two of them. "I want that map."

"Forget it," Melvin said. "I've got a mind to burn the damn thing."

"Why?"

Nelda answered for him. "Because he and his daddy fought over the doggoned thing for years and years. It kind of estranged them—"

"Estranged?" That seemed like a big word for Nelda.

She explained, "I saw a talk show about it. 'Family Grudges and How They Estrange.' Anyway, my Melvin has suffered enough because of that map, and I think you and everyone else should just leave him alone."

Gunter squeezed in a word, "But, Nelda, I have—"

"Gimme, gimme," she said. "That's all you people ever think about. And, I'll tell you, Gunter, this map is worth something. You might just think about paying us for it."

"I'd pay," he piped up.

"Did you hear what he said, Melvin? Did you hear that? I think we should listen to Gunter. He'd pay us."

"No," Melvin said.

"How much?" Nelda said.

"Name your price."

Her beady little eyes squinted as she figured. Her mouth pursed into a bow. How much would be a fortune to Nelda? "A hundred thousand dollars," she said.

"Done." Gunter snapped his small fingers.

After a sharp intake of breath, Nelda groaned. It was an almost orgasmic sound, and her huge body shimmied and quaked. "Oooh, Melvin. Do it."

"No," he said.

"This might change your mind." Gunter reached into his back pocket and produced the diary we'd found at Dental's place. Carefully, almost reverently, he placed it on the counter. "It's an eye-witness account of the alien landing. I guess it actually belongs to you, Melvin, because we found it out at your father's place."

"Looks old," Nelda said, "Is it worth anything?"

"An authentic account from the 1860's," Gunter said. "Yes, I believe it is worth something."

"How much?"

"I have no idea. I can't imagine selling an artifact such as this."

Melvin went to the counter and stared down at the little book that Gunter had carefully wrapped and sealed in a baggy. "Can I look at it?"

Gunter did the unwrapping. "Be very careful. The pages are very brittle."

Using two frankfurter-sized fingers, Melvin lifted back the top cover and read. "This is my diary. Amelia Humpenhoff." He turned to Nelda. "Humpenhoff?"

"What a strange coincidence!" Her entire manner changed. In an instant, she went from loud, brassy, demanding, big Nelda to something smaller, more shy and more vulnerable. At the same time, she took a couple of steps away from Melvin and looked away from him. Quietly, she said, "My maiden name is Humpenhoff."

"Astonishing!" Gunter said. "And you're also from Colorado. Just like the Humpenhoffs who lived here in Morning in the 1860's. Is it possible that you're related to the renowned trapper, Henry Humpenhoff?"

"Gosh, I don't know."

Nelda was uncharacteristically reticent as we all stood watching her. She'd never struck me as a woman who could keep a secret, but I must have been wrong.

"Henry Humpenhoff?" Melvin said. "Who's he?"

Gunter was shocked. "You don't know? Humpenhoff was a famous historical figure. A friend of Kit Carson. Of course, I believe his family moved away from Morning in the late 1800's."

"After the alien had been buried," Melvin said.

"Oh, yes," Gunter concurred. "Much later than that."

Melvin looked at his wife. He was obviously confused by this. "And you're one of those Humpenhoffs?"

If she was, if she had concealed her initial relationship to a local trapper from Melvin, her entire adult life had been based on deception.

"I don't know," she said.

"Bullshit," Melvin said. "You know who you are."

Consulting a phone book was unnecessary. We all knew there weren't that many Humpenhoffs.

"Why didn't you tell me?" Melvin asked.

"I thought you'd get the wrong idea."

"I know what you mean." His voice was low and steady. "If I was a suspicious man, I'd get the idea that you came to Morning and deliberately seduced me. Then, when I was newly out of the service in Denver, you married me. You bore my children and stayed with me for twenty-four years, all for . . . what? To get your mitts on the alien?"

Nelda looked away from him. Her silence was an eloquent admission of guilt.

"Why would you do that? What did you want from me, Nelda?"

Very quietly, she said, "The map. My family knew the alien was valuable, and maybe when I first came down here and met you, I was thinking I wanted to get that map. But then, I fell in love with you, Melvin. I really did."

Alison had moved close beside me and slipped her hand into my own. Her nearness made me wonder how I'd feel if I were Melvin and I found out that my wife, the woman I'd loved, the woman who had borne my children, had married me for nefarious reasons. It was a hard stretch of the imagination for me to think of being in love with Nelda. Though she had one of the most spectacular sets of breasts I had ever seen, similar in size and scope to the Grand Tetons, there was a meanness to her face. And, if I'd been Melvin, I would have covered Nelda's mouth with duct tape twenty-three years ago.

He looked down at her. "Is that all I mean to you? A map?"

"No." She was quiet.

"Tell you what, Nelda, I'm done with this. I'm not going to have that stupid map mess up any more of my life. I'm giving it to you." He marched across the Feed and Seed to the display of yellowed paperback books. In the back of *Treasure Island,* he took out a folded sheet of old paper, wrapped in plastic. "Here it is. I hid it in the books on account of I figured my daddy would never look there unless it was a *Playboy.*"

Melvin held the ragged-edged piece of old parchment out toward his wife.

It was a tense moment in the Morning Feed and Seed. Cliff-hanger thoughts, like at the end of a soap opera, flitted across my mind. Would Nelda take the map? Would she throw away the trust and love of her marriage for a scrap of paper? Would Gunter pay her six figures for the thing? Would she finally have enough money to pay off the mortgage to the Feed and Seed?

Nelda snatched the map and held it to her giant breasts. She glared at Gunter. "The price just went up."

At this most appropriate of moments, Margot—the queen of greed and miserable relationships—stomped through the door, followed by her entourage of Whiney and Monte who had gone back to the hacienda to change and was now, for some inexplicable reason, wearing a kilt.

Predictably, Margot was pissed off at me. "Adam, this is all your fault."

Rather than sit through the entire litany of my shortcomings, starting at kindergarten, I cut to the end. "You're right, Margot. I did it. All of it."

"That's right! You did it!" She pointed at my chest with the scarlet painted forefinger of her right hand. In her left hand, she held the map that I'd stolen from Robinson Crusoe. "Why did you give me this stupid piece of paper?"

"I thought you might want to negotiate with Rob."

"I tried. But he won't meet my demands."

I was curious to know what her demands might be, other than the obvious one that she wanted him out of his sheet. But I didn't have a chance to ask because Nelda had lumbered up to Margot.

"That piece of paper," Nelda informed her. "Is worth a hundred thousand dollars to Gunter."

Margot gazed at the short Viking with a lecherous gleam in her eye. She had never actually met Dr. Gunter Bjornsen because he'd been in Santa Fe during her entire time in Morning. Now, she intended to make up for that oversight. She slithered toward him, more deadly than a rattler, and held out her right hand. "You must be Gunter. Charmed, I'm sure."

Much to his credit, Gunter was not captivated by her charms. As he shook her right hand, he made a little jump toward her left, trying to grab the map.

Margot held it over her head, out of his reach. "Did I hear the number one hundred thousand?"

"Dammit, woman, I'll pay you anything. I want that map."

"Anything?" Margot questioned. "My, that has a nice ring to it."

"Margot, the map doesn't really belong to you," I pointed out. "Besides, I made copies of it. Remember? Gunter can have my copy for free." I pulled the folded simile of the map out of my hip pocket and displayed it.

Gunter was not impressed. "I need the original, Adam. There may be fine line creases that the copier wouldn't reveal."

"Possession is ninety-nine percent of ownership," Margot said.

My sister had very clear ideas on what was hers and what belonged to everyone else. Her theory was, as far as I could figure: What's mine is mine, and what's yours is mine, too.

"I'm wondering," she said, "what this map leads to. What's so valuable at the other end?"

"That's right," Nelda said, "we might be giving up a fortune when he finds the alien."

We all turned when the front door opened again and Consuela darted through. She slammed it hard and began fastening the locks. "I am so sorry, everyone. I must beg the pardon of all."

We could hear other people hammering at the locked door. Loud voices called out.

When Consuela turned toward us, she was a tragic-looking little figure. Her eyes were red and puffy from crying. In her hand, she held a tabloid newspaper. She showed us the headline: Accused Artist Seeks Alien.

"Oh, my God," Monte exclaimed as he took the paper from her. "It's you again, Adam."

Consuela flung herself into my arms. "I am so sorry, Adam. I wrote this article and FAXed it to the people who were waiting. I wanted to be a journalista, but—"

"Nobody cares," Margot said. "Now, let's get back to me. Instead of selling my piece of the map, I'd like a sixty-percent share of whatever we find."

"Me, too," said Nelda.

The hammering on the door grew louder. Several faces appeared in the windows. Cameras flashed.

"Who's out there?" I asked Consuela. "Other journalistas?"

"_Sí._ They have read my words and they have come."

"The media?" Margot asked. "What a perfect time to publicize _Margot, the Mini-Series._ Let them in, Whiney."

We needed a voice of sanity here. Though Gunter wouldn't have been my first choice, he was louder than the rest of us. "Here's what we're going to do. We'll put together the map. We'll divvy up the profits. I guarantee to pay for it. We can't let this opportunity pass by. We must find the alien."

With that, he slapped his third of the map on the countertop. The straight line with the "X" at the end.

Margot went next. Her piece of the map actually looked like a map with topographical features and details. She slipped it into place, fitting the ragged edges against Gunter's.

Nelda thundered toward them. She murmured something under her breath that sounded like, "I'm sorry, Melvin."

Her piece of the map contained a single symbol, representing a compass with the north arrow pointing at a slightly skewed angle.

Using clear tape, Gunter patched the pieces together.

There was silence inside the Feed and Seed as we all stared. And, interestingly, there was also silence from outside.

I was pretty sure that the tabloid journalists had not gone home. As a rule, they were a tenacious bunch.

A loud rapping shook the door in its frame. An authoritative voice boomed out: "It's me, Rob Crusoe. Let me in, Margot."

"He's obsessed with me," she said, rolling her eyes. "Just like Yanni. Honestly, when will these men understand that there's enough to go around."

I went to the door and opened it.

Obligingly, Rob stepped aside, giving me a view of the flat desert landscape outside the Feed and Seed Store. Huddled on the porch, clutching cameras, tape recorders and microphones were more tabloid journalists than had ever showed up for an Elvis sighting. They were quiet and cowering.

Arrayed in a single row in front of the store were the No-Names in their all-terrain vehicles. I was reminded of those scenes in old Western movies when the Indians lined up across a hilltop, preliminary to a bloodthirsty charge. Every No-Name had a firearm of some sort. Every firearm was aimed at me.

Quietly, Rob said, "If there's any goddamned sacred treasure to be unearthed, we're in on it."

Chapter Fourteen

athered among the interested alien seekers, inside the Feed and Seed, I asked the obvious question. "Okay, we have the map. All three pieces. Should we follow it?"

The vote was a unanimous "yes" because Melvin had left the room.

"Next question," I announced. "How?"

"We need to drive," Gunter said. Using a pocket calculator and a protractor, he was busily doing calculations.

"So," I continued, "we need to get past the media vultures and Rob's troops. Which means—"

"Shut up, Adam," Margot said. She turned to Rob. "Call them off."

"I'll give the orders here, Margot."

It would take more than a sheet-wearing general of an armed camp of weirdos to intimidate my sister. She got right up in his face, close enough to sink her fangs into his throat. "Then, do it. I need to find my alien and get to Hollywood as soon as possible."

He made a military pivot and marched to the door. I followed.

Some of the No-Names wore their sheets like ponchos, others had wrapped the sheets like saris, still others were bare-chested and had the sheet wrapped around their heads like designer color coordinated Arabs. Each of them stood at attention beside his or her vehicle. All of their weapons were trained on the Feed and Seed Store.

Rob waved his arm above his head and yelled, "At ease."

I wondered how a guy who had once been a druggie rock star got the authority to act like a military man, but I didn't say anything. First rule of survival among survivalists: Don't piss off the guys with the guns.

When the tabloid reporters on the porch came to life, Rob yelled another order. "Company A, advance."

A group of young men, eight of them including the three kids who had been in the jail cell, came forward and formed a line in front of the Feed and Seed.

A perky blond woman, who I thought I recognized from one of those weird television news-that's-not-real-news shows, bounced up beside Rob. "Excuse me, sir. But I think I recognize you. Could you tell me your name?"

"Names are unimportant," he said, disdainfully.

"How about this troop? Who are they?" She was shivering with excitement, having stumbled upon something that a lunatic might call a scoop. "Are they some kind of militia?"

"We have No Name. Only a symbol." He traced the loopy figure "8" in the air.

The reporter looked at me. "Huh?"

I endeavored to explain. "Like the Artist Formerly Known As Prince."

"Prince?"

Others behind her echoed the word.

And she gushed, "Oh, my God, does this have something to do with Princess Di?"

"Be silent!" Rob thundered.

He strode forth to address Company A. His hands clasped behind his back. If it hadn't been for the sheet and the long hair, he might have been General Patton, pacing back and forth while he issued commands.

"Listen to me, boys, you are about to be tested. Pass this test and you take your first big step toward full-fledged manhood. If you fail, you might as well sign up to sing soprano at the Santa Fe opera because you'll always be girls."

"We can do it," one of the teenaged boys announced.

"Yo, dude. We be men."

In a loud voice, probably the heritage of his former career as a minor rock star, Rob gave the order. "Ready your weapons."

The boys raised their rifles to their shoulders.

"If anyone steps off this porch before I say they can step off this porch, shoot them."

The reporters on the porch began to protest. However, I noticed, not one of them stepped off the porch.

Rob turned to them. "Lack of discipline will not be tolerated. If you must speak, do so quietly."

"Hey, fuck you, man." It was a red-faced cameraman with a skinny neck. "Who the fuck do you think you are?"

Calmly, Rob strolled toward him.

I knew I was going to get a first-hand glimpse of the sort of discipline that Rob dished out to his followers, and I had to admit that I was curious. Somehow, Rob Crusoe had woven a spell over all these people. For some reason, they were willing to obey without question—whether it was a rousing game of nude volleyball or gunning down innocent civilians. I suspected that charisma had something to do with it, but that was a quality I never understood.

Rob motioned for the skinny neck to come toward him.

"No way, fucker. I step off this porch and your goons will blow me away."

Rob waved to Company A. Given the age of the boys, I assumed that the "A" stood for Acne.

"Hold your fire," Rob instructed. He faced the cameraman. "Come."

Rob rested each of his hands on the man's shoulders, near the base of his neck. His grip must have been tight, because the guy winced. Then Rob murmured to him in a low voice. I couldn't hear what he was saying, but his eyes were ferocious. When Robinson Crusoe wanted to, he could be a real scary dude. A fanatic, I thought, and fanatics are dangerous. If he'd gotten it into his head to kill Gunter or to have Gunter killed so that he could have first crack at the alien, it wouldn't surprise me.

Rob forced the cameraman down to his knees, then lifted him up. "Return to the porch."

"Yes, sir."

Rob signaled to Company Acne, and they raised their rifles again.

I walked into the Feed and Seed beside him. "What did you say to that guy?"

"The usual." He shrugged.

Inside the Feed and Seed, we needed to work out the protocol of who was to ride with whom. Logistics were complicated. The D-Day Invasion of Normandy had nothing on the Morning Search for Inter-Planetary Visitors.

Gunter, of course, would be in the lead vehicle because he had the map and the intelligence to read it. And I was determined to stick with Gunter. Though the little professor might feel as invincible as Eric the Red, he was still in danger. There was, after all, a murderer amongst us.

"All right," Rob said. His charm and patience were wearing thin. Even his shiny, manageable hair seemed tangled. "My Jeep

is the lead vehicle. Me and Gunter and Adam are riding together."

"Like hell."

I recognized the voice of my sister and stepped aside. "I'm
riding in the front car," Margot announced. "More than that, I'm
driving."

Rob squared off with her, and I figured it was an almost equal
battle. His ego was practically as large as hers. "Be reasonable,
Margot. If I let you come, I should also make room for Nelda."

"A semi-truck isn't enough room for Nelda," she responded
coolly. "Besides, I'm sure Nelda recognizes this opportunity for
profit. Don't you, dear?"

"There's that whole digging operation," Nelda said. "I think
we're going to be needing shovels and axes and buckets and
blah-blah. Plus the food and blah-blah. Concession stand. Cappuccino and blah—"

"You see," Margot said. "Nelda will be fully occupied. And I
will be riding with you. Driving, that is."

Rob turned to me. "What's your vote? Does Margot drive?"

"Short of a silver bullet between the eyes, I don't see how we
can stop her."

Before we left the Feed and Seed through the rear door, I
spoke to Alison. "I'm sorry about all this."

"You're staying with Gunter so you can protect him, aren't
you?"

"You got it."

"Don't get hurt, Adam." She kissed me lightly on the cheek.
"I have to make a couple of phone calls to Taos. I'll see you at
the dig."

"How will you find us?"

She gestured toward the mob. "Do you really think that will
be a problem?"

Margot slipped behind the wheel of Rob's Jeep and outlined
her plan to Rob who was sitting in the passenger seat, a position

I called the "death chair" when riding with Margot. "Once we've zeroed in on the location," she said, "we'll have to send someone back to get the reporters. This is a natural opportunity to publicize *Margot: The Mini-Series.*"

"I'll decide. This could be a sacred moment for my people."

"Digging up an alien named Lawnchair Yada-Yada? Oh, please!" She circled to the front of the Feed and Seed, slammed the Jeep in park and stood up in the driver's seat. In clarion tones, she announced to the assembled horde. "Synchronize your Rolexes! You may follow us in exactly fifteen minutes."

Rob sat fuming.

She turned to him and smiled. "We'll need people to dig, right? And what else are these mindless geeks good for?"

"These are my people," he said.

"Do you want to find the damned alien or not? We need labor, and I'm not about to chip my fingernails. Are you?"

Apparently, he agreed with her because he rose to his feet. His sheet flapped heroically in the dusty wind. "Fifteen minutes, people. Then you may follow in formation."

Then we were underway, rocketing along the road behind the Feed and Seed.

Gunter, who was in back beside me, said, "Turn right at your next opportunity, Margot."

"That's the road to Mesa Rana," I said. You mean everyone has been digging in the right place all along?"

Gunter stroked the whiskers on his chin as he studied the assembled map. "Not exactly. You see, Rob's portion of the map pretty much indicated Mesa Rana."

Rob leaned into the back seat. "I was right! Hah!"

"But my piece gives the distance," Gunter said.

Ironic, I thought. "So, Melvin's part of the map is irrelevant?"

"Not at all. It is, in fact, vital to finding the location. Melvin's portion of the map has the north arrow. My calculations of the scale and orientation were essentially correct but the north arrow points five degrees further east than the actual magnetic declination would indicate. Probably the result of a faulty compass or an uninformed cartographer."

I knew enough about navigation to understand the consequences of a five-degree compass error. Over a long distance, like the Pacific Ocean, you could miss the Hawaiian Islands by hundreds of miles. But a large-scale map of a relatively small area such as the puzzle-pieced document we now possessed, would probably not throw us off by more than a couple of hundred feet.

"Go toward the hacienda," Gunter instructed.

With wild, off-the-road abandon, Margot obeyed.

After a couple of seismic jolts over potholes, I looked back at the map. "So when you factor the five-degree error and orient the map to magnet north, where does that put us?"

"On the opposite side of the Margot's lands, approximately one hundred and seventy-eight yards from the main house, not far from Whiney's trailer. This is very good because there are only a few places on that side of the mesa where the bedrock is covered with soil deep enough to actually bury something, or someone. We should have very little difficulty in pinpointing the precise location."

To me, the map wasn't much more than a couple of intersecting lines and a few squiggles, but Gunter was highly enthused. Though I'd have to admit the prospect of proving the existence of extra-terrestrial life forms sparked a surge of excitement, the correctness of his assumptions didn't really matter that much. I had a different focus. My primary concern was that all alien hunters in Rio Arriba county gather in one location so I could keep an eye on them. The murderer would surely be among the searchers. Sooner or later he'd make a mistake and tip his hand. That would be enough for me. I could be assured of Gunter's continued safety, I would have avenged the death of Dental Stoker and Gomez-Gomez, and I would have cleared myself of any wrongdoing so I could get back to Taos and try to salvage the remains of my career.

Margot pulled up in front of the house. "Now where?"

"We can walk from here," Gunter said. "It's over by Whiney's trailer."

"Why walk?"

She charged the rutted landscape as if she were driving a tank instead of a Jeep.

"Stop!" Gunter yelled.

With a spray of sandy soil, Margot complied.

The four of us got out of the Jeep without mishap, but the second car—the Cadillac containing Whiney, Monte and Consuela—was not so fortunate. The big car high-centered on a clump of sand and mesquite.

The first one out was Whiney. He scampered toward us. "What are you doing? This is my trailer. You can't lead all these people out here, they'll make a total mess of everything."

Margot folded her arms beneath her breasts and glared at him. "Listen here, Whines For No Reason, this happens to be my land."

"Oh yeah? That's what they always say." He stomped his foot, still wearing my loafer, and winced as he felt the hard earth. "If you want to get technical about it, this is all my land. All of it belongs to my people because we were here first. But, noooo! Nobody wants to give the poor old Indians their due. I have a good mind to call a tribal council or something."

"Feel free," Margot said. "Nelda can sell tickets."

"I took care of your house," he whined. "And this is how you repay me?"

Whiney was practicing guilt on the wrong person. Margot never thought she was wrong, so she never had regrets like other humans. I had always had strong doubts about her inclusion in the species homo sapiens, but I kept them to myself.

Instead, I offered a word of advice to Whiney. "In less than fifteen minutes, all the No-Names and all the reporters and Nelda and her concession stand are going to be set up around here. If I were you, I'd rescue any valuables from my trailer before they get here."

"I never have any luck." He shuffled up to the trailer, kicking at dirt clods in a highly disgruntled manner. "Nobody ever listens to me. Nobody ever pays any attention."

Gunter and Rob were busily pacing off distances and judging the angle of the sun. They first went north, then south, then back north again.

My attention was divided between their calculations and watching the arrival of the No-Names in a rumbling caravan. Nelda was in the front, having loaded her rickety truck with digging implements, and the mob followed, dragging a curtain of swirling dust behind them.

Monte and Consuela stood beside me. The pretty little señorita was whimpering softly. "I wish Shirley could be here to see this," she said.

"She would have arrested all of us," I said.

"It would have made her so happy."

Weeping, she buried her face against Monte's chest, and he did a fairly manly job of comforting her, despite the fact that he was wearing a kilt.

I looked down at his bared knees and raised my eyebrows.

"It was all I had left," he said. "Think of it as Rob Roy conquers the Old West."

"Sounds like a perfect segment for _Margot: The Mini-Series._"

Astoundingly, the No-Names seemed to operate with some semblance of order. They purchased their digging tools from Nelda at outrageously inflated prices and began to work in the general area indicated by Gunter and Rob.

Gunter would not allow anyone to touch the shovel to dirt without hearing him explain archeological procedures. After all this searching, it would be terrible to destroy the little alien with clumsy digging. If anything, they were overly cautious, carefully handling every rock and bringing it to Gunter before tossing it away. Several of them took to filling their sheets with dirt and sifting it before dumping. And so, the search proceeded with agonizingly slow thoroughness.

Behind their ranks, the tabloid reporters set up a camp under the stalwart direction of Monte and Consuela, the two publicity mongers, who gave interview after interview. Though Monte kept trying to drag me in, waving and calling, "Yoo-hoo, Adam," I managed to ignore him.

My plans did not include kissing up to tabloid jerks. I was there to find a murderer. Observation. Sooner or later, the killer would slip, and I would be there to catch him.

A high point during the hot afternoon was when Whiney emerged from his trailer, dressed in a loincloth and high-top moccasins. His face was painted blue. On his chest, he had drawn a moon, a sun and three stars encircling his bellybutton.

Without saying a word, he walked through the reporters and found an open place for himself near the house. He planted a spear in the earth, and drew a long circle. Raising both hands to the sun, he announced, "Let no one step within the sacred circle."

He was actually fairly impressive. Whines-For-No-Reason had the ability to exude dignity when he wanted to. I wondered if I'd ever see my loafers again.

A reporter with a camera crew approached him. "Want to tell me what you're doing here? I understand your name is Whiney."

"No," he said firmly. "For much of my life, I have used that part of my name. Now, you and everyone else must call me Reason."

His name was Reason, but his brain was mulch. I was pretty sure that he was making up his ritual as he went along, but what the hell. Whiney wanted attention, and this was his big chance to get it. Besides, the diggers were gradually coming closer to his trailer and he deserved the chance to protest.

Three camera crews, having tired of videotaping people in sheets digging holes, were now focused upon him. And he started a perky two-step in a circle around his spear. He was chanting steadily, "Ha-da yada yada yada. Ha-da yada yada yada."

"Excuse me, Mr. Reason," one of the reporters interrupted. "Can you tell us what this ritual represents?"

"It's a curse. Yada yada."

"I adore curses," she said. "What kind of curse?"

"May the warts of Mesa Rana descend upon you and cover your feet."

Very colorful, I thought.

"May the spirit of Tonna-Hokay-Pokay-Lawnchair-Yada-Yada piss fire upon your upturned faces."

The print reporters were furiously recording his every syllable.

"May three out of four doctors recommend liposuction."

With the crowd shouting for more, he went into his yada yada dance again.

I watched as another car joined the mob. It was a Fiat, the driving choice of Frenchmen. I had a bad feeling about who was about to arrive, and I was not disappointed. Though Alison popped out of the passenger seat and I was delighted to see her, the driver of the car was none other than Jacques LaFraque. He was accompanied by Dustin from Boston.

When Alison approached, with her two creepy escorts, I noticed that Dustin was walking with a slight limp. Possessively, I snatched Alison to my side.

"How's it going?" she asked.

"Far as I can tell, they haven't found a damned thing."

She explained, "When I called the Sundog, Jacques was there. As was Dustin."

"Peachy," I said.

"He was at the gallery, returning your sculpture," she said.

Obviously, this was proof that Dustin deserved to be the top priority suspect. I really wanted it to be him. The only thing that could have made me happier was if it had been Jacques. But the Frenchman wasn't even a suspect. I knew he could produce alibis 'til the snails came home, most of them from my own fair Alison.

"Bonjour," said Jacques. He hid his disdain for me behind a pair of wrap-around designer sunglasses.

"Yo," I replied. I saw no need to upgrade my image for this guy. As far as he was concerned, I was nothing more than a wine-guzzling Philistine.

I turned to Dustin. "What'd you do to your leg?"

"Oh, the limp? It's nothing really. I stepped off a curb the wrong way and twisted my ankle."

"I'm surprised to see you here. I thought you gave up and went home to Boston.

"Wish I could," he muttered. "Freya is coming to Santa Fe for something to do with the opera. So, she insisted I stay here and work on getting Gunter's approval."

I pointed to Gunter who sat on a lawnchair beneath a striped umbrella overseeing the dig. "There he is. Go for it."

"It's no use," he said. "The old man has hated me from the minute he saw me. I should just wait for Freya to talk sense into him."

"Are you rich, Dusty?"

"That's none of your business." He glanced over at Jacques. "Can you believe he asked me that? Some people have no class."

"And some people have lots of motive," I said. Dustin from Boston had Freya's inheritance to gain if Gunter were deceased. I also thought that the attempts on Gunter were typical of a guy who didn't like to get his hands dirty. A sneak attack at night that had killed Dental Stoker. Dropping the rattlesnakes into the kiva. The booby trap that had snuffed out Shirley Gomez-Gomez.

Dustin sighed heavily, burdened with the weight of a rich white man's woes. "What do you mean? What was my motive for killing that old prospector?"

"You thought he was Gunter."

The prepster snickered and exchanged glances with Jacques who laughed more loudly and said, "Eet ees so sad, Adam. You are, how you say, peesed off becauz Monsieur Dustin has returned your statues, eh?"

"Go suck an escargot, Jacques."

"Why ees thees? I like your work. You, I don' like, but the work? Eet ees manifique!"

Susceptible though I am to flattery, I paid him no mind. I really wanted Dustin to make a mistake, to say something I could hang my suspicions on. The worst part of this was that I knew I had heard or seen something that would implicate him. But I couldn't remember. The alien hysteria had complicated my usually pristine reasoning.

I asked Dustin, "What do you know about explosives? Were bombings covered at law school?"

"Pardon?" he said with that snotty upper-crust accent.

"What about reptiles? Ever taken biology?"

"Never have. I've never been big on the core curriculum."

Apparently, something exciting was going on over by the dig, because there was a flutter of excitement.

Gunter stood on a chair and addressed the crowd. "My calculations were slightly skewed. According to my best figures, the burial site is there." He pointed his stubby forefinger at Whiney's trailer. "Under the foundation."

Still standing inside his circle, Whiney yelled at the top of his lungs, "May your underpants be filled with sand. If you touch that trailer, may you all be cursed with the pain and itching of hemorrhoidal tissue."

They didn't care.

Under Rob's direction, the No-Names surrounded the trailer. On the count of three, they shoved, and the poor, sad, rusted home of Whines-for-No-Reason toppled with an echoing crash.

The newly exposed plot of earth immediately revealed a chunk of metal. For a moment, it seemed to glow, then went dark.

Chapter
Fifteen

"Eureka! We've found it!" Nelda Humpenhoff Stoker charged through the crowd, scattering No-Names and reporters with each sweep of her mighty arms. "I knew it. I knew it was blah-blah-blah."

She was about to hurl her giant body onto the exposed glitter of metal when several of the No-Names caught hold of her brawny arms and held her.

"Let go of me, you idiots. Don't you understand? I've heard about the star traveler since I was a little girl. It was a Humpenhoff family legend. And it exists."

Margot stalked past her. With a disdainful sniff, she said, "Get a grip, Nelda."

Shoving and snarling, Margot positioned herself in front of the small protruding metal corner that seemed to catch the rays of the sun. Rob stood at her side.

Alison took my arm. "They're a handsome couple, don't you think?"

"Sure. When they stand close together like that you can actually see the ego radiating from their bodies."

Still, I had to admit that Rob and Margot were a dramatic twosome, sort of a New Age tribute to self-indulgence. During the dig, Rob had discarded his sheet, displaying his well-muscled, tanned, hairless chest above tight Levi's and the holster on his hip. He raised his arms above his head. "Listen to me, all of you."

Unfortunately, the long afternoon of digging had worn down the standards of No-Name discipline. Two of the teenaged boys, caught up in the thrill of wanton destruction of personal property, performed a victory dance atop Whiney's overturned trailer. Several of the older, more Republican-looking cult gentlemen sprawled in the dirt. They gasped and wheezed, overcome by the atmosphere of rampant greed and notoriety that had so stimulated this crowd.

"Attention," Rob shouted. "Give me your attention."

The reporters and photographers, who had thus far been held at bay, pressed forward, asking obtuse questions and demanding answers from equally obtuse people.

The scene was pretty much chaos, and I kept a careful eye on Gunter who seemed content to sit back and observe, away from the center of hysteria. He had a look of melancholy, perhaps feeling the letdown of an eight-year quest come to an end.

"Please," Rob yelled.

"For Chrissake," Margot said. She whipped the gun from his holster and held it over her head. She fired twice and the explosion of the six-gun brought the noise to a sudden end. Margot lowered the pistol, aiming randomly. "Listen up, people. In case you didn't know, this is my property and you're all trespassing."

"So what?" demanded a reporter.

"So, I shoot trespassers. All of you, back off." She raised the handgun above her head and let go with another shot. "I mean, now."

"You heard the lady." Rob stepped up beside her, his sun-streaked blond hair contrasted with her coal black hair. Her

Wonderbra cleavage matched his. "Move away from the alien."
"Or I'll shoot," Margot said.

The crowd stilled. Obviously, it was the time for a speech, and the leader of the No-Names rose to the occasion.

"This is a momentous . . . moment," Rob said. "We have done what no person has done before. Finally, there is proof of life beyond our own. We have discovered the secrets of the galaxies, of the distant spheres. We have—"

"Can it, Robby," Margot said. "Let's get that valuable little sucker out of the ground and into my house."

He looked affronted, then glanced into Margot's hard brown eyes. Rob Crusoe grinned, "You got it, babe."

Pointing to three of the stronger-looking No-Names, he supervised the last of the dig. The earth beneath Whiney's trailer was darker than the surrounding landscape, and it smelled like the men's room in a downtown bus depot, which might have been how Whiney used the land. But the No-Names waded in bravely and carefully scraped the dirt away from the metal part which appeared to be the brass corner fastenings on a wooden trunk of some kind.

"Gunter," Rob called out. "How should we proceed?"

"They're doing fine," he said. "Take it slowly and carefully. This is a delicate process. They must take care not to scar the surface with the shovels."

It looked to me like this excavation was going to take a long time, and I was glad when Alison pulled me away from the nucleus of the digging. She pointed to Nelda who had gone back to her espresso machine. Silently, the big woman hunched over the tailgate of her truck.

Alison approached her. "Nelda? Are you all right?"

She shook her head. When she drew a sigh, her shoulders quaked, and I was afraid she was going to cry. "Come on, Nelda." I encouraged her, "Don't you want to see what they've uncovered?"

"All these years," she said, "I thought I wanted that alien. I thought the space traveler was my ticket to a wealthy and happy life. But I was wrong." She shuddered. "The alien doesn't matter. I realized that when I went crazy a minute ago. Oh my, I did go crazy, didn't I? I thought I was going to be jumping into the blah-blah-blah."

I was beginning to tune her out when she looked directly at me and said, "I was wrong, and Melvin was right. He was right all along."

Nelda pulled herself up very straight. There was dignity in her bearing. "My happiness and all the wealth I ever needed was right here in Morning. With Melvin."

I was touched by her realization. Dental might have called her big and stupid. Margot might have dismissed her as being a fat lady who was not worthy of notice. But Nelda had a true heart and an earthy wisdom that Rob Crusoe and his No-Names might never find. Melvin was a lucky man.

Nelda tromped around to the cab of her truck and climbed in. "I'm going to find my Melvin. I hope he'll understand."

As she peeled away, the espresso machine fell off the back of the truck with a clatter.

From the mob crowding the perimeter of the dig, we heard excited murmurs. We moved closer and stood beside Jacques LaFraque and Dustin from Boston. We were still about three rows away from the front line and couldn't see well.

"What'd they find?" I asked.

"Eet appears to be a steamer trunk," said Jacques.

"They're calling it a coffin," Dustin said. He was huffy and annoyed. "Honestly, this whole thing seems completely over-blown to me. I can't believe you people wasted all this time and effort looking for this thing. Not to mention the money that Papa Gunter has frittered away."

"Especially the money," I said. "Huh, Dustin?"

"Really, McCleet, your suspicions are growing tiresome. I don't know what you're suggesting."

"Don't you?" I was pretty sure that Dustin was my murderer. All I needed was a single piece of tangible evidence, and I'd call in the cops. "I'll spell it out for you, Dusty. Nice and clear. You're after Gunter's money. Maybe you want it bad enough to commit murder."

"How dare you!"

"Zis eez zee grand insult," Jacques said. He nudged Dustin's arm. "You must not stand for zis."

"He's right," I said. "At the very least, Dustin, you ought to slap my face and challenge me to a duel. Pistols at sunrise? Or maybe you'd prefer rattlesnakes?"

"Zee snakes at sunrise?" Jacques whipped off his sunglasses and stared as if he could hear me better with his bare eyes. "I have never heard of zis. An Americain custom, no?"

I was surprised to see an angry purple bruise surrounding the left eye of Jacques LaFraque. "You look like you've been doing some dueling of your own, Jacques. Where'd you get that shiner?"

He glanced toward Alison, then looked away and returned the sunglasses to the bridge of his nose.

She grinned at me and said, "Jacques and I had a slight disagreement about sleeping arrangements."

"Eet was zee oh-so-small mistake."

"Uh-huh," she said. "You were sleepwalking."

"Oui."

"Naked?"

"Oui. I sleep in zee nude."

"With two wineglasses in your hands?"

"Zis eez possible, I theenk."

I took both of her dainty hands in mine. My little Alison had slugged the Frenchman. She'd given him a black eye. I was so proud. "Honey," I said, "would you like me to cripple him for you?"

"Thank you, dear. But that won't be necessary."

"You are cra-zee," Jacques said. "I must leave zis place. I cannot wait to return to France."

"Bye-bye." I waved. "Give my regards to Jerry Lewis."

Dustin glanced from us to Jacques who was heading toward his car. He limped after the Frenchman. "Wait for me."

As Dustin made his hasty and undignified departure, I noticed a large spot of blood on the calf of his Dockers. "Alison? Didn't he tell us that he'd sprained his ankle?"

"Yes."

"Look at the blood on his leg. You know what I think? I think maybe I hit him when he was shooting at the Feed and Seed with the high-powered rifle."

"Great," she said. "Let's tell Honorio Snead and let him arrest Dustin."

"Not enough evidence," I said.

"A bullethole in the leg? How many other ways could he get a bullet in his leg? And the ballistics will show it came from Melvin's gun."

"It's still not enough. All it would prove is that he was hit by a stray bullet, and I don't want Dustin to get off on some kind of technicality."

There was a better clue, something that played at the edges of my consciousness but would not come into focus.

From the digging, there came shouts of excitement. The three husky No-Name excavators lifted a battered wooden steamer trunk above their heads and marched across the landscape toward the hacienda like Nubian slaves carrying the sarcophagus of the Pharaoh.

"We should go see," I said to Alison.

She frowned. "I feel kind of like Nelda. This all seems anti-climactic."

As if on cue, Nelda's truck roared back on the scene. She pulled up next to us. Melvin was not in the car with her.

"Tell Gunter," she said, "to leave the check at the Feed and Seed. In the lockbox by the door."

She drove off, again.

"Lest we forget," I said, "Nelda's nobility is still slightly tinted by the color of greed." I smiled at Alison. "You really slugged Jacques."

"Oui."

Hand-in-hand, we returned to the hacienda. Though I was Margot's brother, she wasn't going to let me in until Gunter insisted.

"All right," she conceded. "But stay out of the way, Adam. It would be just like you to accidentally knock the alien out of his coffin and break him into a thousand worthless pieces."

The curtains were drawn and the steamer trunk rested on the floor in the center of the living room. The three No-Name pallbearers had been dismissed, and the only people in the house were Rob and Margot, Gunter, Consuela and Monte, and Alison and me. A cozy little group, I thought.

I wasn't sure why Consuela had been invited until Margot said, "Be a dear, Consuela, and bring us a bottle of champagne. I think we may be celebrating."

"I don't think so."

"What seems to be the problem, hon?"

"I am not Consuela the Chief Cook and Bottle Maker, anymore. I am Consuela the Journalist."

"I'll tell you what, Ms. Journalist. How about if I give you an exclusive interview on my next feature film. _Margot and the Treasure of Mesa Rana?_"

"Oh, that would be wonderful!"

"Great," Margot said. "I think we should toast on it."

"Yes, I'll get the champagne."

"Good, you do that."

There was a clatter at the front door.

"Ignore it," Margot said, "they'll go away."

But the door flew open and was just as quickly slammed shut. Whiney, newly renamed Reason, marched inside. Still wearing his warpaint and carrying his spear, he looked fairly impressive.

"What are you doing here?" Margot snapped.

"I have a key, my benefactress."

There was a new sarcasm in his voice, an assertiveness. "There has been damage to my home, to the lands of my ancestors. I will have payment."

"Fine," Margot said. "You can have one percent of my share of the alien. Now sit down and shut up."

He lifted his chin. The proud blood of his ancestors surged through him as he thumped his fist against his bare, symbol-painted chest. Then he began to cough.

"Are you all right?" Monte asked.

"I got a chill," Whiney whined. "And I'm tired. I've been out there all day, cursing up a storm, and I'm hoarse. I might have permanent throat damage."

Gunter knelt on the floor in front of the steamer trunk with a hammer and chisel. Lightly, he tapped at the hasp lock.

"That doesn't look very archeological," Rob said.

"No need to worry about damage," Gunter explained. "This container is unremarkable, only a beat-up piece of furniture from the 1800's."

"Antique?" Margot inquired.

"Not important."

"Then, open the damn thing!"

He tapped the lock and the hasp parted.

"I guess this is it," Gunter said. His voice was strangely sad, lacking in the eager anticipation that characterized his search. "This is what I've been searching for."

Slowly, he eased back the lid.

Inside, there were several large round rocks. And a piece of wrinkled parchment. Gunter lifted the paper and read aloud: "I. O. U. one star traveler. Signed, H. Humpenhoff, Buffalo, New York."

After Margot stopped screaming and Rob had finished kicking the side of the steamer trunk, everyone wandered off to various parts of the hacienda to pout. I took Alison into the kitchen where we toasted each other with champagne.

"No alien," she said. "After all this ridiculous chasing and hiding, there was never an alien."

"Maybe there was," I said. "Maybe Hokey-Pokey-Lawnchair is a roadside attraction outside Buffalo at a gas station with a big sign: Stop at Humpenhoff's and see the Star Traveler."

"The Genuine Alien," she said. "Inside, there might be a gift shop with little commemorative ashtrays and Hokey-Pokey salt and pepper shakers."

I held up my champagne glass. Though the murders of Dental Stoker and Shirley Gomez-Gomez might never be solved, I felt momentarily satisfied. "A toast, Alison. May we always find what we're looking for."

"Yada yada," she replied.

I took a sip of champagne. "Listen, Alison, the other night in Taos, I behaved like kind of a jerk."

"Don't worry about it. Your jerkiness is one of your most endearing qualities."

"I appreciate that. But what I'm talking about is that whole Jacques LaFraque jealousy thing. I should have trusted you. I was feeling a little insecure."

"You're right. You should have trusted me. But a little insecurity in a relationship is not an altogether bad thing. We wouldn't want to start taking each other for granted."

I pulled her close and held her in my arms. Her champagne

spilled down my chest. "The only thing I'll take for granted in our relationship is that you'll always be smarter than me."

"And prettier?"

"If you weren't prettier than me, we wouldn't have a relationship."

Our tender moment was interrupted by the sound of loud weeping from the dining room, and we went to investigate. Consuela sat at the table, sobbing her heart out. Monte and Whiney stood on either side of her. Another bottle of Margot's champagne had been opened and Whiney clutched it protectively before taking a long gulp.

"One percent of nothing," he said. "Everything I own was in that trailer."

"You shouldn't drink champagne like that," Monte said. "You'll get bubbles up your nose."

"May I die of bubble poisoning," he said and drained the bottle.

Consuela wailed again. "My scoop," she cried. "My scoop is no more. I will always be frying bacon at the Morning Tavern, Cafe and Jail. I will have no career. I will never be a journalist."

"Why not?" Monte said, consolingly. "As far as I can tell, there's nothing holding you back. This is America, land of opportunity. You can do anything if you want it bad enough. After all, there's nothing to keep you in Morning now that Shirley's dead."

"Poor Shirley!" She sobbed deeply.

I sat beside her and placed my arm around her shoulder. Instinctively, she buried her face against my chest and wept. I really hate when people cry. It makes a knot in my chest, and the soles of my feet start to itch. But I said "there-there" a half dozen times and patted her shaking shoulders until she began to calm down. When she looked up at me, with her tear-stained face, I remembered how attractive she had been when I saw her at sunset, and we had talked . . .

"Consuela," I said.

"Yes, Adam."

"There's something bothering me. When you were telling me about the information Shirley gathered on all of us suspects, do you remember what she had on Dustin?"

"I do. I have a very good memory."

"Tell me."

"He was married twice. The first wife divorced him. The second died."

"Are you sure?" That was the piece I'd been trying to recall. I glanced over at Alison. "In the jail, when I first met Dustin, he told me that he had never been married, that Freya would be his first wife."

"Two times," Consuela said. "His second wife was murdered."

"Was Dustin a suspect?"

"The husband is always a suspect," she said. "But he was acquitted."

This fell under the category of good background information, but it still wasn't hard evidence.

Margot and Rob strode into the room, hand-in-hand. If Rob's dazed expression was any indication, they had been consoling each other in a carnal way.

"Here's the plan," Margot said. "Rob and I are going to go out on the porch and tell all those media creeps that the alien was stolen."

"Honesty," I said. "That's a novel approach for you."

Under his breath, Monte said, "I wouldn't give Margot any merit badges just yet."

"But first," she said, "we're going to hype _Margot: The Last Temptation._"

"Why not?" Rob concurred. "We might as well take advantage of the publicity."

"So," Margot said. "I want you people to sneak out the back so you won't attract any of my attention."

"Okay," I said. "On one condition. You give Consuela an exclusive on reporting the opening of the steamer trunk. And she gets the I.O.U. from Humpenhoff."

"Sure," Margot said. "Why not?"

She and Rob sailed to the front door.

Consuela looked up at me with wide eyes, beautiful, though bloodshot. "Gracias, Adam."

"You can leave Morning, you know."

"I will."

Whiney roused himself from the corner where he'd slumped and extracted his tongue from the neck of the champagne bottle. "Consuela," he said, "I hope you don't go."

I glanced around the living room. "Where's Gunter?"

Consuela answered, "He was very sad. He said it had all been for nothing. A good man had died for nothing. He said he would make it up to Dental Stoker."

"And then?"

"He left." She shrugged.

I took the Cadillac. Leaving Margot's hacienda and the futility of the alien search behind, I aimed for the location where I thought I would find Gunter Bjornsen. Why had he taken off by himself? It seemed to me that the gunfire at the Feed and Seed, the explosion and the snakes had sent a pretty clear message. Somebody, probably Dustin Florence, was trying to kill the old man.

His disappointment over the damned alien and his belated grief for his friend, Dental, must have overcome his ability to behave rationally. Or maybe he just didn't care about survival, anymore. Maybe he had handed over his future to the whim of the Nordic gods.

When I pulled up at Dental Stoker's shack, Gunter was easy

to find. The first time I'd seen the little Viking, he had been creating a funeral pyre from Formica chairs and tables in the Morning Cafe-Tavern and Jail. That pile-up was nothing compared to the structure he had begun to build at the side of the house. The base was mesquite, easily flammable. Piled on top were two rocking chairs. Stacks of _Playboy_ magazines lined the edges.

He trudged from the house again, carrying Dental's wide-screen television.

"Gunter," I said.

"Leave me alone, Adam. I must do this." With a grunt, he heaved the TV onto the pile. "Dental will need these things in Valhalla."

"You go ahead. Build the biggest damned bonfire you want."

"I intend to. And I don't need your help."

"I'm not leaving. I've spent the last two days keeping you alive."

"Oh, yes." He stared directly at me. "Thank you so much for protecting me from the rattlesnakes."

His point was well-taken. I hadn't always been a great body-guard, but I was trying, damn it, and I wasn't going to let all my hard work go for nothing.

"Just leave me, Adam. If it is my fate to die, then die I shall."

From behind one of the outbuildings, I caught a glimpse of sunlight on metal. To be specific, on the metal barrel of a rifle. It was just possible that I was already too late.

When Gunter shuffled back into the house in search of more fuel for the funeral pyre, I crept around to the rear of the shed. I expected to find Dustin Florence at the business end of the rifle. Though the preppie might be armed and I wasn't, Dustin didn't frighten me too much. As murderers go, he was the sloppiest I'd ever encountered. I could probably take him blindfolded with both hands tied behind my back.

But when I rounded the corner of the shack, I saw Melvin

Stoker. He sat with his back against the shed. His gun was cradled loosely in his arms.

I was shocked. Melvin was the person after Gunter? I'd been certain that Dustin was the murderer. I was amazed at the wrongness of my assumptions.

"Adam," he said.

"Melvin. What's going on, man?"

"You were right about somebody trying to kill Gunter," he said coldly.

He was confessing, but I took small satisfaction in this revelation. It meant Melvin was going to kill Gunter, then probably me. I didn't think I could take Melvin. He was twelve times tougher than Dustin, and he was an armed ex-Marine to boot. If there's one thing they teach in the Marines, it's how to shoot.

"Why, Melvin?"

His forehead furrowed as he looked at me. "Somebody's got to look out for the little guy."

"You mean the alien? There is no alien."

"I mean Gunter," Melvin said. "I figure whoever is trying to kill Gunter is the same person who killed my dad. And I'm going to get 'em, Adam."

I was nodding, but my brain hadn't quite caught up yet. "So, you weren't . . . You didn't . . ."

"What? You thought I was the killer? Hell, Adam, if I want somebody dead, I'm not going to set booby traps and drop snakes and sneak up on them in the night."

"I knew that."

We heard another car pull up, and both of us came out from behind the shed in time to see Dustin Florence approaching the funeral pyre. When he saw us, I could have sworn that he looked disappointed. But he said, "Hello, gentlemen. Is my future father-in-law here?"

Gunter bustled out of the house, carrying a red velvet ottoman that Dental must have purchased from the yard sale of a brothel. He barely looked at Dustin. "It's your business, young man, if you and my daughter want to marry, you need neither my respect nor my consent. Freya is fully capable of making her own decisions."

"All right, sir." He turned to walk away. "But I'm not giving up. I'll be back."

"Dustin," I said, "a question?"

"What now?"

"How many times have you been married?"

He looked chagrinned. "You've found me out, haven't you? Though I have not mentioned my prior weddings to Freya for fear of upsetting her delicate temperament, I have been twice wed."

"And your leg," I said, desperate for something, anything, resembling evidence. "How'd you hurt your leg?"

His expression was boyishly innocent. "I feel rather like a fool in saying this. But I was experimenting with a new gun I'd purchased and the damn thing went off. Shot myself in the calf. It's nothing serious, only a flesh wound."

"Yeah," I said. "Well, what about—"

"Honestly, you people are so—"

"Hold it! I remember another of your condescending 'you people' speeches. We were at Gunter's teepee the day before it got blown up, and you said that we people talk to animals."

Dustin said, "I do tend to generalize that way, but—"

"The only animal I've talked to lately was Dental Stoker's burro, Laddie. And the only way you could have heard that conversation was if you were standing behind me with a club in your hand."

"This is absurd."

"You only made two mistakes, Dustin. In the dark, you killed Dental instead of Gunter. You couldn't tell one dusty old codger from another. No offense, Gunter."

"None taken. What was his second mistake?" Gunter eyed me warily.

I poked Dustin's chest with the tip of my index finger. "You pissed me off."

"Why would I want to kill my future father-in-law?"

"Gunter, doesn't Freya live on a trust fund?"

"A generous allowance," he said. "But when I die, she'll inherit my entire estate. An amount in the millions."

"You just couldn't wait, could you, Dustin? Who were you going to kill next? Freya?"

"This is all conjecture," Dustin said, sounding like almost a lawyer. "Circumstantial and worthless."

From the road, we heard the purr of a perfectly tuned car engine. A white Jaguar appeared like a mirage and cruised to a stop at the front of the humble desert shack.

When Dustin turned and looked, his tennis tan faded to stark white. His confidence faltered. "Freya," he said.

The woman who disembarked from the Jag was incredible. She must have been six feet, three inches tall. Though her shoulders were broad and her hips were full and curvaceous, there didn't appear to be an ounce of fat on her statuesque frame. White-gold hair flowed straight and shining to her narrow waist. This was Freya?

She was dressed in a sleeveless white sheath, and it suited her because I could tell at a glance that Freya Bjornsen was an ice maiden. There was no warmth in her blue eyes, almost a total lack of expression as she went to her father, bent his head toward her and kissed him on the crown. "I have missed you, Gunter."

"My lovely Freya. You look well."

"And in fine voice," she said. "I'll be singing a small role at the Santa Fe opera."

"I am proud of you, Daughter."

Weakly, Dustin said, "Me, too. Great to see you, darling."

Her blue eyes shot ice cubes when she confronted him. "Dustin, my dear, I am concerned."

He seemed to be breaking out in a cold sweat. "Why is that, honeypot?"

"I had a call from my credit card company about some unusual charges, Dustin. Three thousand dollars for a sculpture."

He took her arm, "I returned it, Freya."

She shook free of him. "I'm not finished, Dustin. There were also charges for four rattlesnakes, a half pound of TNT and an SKS assault rifle."

There it was, all the proof I ever needed. Right there on the credit card bill. It was enough hard evidence for a solid murder conviction in any jurisdiction in the land, with the possible exception of Los Angeles county.

Dustin realized the same thing. He made a grab for Melvin's gun, but missed, and the big guy used Dustin's forward motion to propel him. Dustin stumbled and teetered on the edge of the kiva where, I assumed, two of his purchases were still coiled in the shadows.

I made a lunging grab for the front of his shirt, but missed.

With a loud yelp, Dustin toppled backwards. He didn't handle the situation well at all. His screams of fear echoed in the desert like the howls of a lone coyote.

We gathered at the edge of the kiva pit and looked down.

"You'd better get out of there," Gunter said. "Those snakebites can be quite nasty."

"Help me, please," he shrieked. "My arm is broken and I've been bitten."

"Gunter's right," I said. "You'd better use the ladder. I don't think any of us plan to come down there after you."

In spite of his broken arm, he struggled to his feet and scrambled up the ladder with remarkable agility. He emerged from the hole and flopped onto his back, gasping. The fang punctures on his cheek, just below his right eye, looked particularly painful.

Melvin pressed the barrel of his rifle against Dustin's forehead and tensed his trigger finger. "You're going to die, you little fuck."

"Melvin, don't do it," I said. "It's murder."

"He killed my dad. The spineless little snot doesn't deserve to live."

"You don't want to go to jail for this coward, Melvin."

"Why not? There's nothing left for me in Morning."

"There's Nelda," I said. "She took off before the alien was uncovered. She's looking for you, man. She doesn't want to lose you."

"Nelda said that?"

Nelda said a lot of things, but I didn't even try to repeat her exact words. "She's sorry. She said you were right about the alien and that you're all the happiness and wealth she needs." I did not add that she was more than willing to accept Gunter's check. "She loves you, man."

"Nelda's a good woman," he said, handing me his gun.

Dustin flailed on the ground. The hemotoxic venom was beginning to take effect. "Please. I need a doctor."

We did not do him the honor of taking him to *la curandera*. Instead, we called the police and allowed him to take his chances with conventional medicine and justice. And as he was being hauled away, I clenched my hand around a certain small, glowing item in my pocket. I'd just have to make sure all of the loose ends of this adventure were dealt with appropriately.

Chapter
Sixteen

E ight months later, Alison and I returned to New Mexico with an original sculpture Gunter had commissioned to commemorate the alien and to serve as a memorial for Dental Stoker and Sheriff Shirley Gomez-Gomez.

When we arrived in Morning, we noticed that the former Cafe-Tavern and Jail had had a minor facelift and a new sign that read: Morning Cafe-Tavern and Art Gallery.

Gunter and Freya were waiting, and the little Viking greeted us enthusiastically with warm hugs. Freya, who was dressed in a white shirt and pristine white Levi's, bent down to shake my little hand.

"Would you like some help unloading the statue?" Gunter asked.

"Yes," I said, lowering the tailgate.

While Freya helped wrestle the two-hundred-pound sculpture off the truck, Gunter and Alison sat down on the steps of the cafe porch.

Alison asked, "How is your latest archaeological project coming along?"

"Extremely well, now that Freya is here to help me. Although we never found the Star Traveler, we know he existed. This serves to reinforce my theories about the mysterious disappearance of the Anasazi."

Freya and I dragged my sculpture to the concrete foundation that had previously supported the defunct gas pump. I was winded and gasping, but Freya was fresh as the north wind. She tossed her head and whispered, "Papa has found an arrowhead that glows in the dark."

"Hush, Freya," Gunter said. "You mustn't reveal our secrets."

Yes, I thought, please don't tell me this stuff.

Alison asked Freya, "Are you working with Gunter full time now?"

"Certainly not," Gunter responded. "I would never allow Freya to abandon her dream."

"I'm singing with the Santa Fe Company," she said. "But we're close enough now that, when I'm not performing, I can help my father with his research and fieldwork."

"That's wonderful," Alison said. "Isn't that wonderful, Adam?"

A booming voice rang out, "Well, it's about time you two got here. We've been waiting since blah-ditty-blah-blah."

I turned to see Melvin and Nelda walking toward us, hand in hand, looking like gargantuan lovebirds. But Melvin was doing all the talking as Nelda gazed adoringly at him.

"Where's that sister of yours?" Melvin demanded. "She sure did stir up a hornet's nest when she was blah-blah."

"Rob and Margot send their regrets," I said as I shook Melvin's hand and endured a bone-crushing hug from Nelda.

"They're in Hollywood taking meetings," Alison said as she danced away from Nelda's outstretched arms. "Rob's a producer now. His first project is *Margot: The Epic.*"

Gunter strolled toward the canvas-wrapped sculpture. "When do we get to see it?"

"Now, I guess." I started to cut the jute strings that held the covering in place.

"Wait," Alison said. "I had hoped Whiney would be here."

Melvin turned his head and bellowed, "Hey, Sheriff. Get on out here. There's some folks who want to see you."

"Sheriff?" Alison and I said in chorus.

Melvin explained, "After Alison got to selling Mr. Reason's art, he got a little of his self-worth back and he joined up in one of those twelve-step programs."

Nelda piped up, "We were his support group. It was tough going for a couple of months."

Melvin said, "But before we knew it, he'd pulled himself up by his moccasins and become Morning's most upstanding citizen. He took over the Cafe-Tavern and converted the jail into a showcase for his paintings."

"Isn't that wonderful," Alison said.

"Sheriff is really an honorary title," Melvin explained. "We just call him that because we can't get used to calling him Mr. Reason."

The screen door to the cafe swung open and out stepped a tall, handsome, dark-skinned man with clear brown eyes and shining raven hair tied back in a ponytail. A turquoise headband matched his shirt, which was cinched at the waist with a silver concho belt. He wore his faded Levi's tucked into a pair of pristine knee-high buckskin moccasins.

He held up his hand in greeting. "Adam. Alison. My heart soars."

Whiney really had changed. Eight months ago, he would have said: My heart is sore.

"It's good to see you, Whin—" Alison corrected herself. "Sheriff."

He laughed. "It's okay, Alison. You can call me Whiney. You changed my life. You can call me anything you want. Just don't call me late for my AA meeting."

"Can we get on with this?" Gunter said. "I'm anxious to see the statue."

We gathered around the statue, and Whiney said, "Wait. I have to get Consuela's camera."

As he strode back into the Cafe-Tavern and Art Gallery, Melvin confided, "Consuela is Mrs. Sheriff, you know."

"Married to Whiney?" Alison questioned. Apparently, she was at a loss for words because all she could mutter was, "How wonderful."

"Got hitched two weeks ago," Melvin said. *"La curandera* performed the ceremony."

"It was magical," Gunter said, "Truly magical."

Whiney returned with the camera. "Consuela really wanted to be here, but she's on assignment. She had to go over to Truth or Consequences to cover cattle mutilations for *The Enquirer."* He held the professional-looking, black-bodied 35mm camera to his eye. "Go ahead, Adam."

I felt the familiar queaziness that always comes when I'm about to present a commissioned piece. "I hope you like this. I call it *Still Life."*

I pulled off the tarp and held my breath for the half-minute of silence when the viewers formed their first impressions.

The sculpture was four feet tall, polished stainless steel and brass. The metals intertwined in graceful curves and twists. In the harsh light of day, from various angles, it looked like the crest of an ocean wave. But, in the constantly changing spectrum of the infinite New Mexico sunset, the edges would capture light. I had intended for the sculpture to resemble a thing from another world, a hovering starship. The crowning touch was a single, indestructible screw that held the sculpture in place and glowed in the dark. The people of Morning would never know just where it came from, or what it cost them.

"It's magnificent," said Freya.

The others echoed her opinion, and I breathed more comfortably.

Gunter asked, "Why do you call it *Still Life?* "

"I just made up the title," I said. "Because there's still life in Morning, still life in all of you. And there's still life in me."

Whiney said, "Shall I break out the sparkling cider?"

"Not yet," Gunter said. "I have the feeling that we haven't quite completed this ceremony."

"I know what you mean," Alison said. "After all we've been through, we need some kind of closure."

"Yes," Whiney said. "We should process our feelings."

"How about this?" I suggested. "We came to New Mexico as strangers and left as friends."

Melvin said, "Or maybe we should mention how Adam captured Dustin and ended his reign of terror."

I liked that. It made me sound like some kind of superhero.

"Or," Alison said, "we could mention how, as a result of the show at the Sundog Gallery and the coverage in the tabloids, Adam is now an international artist with a large display in Paris at Jacques LaFraque's Rue des Rudes Gallery."

I shook my head. "Somehow, it still doesn't feel like it's over."

"I know how to conclude this ceremony," Gunter said. "Freya will sing."

She laughed gracefully. Then, in a crystal-pure soprano, she sang "Over the Rainbow." On the second verse, Nelda stepped in and harmonized.

"Now, it's over," I said to Alison.

"Why?"

I gestured toward Nelda. "The fat lady sings."